THE KISSING BOOTH GIRL
AND OTHER STORIES

LETHE PRESS
MAPLE SHADE. NEW JERSEY

The
KISSING BOOTH GIRL
and OTHER STORIES

A.C. WISE

Published by Lethe Press
118 Heritage Ave, Maple Shade,
NJ 08052
lethepressbooks.com

ISBN 978-1-59021-633-0

Cover Art by
Reiko Murakami

Cover and Interior Design by
Inkspiral Design

For JANIS MORROW who showed me the path under my feet, and for JILL ROLLINS who encouraged me to keep walking it.

TABLE OF CONTENTS

THE POET'S CHILD

Oranges, Age, and Regret

The poet's child awoke to discover the loss of a word for fruit so bright its skin is like the setting sun, its juice so bitter-sweet that it is all of summer and winter in one mouthful. The child rose, and seeing the day was already late, went downstairs. The poet sat in the glassed-in porch, cat-curled into a chair before the table placed in the center of the room.

The room was an eye, and on three sides its windows gazed out over rolling grass — painfully green — and trees swaying under a sun the thick-gold of weak tea or strong honey. The land surrounding the house was a painting — too beautiful and unreal to be true. The poet's child gestured beyond the glass.

"Those trees, I used to know the name of the fruit growing on them."

The poet looked up, face holding an expression that was perhaps not as remorseful as it might have been. The child saw that the poet had been chewing the pen again — that the bone-colored quill had begun to splinter under the constant gnashing of teeth. The poet's lips were stained black with ink soaked deep into the cracks in the skin.

Slanting sunlight caught the poet's hair and illuminated eyes, which were a green far less painful than the grass, but no less dangerous. The poet shrugged, a slight movement lifting winglike shoulder bones.

"It's a poem about the countryside, about this house, and the land," the poet said, as though no more explanation or justification was needed for the theft of words. The speaking showed stained teeth behind stained lips, fissures of black scored into panes of ivory.

The poet held the child's gaze for a moment longer, then resumed chewing the pen. The glass room, which trapped sunlight and kept out the world, filled with the skritch of quill over paper; it filled with the sound made by the end of the feather that had once been buried in a goose's flesh, breaking.

Watching the poet, the child came to know the loss of a score of other words, like the way for counting the number of years one has been alone. The child knew only of being neither too old, nor too young for heartbreak.

"I used to bring you plums," the child spoke, thoughtful, looking out over the wide lawn. It hurt, choosing words so carefully. It dug at all the places where the words weren't, where holes in memory had stolen things that mattered, things the child used to love. "I used to bring them in a wide ceramic bowl, chilled so that they still carried the imprint of a breath like frost on their dark skin. Do you remember?"

The poet shrugged once more. The child tried to summon something — a feeling for not taking joy in what had been lost, but that word was gone too, devoured by the poet's pen. The poet didn't look up, but bent further to the poem, fractured quill scratching paper as thin as skin, stained lips shaping words without sound. The poet's child turned, leaving the poet and poem alone.

✄

Desire, Sex, Tears, and Rain

The poet's child walked out beyond the windows, looking back at the house and the poet bent over the poem only once. The child climbed up the low hills rolling above the house and bucking like the sea. The breeze blew through olive trees — a fruit with a name the child could still hold on the tongue, like the taste of olives themselves, salty and soaked in brine.

The poet's child remembered that flavor, lingering like a ghost, but had forgotten another word in its place. It was the word for the thing that so often comes between people, but also brings them together, closer than skin on skin. The word, the poet's child knew, brought a host of other things tumbling in its wake — similar, different, separate and not, chromosomes, just slightly off-kilter from each other, creating rifts universe-wide, or things so achingly the same that everything came crumbling down between them when they touched.

Every word the child could remember to describe that lost thing was mundane, clinical and cold, expressing nothing at all. There was so much more, something the child could almost touch. A memory snagged in the trees, in the leaves flipped silver by the blowing wind. Someone else, maybe more than one person, had stood here once.

The child could almost remember eyes like the poet's — just as green and just as dangerous. Where the child stood now, someone else had stood, close enough to press hand to hand. The poet's child remembered sun-warmed skin, but none of the names spoken into the air between the trees. If the wind-silvered leaves were frosted in the ghost-skin of memory, they spoke nothing of it and kept their secrets.

The poet's child had forgotten many things.

From that vantage point on the hill, looking away from the house, the poet's child could just catch a glimpse of the sea. Between the trees, far more distant than the ones whispering indecipherable things overhead, water sparkled — mirrored drops of silver, cast hopelessly adrift on the blue.

Turning, the poet's child descended to the house, which squatted among lengthening shadows. The hills made a bowl and the house nestled in it, like frosted plums in concave ceramic, set next to a parent's hand.

The poet still sat at the table, legs bent the same, pen to lips, staring. The poet did not look up, as the child crossed the room, and the child peered over the poet's shoulder.

The poem sitting on the table was written on air, a melting insubstantial thing. The paper was made of shed flesh and snow destined to melt. The words were all strange; the child had lost them long ago.

"I used to know a word," the child said, "for wanting a person, or a thing above any other thing in the world. Only it was more than wanting. The word was a key, heavy on my tongue, tasting of brass and iron, marrow and blood. It unlocked a heart that wasn't mine."

The poet didn't look up, but raised shoulders in a barricade of bone. The poet hunched closer to the poem with sheltering arms, as though the words dripping from the child's mouth were a rough downpour that might damage the fragile thing the poet had created. Silence stretched, pressing against the glass walls to shatter them. When it was too much to bear, the poet finally looked up.

"It's a poem about love," the poet explained — insufficient, but offering nothing more. "It's a poem about losing things, and sadness, and letting go."

The poet's eyes were infinite — the green of deep wells where moss grows and never sees the light. The poet had stolen the words, but lost the essence of their meaning — a linguistic vampire, unwarmed by the blood of others. There was no pity in the poet's fathomless gaze.

Turning, the poet flicked one hand, dismissing the child with long, thin fingers scarcely more than bone. Those fingers were the same shade as the quill, stained with as much ink. Poet and pen formed one thing, inseparable, indivisible and absolute. The poet's skin, the child realized, was very much like the paper; the language written there just as unknowable and strange.

The poet's child drew back, but at the door, paused and turned. In the room, shadows lengthened — plum-skin and bruise purple, lying so thick the poet could scarcely be seen.

"There used be another...person here, didn't there?" The child stumbled over unfamiliar words, tongue ungainly in the face of so much loss. It was like trying to express a thing never seen, trying to see a whisper in the dark, or trying to feel a color at the bottom of the ocean. "You used to be...not alone."

The poet looked up, those dangerous green eyes still visible in the dark. They were more than the color of moss; they were also the shade of sunlight on a forest pool. They were gold flecked over deep water, dampness and stones. They were the memory of things past, never to be caught again.

The poet shrugged — a favorite gesture. It made the child think of flayed skin and exposed bone and terrible angels.

"I used to bring you fruit that tasted like winter," the poet's child murmured.

Stars pinpricked the black as the child climbed the stairs — sky mirroring the water as seen through the distant trees. The poet's child was tired, though a memory of waking with the dawn lingered, a memory of not lying down to sleep until long after the moon had crossed the apex of the sky.

"I'm tired all the time now, I sleep all night and all day," the child said to no one. It was good to speak aloud, words were so precious and few. Yet each word caused pain, bruising lips as they fell into a house of weird silences.

Sitting on the bed, the poet's child could see out the window to the gentle hills and the silvered olive trees, now star-touched. The place between the trees where no one stood, where absence was a palpable thing, shone with moonlight. Alone on the bed, the poet's child almost felt the touch of a long-gone hand.

Once upon a time, there was a word that went with the word poet — other and together — fitting things into a whole. The poet's child wondered what the poet had lost, what else had been given up in service of the poem. Was it anything like what the child had lost?

The child wondered about eyes the green of olives, and kisses with the same salt-brine taste as that fruit. Once upon a time, the child had known a dozen words for goodbye and a dozen reasons to say them. But the poet's child had forgotten them now, along with the words for water falling from the sky, or falling from the eyes of someone who is gone.

The poet's child trembled, full of frustration and the pent-up need to express the inexpressible. What could be worth this? Would the poet's scratching pen circumnavigate the world, bind it in ink and vellum skin? Would the poet wrap up all the words ever spoken to keep them safe, to banish memory and feeling?

Would it be a kindness, the poet's child wondered, or a cruelty, stealing words, one by one, and taking their meaning away? In the terrible silence of the house, the poet's child felt the splintered pen, goose quill, ink stained, scratching at the walls, scratching over skin and bones.

Forgiveness

The poet's child wakes under the eye of night. It is cold in the house and utterly dark now. The child cannot remember the last time of waking without the sun. The lawn around the house is not green anymore, but black, slaughtered by the moon and turned into a fathomless sea where they will drift forever — poet and child.

The child rises, feet chill on the stone, and creeps downstairs. Ghosts crowd the space between the walls. The poet's child slips into the room once suffused with sunlight, now heavy with the moon.

Three glass walls show the poet in silver light, dark hair feathered against pale skin, one cheek pillowed on a too-long hand. The pen is still, gripped over the vellum skin of the page. The tip is utterly splintered now, and the poet's lips are as pure black as the sky.

The child crouches, catching the poet's breath as it passes sleeping lips.

There are inky words imprinted on the poet's tongue. The child can almost see them, inhale them like phantoms, allowing understanding of everything lost and gone.

More words have slipped away in the night — more than sun-bright fruit, and need like a key slipped between skin and bone to let someone on the outside in. The words that are lost are much more terrible now. They encompass caring for another person enough to protect them even after they have hurt you; they hold pain in the soul, and the word for growing from that pain into something that makes it close to okay in the end.

The poet's child rises and slips the poem from beneath the poet's sleeping hand. The poem has almost outgrown the table, spilling onto the floor, and there is still blank space at the bottom, a place where more stolen words will go. The half-shattered pen catches on the frost-thin sheet, almost but not quite tearing it. There are still a few words the poet's child remembers — words like match and fire and burn.

The smoke is acrid in the closed room, but not enough to wake the sleeping poet who breathes out inky dreams that would turn the color of drifting ash if they could take solid form. The poet's child turns away, gliding out the door like a ghost and out into the world.

Footprints mar the dew, moving away from a place of shadows cradled in a bowl of hills. There is a word the child can almost remember. It is a word spoken between people who have caused each other pain, but are bonded by something bigger than that pain, big enough to swallow that pain and keep surviving in its wake.

But the poem has devoured that word, stealing it from both poet and child. All that is left between them in its absence is this: going away and never looking back again.

JULIET AND JULIET(TE): A ROMANCE OF ALTERNATE WORLDS

The day she meets Juliet, Juliet(te) changes the spelling of her name. It's a simple act, but it's monumental at the same time. It sets her apart and makes her part of something larger. Juliet + Juliet(te) = forever and irrevocably changed.

That's what love (though neither of them has used the word yet) does: it changes you. For instance, when Juliet first sees her she finds herself considering what Juliet(te)'s mouth will taste like. And Juliet(te) finds herself considering the way Juliet's hands will feel resting on the curve of her waist. For the rest of the night, they are no longer separate people, they are satellites orbiting each other, constantly succumbing to the pull of gravity and drifting ever closer to their moment of impact.

On the day she meets Juliet(te), Juliet is mooning over a girl named Rosa who won't even give her the time of day. Just when she's decided she's done with love, she spots Juliet(te) across the room, and the whole world flips upside down. The music in the club at the resort where they're both spending spring break thumps blood hot. Bodies pack tight, sweat-slicked and scattered with broken light. For one split second, they all stop.

Juliet doesn't give herself time to doubt or regret. Rosa? Who's that? Juliet crosses the packed club, takes Juliet(te)'s hand, and discovers her mouth, in fact, tastes like salt and lime from the tequila shots she's been pounding.

Juliet puts her hands on Juliet(te)'s waist, and they both agree without saying it aloud that they're not going to think beyond this moment. Not until last call, last dance, and the moon rolling over the horizon into dawn. They're young, and forever isn't a word in their vocabulary.

When the sky finally starts to pink, Juliet takes Juliet(te)'s hand again and leads her outside to see the last of the stars. After the heat of the club, everything is silent and still. There's a little path winding through the sea grass that leads them to the dunes overlooking the beach. In the not quite dawn, the sand is silver-gray and the water is the restless color of a bruise.

"It looks like an alien world," Juliet(te) says.

Breeze whips her long red hair into a comet's tail. Juliet's hair is stiff-dyed spikes of darkness, somewhere between black and blue. Willowy Juliet(te) wears a tank top and cut-off shorts. Stocky Juliet wears a button-down shirt with the sleeves rolled, and laced-up boots scornful of the sand.

A single star shakes loose of the firmament and streaks across the sky. A moment later, a second star falls in the opposite direction.

"One for each of us," Juliet(te) says. "Make a wish."

"I don't believe in wishes," Juliet says. "Just like I don't believe in destiny. Each moment is what you make of it."

"What do you want to make of this one, then?" Juliet(te) asks, smiling a little sly. She's already made a wish of her own, and she holds it close to her heart, never speaking it out loud.

"A race," says Juliet, squinting a little bit against the rising sun. She's slightly drunk, but mostly sober, though the world is blurred at the edges.

"To where?" Juliet(te) asks.

"Anywhere and everywhere. To the past, to the future. Let's see where the moment takes us."

This time, Juliet(te) takes Juliet's hand. "Let's start with to the water." She doesn't wait for an answer. They charge the edge of the dunes. They jump. And hand in hand, they run.

≫≪

None of this can end well. They know it in the core of their beings. The fate dictated by their shared names (even though Juliet doesn't believe in fate) says one of them must die, if not both of them. Because that's what happens to girls in stories. That's what happens to girls who love girls, and sometimes girls who love boys, or boys who love each other, and even the rare people who realize that labels and names are passé.

Juliet(te) asks Juliet about it as they sit on the beach, sipping frozen margaritas through pink plastic straws. They've been up all night, extending their just-for-now, getting around to talking about the similarity in their names and classic English literature at roughly noon. Juliet snorts.

"You think we're the reincarnation of ancient doom, fated to play out some sad-ass love story with a bullshit end?"

Juliet(te) is a little embarrassed by Juliet's scorn, but she doesn't back down. "Could be," she says, slurping and looking sadly at the bottom of her empty glass.

"Fuck that noise," Juliet responds. "I don't roll that way."

Juliet(te) looks up; a grin spreads slow. Hope blooms somewhere in the center of her chest, making her limbs warm in a way that has nothing to do with the intensity of the sun. Juliet's jaw is set, her eyes on the horizon.

"Amen!" Juliet(te) says. She jumps up and punches Juliet on the arm; her heart beats harder still. She's never dared not to believe in fate before. "So what do we do instead?"

"We do better," Juliet says. "The day is young and ripe for adventure. We'll build a time machine. Jump to a different world. Jump to all of the worlds. We'll run away."

"You serious?" Juliet(te) asks. She's feeling a little drunk. The tequila is playing catch-up. Her lips still feel frosted salty-sweet from the night before.

Juliet thinks about it. "Why the hell not? Stranger things have happened."

"Fuckin' A!" Juliet(te) punches the air. "Not forever," she adds, in case her enthusiasm scares Juliet away. "Just for now."

"Just for now," Juliet agrees, though she means it a little less than she ever has before.

⊰✄⊱

"Future," Juliet says, "or past?"

"Future." Juliet(te) grins. "There'll be time for yesterday tomorrow."

"Fuckin' A." Juliet borrows the phrase from her lover's mouth, liking the way it tastes on her tongue.

Juliet rigs electric switches and dials, geegaws and doodads. She doesn't know anything about building time machines, but how hard can it be? She knows everything about tearing down and rebuilding motorcycles, after all.

When the time machine is primed and ready to go, Juliet(te) does her make-up in the not-mirror of Juliet's face. She smears her cheeks with glitter and her eyes with kohl. She stains her lips improbable shades, colors that linger in the cracks of her chapped skin. Juliet welds neon to the soles of her boots so they flash and shine, space-pirate-style.

"Ready?" Juliet(te) asks.

"Fuckin' A," Juliet says, and throws the switch.

They hurtle through space, out past the rings of Saturn. They hurtle through time to a when where humans and aliens live side by side among the stars. They dock their improvised time machine on a space station with a thousand kinds of life speaking a thousand languages they don't understand. They find a part of the station that doesn't spin, and in zero-g, they fuck for the first time. They learn the ways their bodies fit together, and the ways they don't. They laugh as they crash into each other, and crash into the walls, getting it right more often than they get it wrong.

When they're good and bruised, happy and sore, they web themselves in a hammock tethered to the wall. They feed each other dishes they don't recognize, coming up with their own names for the alien spices that stain their fingers strange hues.

"Where next?" Juliet asks, drifting on the edge of sleep.

Part of her never wants to leave. This future is too perfect — and it still counts as just for now when you have a time machine. It's not even tomorrow yet, Juliet thinks. That makes it okay to think about falling in love.

※

Back on earth, they become maenads in a post-apocalyptic motorcycle gang, hoarding gasoline and devouring their enemies with mirror-bright teeth. Juliet's skills come in handy, and she teaches Juliet(te) the art of motorcycle repair.

When the future becomes passé, Juliet(te) tinkers with Juliet's time machine, rigging it to take them from might-bes to never-weres. They become goddesses on a sun-drenched island in the Mediterranean, benevolent rulers of a land populated with centaurs and minotaurs.

When their skins begin to itch from too much sun, Juliet(te) and Juliet become queens of an underground realm, co-ruling the land of the dead. From

there, they slip beneath the waves, growing gills and shedding their skin. At
some point, they learn to fly.

"Do you need a break?" Juliet(te) asks one day, shaking free a storm of
feathers from her sun-scorched skin. They dared too close to the sun, but both
of them declined to fall.

She's afraid of what Juliet's answer might be. Just for now has become a
year, or maybe more. It could be centuries since they first met by the sea. It's
easy to lose track with a time machine.

"I'm game for another round if you are," Juliet says. She's afraid of
Juliet(te)'s reason for asking. The idea of letting go, even for a moment, is more
than she can bear

Juliet(te) raises her hands, palms out, in front of her. "I want to try
something,"

Like a mirror, Juliet puts her hands against her lover's skin. Between
them, there is warmth, and their pulse is a steady beat keeping time. They lean
together until their foreheads touch. If they can build a time machine, a myth
machine, why can't they live inside each other's skin?

For an entire year, Juliet(te) becomes Juliet and vice versa. They circle
each other, learning their bodies anew. Everything is different from the outside.

Juliet dyes Juliet(te)'s hair the color of cold water and plums, tangling it
up in a thousand complicated braids. She pierces Juliet(te)'s lip and her left
eyebrow and her belly button. Because that's what love (she still hasn't used
the word aloud, and so she manifests it physically in silver and niobium) does.
It breaks you open and transforms you; it enters you and it makes you shine.

Juliet as Juliet(te) lies nude on a tar-paper rooftop under the stars and
makes Juliet(te)'s body come with fingers that aren't quite hers. She does it
again and again until she can't breathe for the beauty of it all.

Juliet(te) takes Juliet's body to night school and flirts with boys. She earns
Juliet a certificate in computer engineering and travels to Rome where she

almost falls in love with a vestal virgin. She enacts all the scenarios of letting go she can imagine, the ways she and Juliet will fall apart in the end. She casts these futures like sympathetic magic. She does this to banish every single one.

Juliet uses Juliet(te)'s body to learn yoga, something she's always wanted to try, but has always been afraid. She takes up rock climbing, and quits it immediately. She drinks too much and induces insomnia, watching late-night television and eating frozen dinners that are terrible for her. She considers adopting a cat. She spends a whole month not speaking at all. She practices living alone.

After a year, Juliet and Juliet(te) crash back into each other on the dunes above the ocean where they first met. Bruised and battered, starved and confused, they devour each other. Neither can remember where one starts and the other begins, or what they were so afraid of; they see there's no need to let go. Juliet and Juliet(te) entwine hands and limbs, and lie exhausted side by side.

"Are you me, or am I you?" asks Juliet(te).

"Does it matter?"

Anything is possible, even forever not being a terrible thing.

Doomed love doesn't have to die young. They can live on the edge of annihilation, refusing destiny in the name of their own narratives. They will burn twice as bright, and fly twice as far, setting the night on fire in the brilliance of their wake.

"Keep running?" Juliet(te) asks.

"Fuckin' A," Juliet says, slipping into sleep, still holding her lover's hand.

✄

They travel everywhere — ancient Sparta, far-future Lisbon, the moons of Jupiter, and the deep undersea caves of worlds waiting to be discovered. They are myth, possibility, and actuality all rolled into one. They tell their own stories, rather than letting fate tell one for them, something Juliet(te) never thought was possible.

They travel nowhere. They take up knitting. They plant a garden, nothing edible except to bees. They go to the market on Sundays, and consider learning how to keep the bees that have been lingering longer and longer at their house. They learn to enjoy silence and stillness, something Juliet never thought they would do. They learn to stop being afraid of standing still.

It's been only a moment since they met, and it's been a thousand years, when Juliet finally speaks the word love aloud. She whispers it into the fire of her lover's hair, and Juliet(te) offers it back to her in the same breath and heartbeat.

"If you could choose any future, any past, out of all the ones we've visited, which one would you choose?" Juliet asks. She has a smear of honey on her chin from their pancake breakfast.

Juliet(te) smiles because the answer is so simple (why haven't others realized this?): "One with you." The pad of her thumb rubs that smear like errant lipstick.

✳

Juliet and Juliet(te) wake to the crash of waves. They roll toward each other in their bed in their little cottage by the sea. Roses climb the walls, curling around the windows; everything smells of salt and glory, winter mixed with spring.

As they have every morning since they met, they examine themselves in the mirror of each other's faces, and smile at what they see. Their hair is the same storm-tossed shade of gray these days. Their wrinkles are very much the map of each other's lives. Some people mistake them for sisters, for twins. Those same people look away with pinched mouths when the two old ladies reach for each other to lock gnarled hands, or giggle like teenagers, or kiss like the same.

"Young love is grand, isn't it?" Juliet(te) asks Juliet in their cottage by the sea.

"Fuckin' A," Juliet agrees.

One day, they may die in each other's arms, perhaps in sleep, perhaps before bed as they each slip soft nightgowns over the other's familiar body, but it won't be tragic this time. As Juliet once said to Juliet(te) — fuck that noise. There are better stories to tell, and the only moment they care about is this one, right here, right now.

AND IF THE BODY WERE NOT THE SOUL

Ro shoulders the courier bag, leaving the bike chained at the entrance to the Zone. Even here, at the edge, dampness permeates the air green like a receding tide. The pavement is patchwork. Brick and stone show through tears in the asphalt, wounds no one bothered to heal once the aliens moved in, once it was clear humans would never move back into the neighborhood and it became the *Zone*.

Weeds grow in the gaps, flourishing in the damp. Ro places each boot carefully, avoiding the puddles reflecting sodium streetlights. On either side of the street, buildings stand with their doors shuttered against the gathering twilight. Some are ragged against the emerging stars, top layers blown away, evidence of the violence that emptied the neighborhood, made it unfit for human habitation, and eventually turned it into the Zone. But close to the ground, the world is still whole. If Ro doesn't look up, it's as though nothing has changed.

Except the Zone is haunted by waiting. The sense of impermanence is palpable — like the refugee camps and shanty towns of the early century, the ones the government planned to empty after the last great flood, or hurricane, but never did. The Zone was meant to be a way station, a temporary solution until the Immies (the word tastes dirty even in Ro's mind, hateful, ugly, but there isn't a better one because the aliens have never given the humans their true name) could be fully integrated into life on Earth. And yet...

Ro shrugs against the weight of emptiness and broken promises. At least Xal's light is still on, welcoming. A bell over the door jangles; stepping inside, Ro can't help smiling at this incongruously human touch. It's like the shelves behind the glass counters, crammed floor to ceiling with human knickknacks and oddities no Immie could possibly want, and no human would come here to buy. Charming, but sad in a way, too. Lonely.

It takes Ro a moment to pick out Xal's form against the crowded shelves. Today, Xal's flesh is the color of sand. It reminds Ro of the fish that disguise themselves from predators by lying flat against the ocean floor. There are variations, tiny glints of light. It is brown only in the way pigeons are simply gray, full of tones unseen until it is pointed out they were there all along.

"Hi." Ro sets the courier bag on the counter — this time full of gamboling ceramic kittens — and places the delivery slip on top.

Xal doesn't respond, which isn't unusual for an Immie, only for Xal. Ro hesitates. Payment is stacked neatly on the counter, as always. Perhaps Xal simply doesn't want to talk. Ro turns, hiding disappointment.

::Tone — Plea/Imperative: Ro. Wait.::

Xal's voice is changeless, only the tone-statement betraying the edge of panic. There are no human or even human-like features to convey pain. But now that Ro looks closer, it is written in the restless knotting of limbs hanging beneath the bulk of Xal's body.

Ro steps forward. Xal shifts, flickering in and out. Barely visible one moment, then sharply outlined the next. Sinuous lines gleam damp, twisting through a host of colors Ro can't begin to name. Ro's breath catches. There, an extra wetness, almost hidden by the tangled lines, a gash leaking fluid, smelling of salt.

"What happened?"

::Tone — Statement/Fear: An accident.:: Ro hears hesitation in Xal's tone; in a human, it might sound like a lie. ::Tone — Statement/Honesty: An attack. In the human district, not far over the line. Just looking.::

Colors roll; Xal fades in and out again.

"You were attacked?"

::Tone — Affirmative/Sorrow: Yes.::

"What can I do to help? Is there someone I can call?"

::Tone — Alarm/Negative: No.::

"Okay." Ro holds up hands, palms out, hoping Xal will understand the human gesture and feeling helpless.

Xal's body clenches, shuddering, furling tight around the wound. A sound like keening, like an in-drawn breath, like music, traces Ro's jaw and spine. Then the sound stops and Xal unfolds, becoming more solid.

The wound already looks less, but still, a tremor ripples out from Ro's center. Disgust. Ro clenches teeth against the reaction, a reflexive hatred for the uselessness of all flesh. It isn't fair; Xal is wounded, Xal needs help, and this isn't the time. And yet the bone-achingly physical reaction remains, rooted in the very thing causing the revulsion. Flesh. Ro shudders, stepping closer to the counter as if to step away from skin, from muscle, leaving disgust behind.

::Tone — Statement/Sincere: The pain is less. Ro. Thank you for staying.::

A limb uncurls, a jerky, reflexive motion as though Xal is not entirely in control yet. It brushes Ro's hand, braced against the countertop. A new sound, a new quality of pain, laced with surprise. Xal draws back, but not before the touch sparks — a snap like an electric shock and a taste like lemons.

A scream locks in Ro's throat. A sensation of dislocation without motion. A space of falling or flying, existing between the moment of contact and Xal's touch withdrawn. Ro blinks away patches of violet light until the shop comes back into focus, bracing for a horror that never comes.

The lightness of Xal's touch, unlike anything human. Ro lets out a breath, coming back to center.

Xal's limbs are knotted in a new pattern now, anxious.

::Tone — Statement/Fear: Ro. Apology. Pain was not intended.::

"No. I..." Ro's breath — ragged — calms, but not fast enough. "It didn't hurt. I don't..."

Flying. Falling. Ro struggles to process the sensation of Xal's limb, solid yet ephemeral. The memory of the touch remains, like a lost tooth wanting to be probed. It is a moment of slipping out from under the weight of skin and bones, of being somewhere else, yet wholly here.

Ro tries to draw back from the sensation, but there is nothing to withdraw from.

::Tone — Query/Fear: Not hurt.:: Xal's voice again. Ro's mind thrums to an absence, reaching again for revulsion where there is none.

"No. I should just... I'm sorry."

Ro turns, bell jangling. The green scent of the streets is an assault, the slickness underfoot designed to trip uncareful steps. Even the shorter buildings lean in, edges all jagged. They outline an empty space, something that cannot be defined.

On the edge of hyperventilation, Ro bursts out of the Zone. Leaving the bike behind, leaving everything. Not questioning the source of the fear, just running. Then stopping, leaning against a building, a stitch lacing between two ribs.

"Ro?"

Ro looks up, blinking, human buildings and a single figure resolving. Audra slows her bike, dropping one foot to the pavement. The courier satchel at Audra's hip is empty; Ro remembers the bag left with the delivery in Xal's shop, the bike chained to a post at the entrance of the Zone.

"Are you okay? You look like you're about to faint."

"I..." Ro falters, tries again. "Something happened."

"What?"

There are no words. Only lemons and the snap of electricity. Ro rubs the spot Xal touched, chasing ghosts.

"Come on." Audra swings her leg over the courier bike, twin to the one Ro left behind. A tilt of her chin indicates the café across the street, glowing warm in the twilight. "We're getting some tea into you. My treat."

Audra keeps a space and silence between them. Ro is grateful. But Audra's gaze still slides in Ro's direction, questioning. Inside the café, Audra pushes a cup of tea across the table.

"What happened?"

"I was making a delivery to Xal." Ro hesitates, seeing an expression of distaste Audra is not quick enough to hide. "Xal was attacked, outside the Zone."

The muscles between Ro's shoulder blades tense, waiting for Audra to ask what an *Immie* was doing outside the Zone. But the question doesn't come, and Ro swallows guilt at putting venom in Audra's mouth before continuing.

"Xal was hurt and...accidentally touched me."

Audra's eyes widen. Small fingers of panic tap at Ro's ribs from the inside. Xal's tone-statements make things so much simpler. With Audra, Ro is lost. Is she jealous? Angry?

At last year's office holiday party, Audra drunkenly tried to kiss Ro. They had only known each other a short time, and so it was Ro who mumbled apologies and made the effort to explain.

It's not you, it's me. I'm not.... I don't really date. I don't like... And there, the explanation faltered. Because what could Ro say that Audra would understand? Audra was wholly comfortable in her skin, more so than anyone Ro had ever met. She dated men and women in equal numbers; affection — casual and intimate — came to her as naturally as breath. She drank the world in through her fingertips and remained thirsty for more.

So how could Ro explain a hatred of touch, of flesh? The discomfort of even having a body, let alone one identifying with a single, narrow gender and responding to others sexually?

How could Ro explain it then? How can Ro explain it now? How that night Ro hadn't fled, but had remained horrified. How this night Ro had fled, but wasn't disgusted.

Audra shakes her head. Amazement? Ro still can't tell. Xal's touch was accidental; would emphasizing that help? Audra has been kind, understanding; Ro doesn't want to see Audra hurt, but the gulf between them is so vast.

Audra wraps her hands around her mug. Steam rises between them. She does not look at Ro.

"So what happened?"

"It tasted like lemons. And it was like being somewhere else."

"Xal tasted like lemons?"

"No. I mean. I don't know. Haven't you ever smelled something and had the taste hit you at the same time? I'm explaining it badly."

"No." Audra draws the word out. She looks at her hands, her expression guarded, like she wants to say more, but silence stretches between them.

Ro feels a pang of guilt, threaded with a flutter of panic, imagining Audra wants to put her hand over Ro's. A comforting gesture; it's what Audra would do if she was sitting with anyone else. Ro has seen it, the way Audra leans into their other co-workers — a nudge from her hip to emphasize a joke, a sympathetic hand on an arm, a head comfortably resting on a shoulder. Even when it isn't sexual, Audra is so casual with her body; Ro can't begin to understand it.

"I have to go back for my messenger bag," Ro says, abrupt, standing.

"But…" Hurt flickers in Audra's eyes, this time unmistakable.

"I'm sorry," Ro says.

It feels like fleeing again. The phantom of Xal's touch lingers, but it doesn't have half the weight of Audra's gaze. Still, Ro rubs the spot again, pushing out the door. A light drizzle mists the air. Hairs rise on Ro's arm, catching the moisture. Ro rubs harder, half expecting to see translucence and hollow bones like glass — flesh both there and not there in the aftermath of Xal's touch.

Instead of going back to the Zone, Ro goes home, climbing three flights to a small apartment, boots heavy on each step. Guilt prickles, and with it, something else. Curiosity.

Ro crosses to the window, touching the glass. It's cool, and condensation forms a halo in the shape of a hand. When she draws away, there is a space left — defined by the imprint of four fingers, a palm, a thumb. And in the place of flesh, droplets of water cling to the window, heavy with the light and shimmering like stars.

❧

Nerves flutter in Ro's stomach. The memory of rain glistens on the bike, still chained at the Zone's entrance. Ro brushes fingertips over the metal frame in passing. Never has the walk to Xal's shop seemed longer. Never has the jigsaw of uneven pavement, brick, and stone seemed such an impediment.

Ro tries to think of anything written or said about physical contact between humans and Immies, but comes up empty. If it's done, it's a private thing. Does everyone taste lemons, feel the snap of electricity? The Immie community is so small. Maybe Ro is the first, the only one.

But who is there to ask? The other couriers don't travel into the Zone. Scarcely any humans do. Ro has never seen another human walking the shattered streets. Which makes the kitschy human ornaments crowding the walls in Xal's shop even sadder.

Ro pauses, wondering if Xal has ever made a sale, if the shipments Ro regularly delivers ever leave the shop again, or only sit there gathering dust.

Why, Ro wonders. Aliens came to their world. Shouldn't people be excited, curious? But they don't seem to be. It's not fear exactly, but more a way of not seeing, Ro supposes. Turning a blind eye to what is inconvenient, uncomfortable. Like the government pretending the Zone is only temporary. Like the refugee camps that never empty. Like racial tension, poverty, homophobia. If the problem is ignored long enough, perhaps it will simply go away.

Ro pauses before pushing open Xal's door; the bell jangles. The courier bag, now empty, waits on the counter. And Xal waits behind it, limbs no longer bunched in pain, but held inward, careful, betraying tension. Ro's throat is dry; it takes a moment to get the words out.

"How are you feeling?"

There's no sign of the wound. Ro can't tell whether it's healed completely, or whether Xal is simply hiding it. Limbs fold and unfold, a rippling effect unsettling the first time Ro saw it. Now it's almost comforting.

Today, Xal is gray-green, but with shades of violet. Ro thinks of sea anemones, rocks grown over with lichen, algae stirred by gentle waves.

::Tone — Relief/Query: Unhurt, now. Are you well.::

Ro nods.

"I'm sorry for running out yesterday. It's just…" Trying to explain things to Audra was awkward enough. They share common language, context.

"I forgot my bag." Ro points; it is a cowardly change of subject, but safer ground.

Ro touches the bag, but makes no move toward the door. Xal seems watchful, even without visible eyes. But what else? Hurt? Confused? Ro is suddenly aware of standing stiff, one arm crossed to hold the opposite elbow, lips parted as if to speak. Flesh again — bodies speaking a language Ro can't understand. It's all so useless. So…

"I want you to touch me again." The words come in a rush too quick for regret. Heat suffuses cheeks, another betrayal, and Ro almost flees.

But the shop bell stays silent. Ro's boots remain planted on the floor.

"I mean if…it didn't hurt you? If…if it's okay."

Pulse beats under jawline, at wrists and elbows. Xal furls and unfurls, the there and not-there-ness coming across as deliberation, physically rolling and weighing the request.

::Tone — Hesitation/Query: It does not hurt. Why do you want this.::

"I don't know."

It's the most honest answer Ro can give. A paradox blooms, a strange, fractal bruise centered at the site of Xal's last touch. It spreads outward, rewriting Ro's hardwired code. Ro *wants* this. No, Ro *needs* this.

"What was it like for you?" Ro's eyes slide closed; it's easier to speak this way, even if it means having to ignore the extra weight of tears just starting to frost lashes. "I don't want to impose, is what I mean. I don't normally like… But this was different. I tasted lemons."

The ache is physical — a desire to step off the edge, precisely because it is unsafe, unknown. There are blank spaces defined by broken buildings, by the ghost of a handprint. They are defined by lack — not by something missing precisely, simply by something not there. They are possibility, made manifest.

In that brief moment, Ro had the sense of Xal's touch being like the ideal of falling into the night sky, being weightless and rushing so fast between stars their light draws blood. That paradox bruising Ro's skin — the contradiction of making the unknown known and erasing the infinite possibility — is too attractive.

"I can't explain." Ro's throat aches around the inadequacy of words.

A heartbeat. A space of silence. Eyes open. Ro consciously remembers to breathe. Xal is watchful, even without eyes. There is the same sense of consideration in the roiling movements, colors flickering, limbs furling and unfurling.

::Tone — Statement/Uncertainty: It is curious. No other humans come here. To touch would be to know more.::

Ro lets out a rush of breath.

"You're sure?"

::Tone — Anticipation/Fear: The store is closed.::

At first, Ro doesn't understand. Then Xal touches a switch and the lights dim, leaving only the faint glow of emergency lighting. Understanding crashes in: This is agreement, consent. Xal is giving them privacy.

::Tone — Anticipation/Fear: Ro. Put your arm on the counter.::

Ro hesitates only a moment, breathes out, then rests both arms, wrist up, on the glass. In the dimness, Xal is both easier and harder to see. Red light from the emergency-exit sign traces contours and makes flesh the color of water over gray-green stone glow.

Ro tries not to flinch, pressing arms against the countertop to keep from shaking. Xal's...arm? Leg? Is there a human word for it? Extends slowly, waits the space of a heartbeat, then surrounds Ro's flesh, passing through and into it.

The shop tilts. A scent like violets and seaweed, like gunpowder, fills the air. There is no weight to Xal's touch, yet pressure builds in Ro's bones. A sense of fullness pushing outward, but without pain.

Xal flickers, slow, slow, fast, slow, unfolding, folding, turning. There and not there. Ro feels it too, absent and present, within the shop and elsewhere. An elsewhere that cannot be described.

Part of Ro reaches for something to anchor to in the here and now — long division, the names of past presidents, a list of capital cities. The larger part spins outward, spiraling from a weightless center, out through rings of stars, arms flung wide against the dark. Fragments of unknown worlds tumble past. Everything is vast and Ro is small and for a moment the sense of it is crushing.

"No." Ro jerks back, the word slipping out.

::Tone — Query/Concern: Ro. Are you hurt.::

Xal's shop snaps back into focus. Ro crashes back into a body too small to hold the sense of stars, and their loss is just as terrible as their presence.

"I'm…" A ragged breath. Ro places a hand over the skin Xal touched; it is solid, real. Colors ripple across Xal, the salt-scent in the room intensifying.

::Tone — Shame/Sincerity: Apologies. I did not mean to cause pain.::

"No. You didn't. I'm sorry. I shouldn't have…"

Under the salt-scent, the smell of violets and gunpowder. Ro's flesh prickles, as though swept by a cool breeze; the hairs rise. A sense of pressure, reaching, but never quite arriving, haunts the space between Ro's bones. It isn't desire — that's too simple a word, too human. But there is wanting, need unfulfilled.

"I want to try again. Please."

::Tone — Statement/Confusion: You were hurt.::

"No. It didn't hurt. I was just scared. But I want to try again." Ro's pulse thumps, arms trembling as they are pressed against the counter once more. "Please?"

Color and movement speak doubt as they roll across Xal's flesh — storm clouds, and the scent of oncoming rain. Dust — Ro can almost taste it. The same doubt fills Ro, but it can't end here. Ro reaches after something to keep the moment from slipping away, and lands on Xal's curiosity.

"What did you feel?"

::Tone — Statement/Uncertainty: Sunlight. A plank of wood. Many planks of wood. Water. Sunlight on water. The sensation of limbs in water. Smoke and charcoal.::

Hesitation between Xal's words, searching for concepts to capture such simple, human things. The memory comes rushing back to Ro, sitting on a dock at the lake, toes trailing in the water, a grown-up grilling hot dogs in the background and the air filling with shrieks as other children dove and splashed in the water. A slice of childhood, pulled through Ro's skin and transferred into

Xal's mind through touch.

"You saw my memories?"

More hesitation, then, ::Tone — Agreement/Affirmative: Yes.::

The information makes Ro's head swim. Could it work both ways? An alien childhood, if there is even such a thing, slipping into Ro's skin. There's so much Ro doesn't know about Xal, about the Immies in general. The need to know is overwhelming.

Ro looks to where Xal's eyes would be on a human, trying to communicate need. The absence of Xal's touch is a pressure as great as the touch itself. It's only a matter of quality, of flavor — not better, or worse, just different.

Xal reaches out again. A sigh, a musical tone so unlike the sound of pain from the night before traces the length of Ro's spine, the curve of Ro's jaw. Touch.

A needle, a thread draws through Ro's skin, stitching it with the light of the universe. The taste of bitter greens, the feel of velvet, the scent of woodsmoke. Ro's mind substituting human concepts for unimaginable things. Nebulae bloom against Ro's closed eyes.

"Oh." The word escapes in a breath. Language and thought failing. Space simultaneously narrows to the point of contact between them, and expands beyond calculation.

"Oh." There are no other words. "Oh."

Again and again as the world spins away from them and Ro flies and falls.

⚛

"Hey."

Ro turns toward Audra's voice, still holding the coffee pot. The scent of it, just on the edge of burnt, fills the small courier office above the shed where their bikes are racked.

"Careful. You're going to spill." Audra points, and Ro starts, realizing the coffee is perilously close to the edge of the mug.

Even before the first sip, Ro is shaky, nerves taut and singing.

"Sorry." Ro replaces the coffee pot, sips scalding heat.

"Are you okay?" Audra frowns. "You look exhausted."

Ro doesn't remember returning to the apartment last night, only waking in a tangle of sheets this morning, eyelids sticky, limbs heavy. The world keeps wanting to slide away; the edges of Ro's vision glimmer with light, like a migraine coming on, only without pain.

"Any new jobs come in since yesterday?" Ro asks instead of answering Audra's question.

Even seen peripherally, Audra's concern is clear. There are no mirrors in Ro's apartment, but Ro imagines the shadow-bruises of sleeplessness, improperly combed hair.

"A few." Audra hands over the clipboard before pouring her own mug of coffee. Her knuckles are white, gripping the handle. It is a gesture of restraint; Ro has seen it before. If Audra doesn't anchor herself to her mug, she will reach out a comforting hand to touch Ro's arm.

Evasion tastes as sour as a lie. Audra only wants to help, but what can Ro say? Audra might understand, but she might as easily be hurt. She might think Ro is sick, wrong for wanting this inexplicable thing, and that would be unbearable. It's not that kind of desire, but it's too hard to explain. There are no words for what it is, at least none that Ro knows.

"Mind if I take the Thayer Street drop?" Ro's voice cracks.

The sound is covered with more sips of coffee — too quick. The heat doesn't help the flush coming to Ro's cheeks. The truth must be written everywhere on Ro's skin, the evidence of Xal wrapped around and through, highlighting the translucence of bones, hollowed like glass.

Ro is clattering down the stairs to the bike shed almost before realizing it.

"Ro!" Audra follows, and Ro isn't quick enough — fingers shaking and clumsy — to strap the package to the back of the bike and leave before Audra blocks the door.

"What happened?"

Ro doesn't answer. Can't. Tears sting, hot and bright, but don't fall.

"Ro." Audra's voice is soft. She weaves between the bikes, comes within a few inches of Ro, and reaches out. But at the sharp intake of breath, she stops, her fingers falling short of brushing Ro's wrist.

"Sorry. I forgot." Audra looks down, then back again. The hope in her eyes is crushing.

Ro shifts, putting the bike between them, and feels guilty doing so.

"I went back to see Xal." Ro swallows, gripping the bike.

Audra's eyes widen, drawing light from the gaps where the door of the shed doesn't quite fit. All the darkness in them reminds Ro of falling through the stars. There is a sound that isn't quite a sob, and it takes Ro a moment to realize its source.

"Are you hurt?"

Ro gives a shake of the head, slight, but easier than words.

"What happened?"

Ro's lips press tight, fighting the sense of being overwhelmed without understanding its source. The loneliness of being trapped in a single body with its weight of flesh — Ro has always known it, but until feeling the alternative offered by Xal, it was bearable. Now the world is open, a wound no amount of thread can stitch closed.

Audra's fingers circle Ro's wrist, insistent this time. Ro's mouth flies open, but Audra's grip tightens.

"Please. I want to understand."

The need to touch is written clearly in Audra's eyes, as clear as Ro's desire to pull away. Ro lets out a shuddering breath, doesn't move. Pulse beats between them, in Audra's fingertips, in Ro's wrist. Maybe this is a language Audra can read; maybe Ro doesn't need to say anything at all.

Audra exhales, letting go, and Ro's pulse falls back into a regular rhythm. How can Xal's touch soothe, being so alien, while Audra's induces only panic? Most of the world would consider it wrong, broken. But Ro knows it isn't. There is no weight to Xal's touch, no expectation.

"I'm sorry," Ro says, and at the same time, Audra says, "I'm sorry."

Breath and silence fills the shed. They look at each other across the bike between them. The light coming through the gap around the door shifts, leaving Audra's face in shadow, stealing the illusion of stars from her eyes, but catching sylph-like in her dark curls.

Ro's chest tightens. There are no words that won't make things worse. *It's not you, it's me*, will only give Audra the impression Ro thinks the opposite.

If human touch could communicate the way Xal's does, Ro would understand. And maybe, for Audra, it does. Maybe Audra experiences the world through the tips of her fingers, gives away pieces of herself with each touch, but gains just as much in return, never diminishing.

But Ro cannot say this, cannot ask without fear of giving Audra hope. It's not that Audra has ever pressured Ro, or implied that maybe if Ro just tried it, met the right person, then things would be different. It's that sometimes, Ro catches Audra looking and thinks there is a glimmer, faint, but wistful — wishing things were different between them — and it makes Ro's heart ache.

"Tell me," Audra says, taking a step back, putting more space between them. She crosses her arms, holding herself in, holding back.

But Audra isn't running away, and relief surges through Ro. Whatever else they may be, at the core, they are still friends. The realization that Audra won't leave, won't shun, no matter what, brings a surge of emotion. It's almost like love, vast and complicated, but even the thought of the word comes thick with ghosts — meanings and expectations layered upon it by all the lips that have spoken it before. Ro pushes it away and, halting, tries to explain. Audra listens, never interrupting.

"Do you think there's something wrong with me?" Ro asks, needing to hear the words aloud, needing to taste them in order to let them go.

"No." Audra's tone is firm, but she looks lost as well. Scared. "I just don't want you to get hurt, okay? Promise me you'll be careful?"

Audra hugs herself tighter. Ro nods, pressing lips together, tasting salt even without tears. The promise means nothing; they both understand. This is unknown territory, and there is no way to travel it without gathering bone-deep scars.

⨯

Sirens shatter Ro's sleep. Pulse jack-rabbiting, pushing away sweat-tangled sheets and the remnants of a dream, Ro stumbles to the window. The sound is tied to the dream — one of being very far away, but very close, stretched thin, no blood or bone, no muscle, only skin and nerves pulled taut like a sheet over the world.

On the street below, red and blue lights spin in time with Ro's pulse. A sudden spike of pain. Ro clasps the wound, but there's nothing there.

Xal.

Pain arcs again, bringing flashes of violence, memories not Ro's own.

Xal.

Jacket and pants pulled over rumpled pajamas. Feet shoved into unlaced boots. Clattering down three flights of stairs. Ro's courier bike leans outside the apartment's outer door. Grabbing it, Ro is gone. Falling. Flying. Pedaling madly into the night, toward the flashing lights.

The whole city is wet, smearing in Ro's peripheral vision. Two cop cars park askew across the main entrance to the Zone. Ro stops the bike, lets it fall. A knot of people huddle, pointing. The cops struggle with a man whose hands are secured with a plastic zip tie. He thrashes, resisting as they push him toward the nearest car.

"Fucking Immie got what it deserved, slurping and lurking around our streets. They need to fucking stay where they're told or go the fuck home."

Light skips off shards of broken glass, blood red and deep blue. The man throws his head back; the cop's nose makes a sickening crunch as bone connects with bone. Swearing, the cop lets go, but her partner is quick, sweeping the man's legs and dropping him. The second cop gets a knee in the man's back, holding him down against the tongue of uneven pavement extending from the mouth of the Zone. The man continues swearing, lips spit-flecked.

"Fucking Immie. I hope it's dead."

Ro breaks into a run, ignoring a muffled shout from the cop with the broken nose. The door to Xal's shop hangs open. Ro nearly slips in slickness trailing across the floor. Xal never made it to the safety behind the counter, and instead lies knotted in front of it, limbs drawn together in the universal language of pain.

There is no hesitation. Ro kneels, folding around and over Xal. Shock waves of pain radiate outward, but Ro doesn't let go. Stars spin, razor bright. The smell of matches, freshly-struck; a taste like a battery held on the tongue; the persistent thrum of rain.

"It's okay. It's okay."

Ro repeats the words, trying to stay conscious, trying to soothe. Xal's pain is overwhelming, an assault of sensation. Lighthouse flash. The taste of apples. Green-wet stone. Stairs spiraling down.

Desperate, Ro tries to pour sensation back into Xal — more childhood memories — introduce a new thread into the loop of feedback flowing between them. But the images keep coming, pounding Ro like fists, like stones. It's impossible to concentrate. The rasp of wool, black crayons melting in the sun, the taste of cherries. The touch-taste-smell correlation stutters. Xal's control slips, no longer translating sensations into human terms.

Ro screams. A note, sheer sound, shearing bone from bone, sloughing flesh. Ro's mind reels, trying to process what there are no words for.

A body — Ro's, Xal's, both, shudders. Collapses inward. Spins outward. The rush of wind, hot and dry and wet all at once. The crushing cold between stars. Stretching impossibly thin-fast-long across a cord of silver and all of it is everything all at once. Then, nothing.

⊰⊱

Scraps torn from a quilt, broken fragments of a mirror, numb fingers trying to piece them back together and failing. Surfacing. Ro approaches a reflection etched on the underside of waves, surrounded by a distorted view of sky and trees and sunlight on the other side. Lips almost touch lips — reality kissing reflection — then Ro sinks again. A stream of bubbles, like pearls, like laughter, trail behind.

Hands. A voice. Audra's?

Wheels hum fast through sterile corridors; too-bright lights overhead. Sharp-jabbed needles. Medicine smell. The steady pulse of machines. Then nothing again.

⊰⊱

Ro comes back from very far away. The simple task of cracking open an eyelid is monumental. Dry lips part.

"Water?"

A straw touches swollen and bruised lips. Ro sucks greedily until the straw is withdrawn.

"Not too much too fast. The doctors said."

Ro turns, head even heavier than eyelids. Audra perches in a chair next to the bed, holding the water glass awkwardly in her lap. She looks as though she's about to cry, or has just stopped.

"I should call the nurse."

"Wait." Ro tries to remember — in the haze of moments between then and now, was Audra's name spoken in answer to the nurses asking if there was someone they should call?

"What happened?" Ro tastes blood from cracked lips.

Audra holds the water out again, automatic.

"The police found you and Xal curled together on the floor. It looked like you'd been beaten to a bloody pulp. They thought you were dead."

"I don't remember."

"Were you attacked?"

"No. Xal was hurt. I…" There is no word for it, but Ro feels one trying to take shape on a tongue not meant for such sounds.

"You have to stop this. Promise me you'll stay away from Xal."

"I can't." It isn't what Ro means to say, not meaning to say anything at all.

For a moment, Ro is afraid Audra will storm out, but she only crosses her arms tight around her body.

"Ro, what are you doing?"

"I don't know." Ro's voice cracks. "I really don't."

Ro lies back on the pillow, closing eyes before they snap open again.

"Is Xal okay?" It hurts, but Ro turns toward Audra.

"Xal is fine, as far as I know." Audra stiffens, her tone brittle and sharp. Hurt shines in her eyes. Her mouth opens, but she closes it again, standing. "I'll go get a nurse."

Audra's shoes click and silence falls in their wake. Weary and bruised in ways that have nothing to do with skin, Ro curls into a ball, trying to recreate a knot of limbs so woven over and under and through each other they become one.

✖

Ro toys with the hospital bracelet. It's been three days, and Ro's wounds have vanished as though they never existed. Still, Audra insisted on riding in the cab back to the apartment, and now perches on the arm of Ro's battered couch, watchful.

"What exactly did Lena say?" Ro paces to the window.

"She just suggested you might want to take some time off, for your health."

"And she couldn't be bothered to tell me in person?"

Ro glances back as Audra shrugs, looking uncomfortable.

"I'm sure she's just worried. We all are."

The slope of Audra's shoulders and the way she studies her feet keeps Ro silent. *Don't shoot the messenger.*

"I'm not fired?"

Audra shrugs again. Of course word has spread. Ro declined the opportunity to talk to reporters doing follow-up stories on the attack, but it doesn't matter. The stories are still out there, painting Ro as a misguided loner, the victim of an alien attack, a pervert. Maybe Lena is right to be wary, the other couriers right to withdraw. All except Audra.

"Come with me," Ro says.

Audra looks up, alarmed. "What?"

"Come with me to see Xal."

If others understood what Ro experienced, maybe they wouldn't be afraid. Maybe things can change. And where better to start with than Audra, living through touch — hand brushed to arm, palm squeezed to palm? Maybe this is something Ro can give Audra, like a gift. Something to bring them closer together in a way that balances both of their needs. And Xal, lonely, hungry for human experience. Ro's pulse speeds with the thought.

"Please? Trust me?"

Ro knows it isn't fair. Audra has offered so much, unasked — what right does Ro have to ask this in return? Because there's no way to explain to Audra without showing her what it is Ro is trying to do.

"Okay." Audra stands.

"Now?"

"Sure." Audra's smile holds an edge of sadness. "Why wait?"

The streets are silent, dusk just starting to fall. They walk with hands in pockets, watching their feet, watching the streetlights increasingly reflected as they draw closer to the Zone. Ro hears the hitch in Audra's breath as they cross the line.

"It's okay." Ro glances back, trying for a smile. "It's an imaginary border."

Audra nods, looking sheepish. Ro tries not to hold too tight to the fragile ball of hope, lest it shatter.

The shop bell jangles; behind the counter, Xal unfolds — a gesture Ro interprets as turning to face them.

::Tone — Alarm/Joy: Ro. You are not hurt.::

"Not anymore."

Xal knots and unknots, an anxious gesture.

"This is Audra, my . . . friend. Is it okay that she's here?"

::Tone — Formal/Greeting: Audra. Welcome.::

"Hi."

"I brought her here…" Ro falters under the combined weight of Audra and Xal's attention. "Audra is worried about me. I want her to understand. I thought…" Ro tries not to blush, tries not to panic.

Audra comes to the rescue, stepping forward while keeping careful space between her body and Ro's. Her voice carries a hint of nerves, but not outright fear.

"What happened the night you were attacked?"

::Tone — Statement/Query: It is not fair to be restricted. Why cross the stars to see only one small corner of a different world.::

Ro's breath catches.

::Tone — Statement/Anger: Your government promises change. We will be free to go where we please. Nothing changes.::

Xal grows, unfolding new dimensions. Ro's heart trips on the truth of the words, cracking. Again, it is a sensation too big to express, to hold. Human words are all too fraught. Ro needs an anatomy like Xal's, one to unfold and express everything mere flesh cannot contain.

Audra glances at Ro, eyes shining but cheeks dry. Ro holds her gaze, then nods, heart cracking again. There is understanding in Audra's eyes, not fear. The way Audra and Xal both watch Ro is like being rewritten — blood and bones, skin and heart. Ro is most surprised by Audra. Humans, it seems can unfold to reveal new dimensions, too.

Audra pushes her sleeves up and rests her arms on the counter.

"I want to understand."

Xal flickers, shifting attention to Ro, asking an unspoken question.

Ro's voice shakes slightly, addressing them both. "It's okay. It's safe. No one will get hurt."

Xal unfurls, encompassing Audra's arms. Ro releases a breath at the same time Audra sucks one in, sharp, but containing more surprise than pain. It is the sound of plunging into a cold lake on a hot day — pleasure and shock rolled into one.

Audra blushes, the non-colors of Xal rippling across every bit of exposed flesh. The back of her neck is a sunset in deep sea shades; her arms are the color of starlight on a pond. She is there and not there. The scent of cherries and running water leak into the air.

"Can I…?" Ro doesn't finish the sentence.

Perhaps Ro closes the space, or perhaps Xal and Audra entwined unfold to welcome Ro — a circle, a thread, a knot without beginning or end.

Sparks jump the gap between Ro's bones, suffusing flesh with light, like an x-ray, only brighter, more beautiful. Ro feels Audra's body, Xal's, all three occupying the same space and time. A moment of suffocation, a moment of panic, then everything opens with a smell like just-damp laundry snapping in the breeze. The shop warps, new segments forming like fractals of water freezing into ice.

A pulse beats, not Ro's own. A sensation belonging to — it must be Audra, because the memory — sharp and present — is so human. A bicycle, fiercely pedaled with bare feet to the crest of a hill before hands and feet are removed. It's like flying — the glorious, stomach-dropping feeling of the world falling away, the rush of wind, the warmth of light and being suspended beautifully between earth and sky. Ro feels it, filtered through Audra's flesh; from within, her body doesn't feel like an impossible weight against her bones. Ro understands, viscerally, how Audra revels in being blood, muscle, bone.

"Oh." Ro wants to dig fingertips into Audra's flesh, into Xal's, and hold onto this moment forever. But too soon, the connection is broken.

"Wow." Audra is the first to step back. "That was…intense."

Her pupils are dilated, her breath fast. Ro steps back as well, chill with a fresh awareness of the space between them. Something in Ro aches to close the gap, but the familiar horror is there as well: it wouldn't be the same, couldn't ever be the same, inside this skin.

"You're glowing." Audra smiles.

Bits of light dance at the edges of Ro's vision.

"It's beautiful." Audra takes a half step, but stops.

Ro's throat is closed — thick. Eyes squeeze shut, a deep breath, then Ro looks at Audra again just in time to catch the tail end of disappointment, the smile fading. The back of Audra's neck blushes, just blood colors now, the deep sea faded as she turns to Xal.

"Thank you." The faint quiver in her voice might be the aftershock of touch, or something else.

::Tone — Formal/Pleased: You are welcome. Audra. Thank you for sharing memories and experience of your world.::

The ache lessens in Ro's throat, fading to a sensation more like a bruise than a fresh wound.

"The night you were attacked, the first night, it wasn't the first time you left the Zone, was it?" Audra's question surprises Ro.

::Tone — Statement/Truthful: No.::

"How many times?"

Ro grips the counter, watching Audra and Xal. How is it they understand each other so well, so quickly? Or is it only that Ro's own curiosity blocked out certain aspects of Xal? Or perhaps because Audra is more used to processing sensation, she was less overwhelmed. Now that Ro thinks about it, it's obvious. How could Xal have been happy — how could any Immie be happy — confined to the Zone? All the times Ro traveled to Xal's shop, never once thinking Xal might want to leave, experience the wider world. Ro's skin flushes hot, but neither Xal nor Audra is paying attention.

::Tone — Statement/Truthful: The attack happened the fifth time.::

"Where were you going?" Audra leans forward; Ro leans, too, gravity pulling them both toward Xal's center.

Concentric rings spread across Xal's flesh, as though from a dropped stone. Now Xal is the color of moss, of sunlight, filtered through pine trees.

::Tone — Statement/Confidential: Some are patient, but not all. There is a group who would see the Zone change, the border gone.::

"Who?" Both Xal and Audra turn as though they'd forgotten Ro.

::Tone — Statement/Anger: It is a small group. One is in your city government, working to change things from within. But it is too slow. Others would wait. Not all are so patient.::

Not all, Ro thinks. Like Xal, restless, hungry for change.

"Is that why you've been leaving the Zone alone? Trying to start fights?"

Again, Ro is surprised at Audra's words, her insight. How willfully blind has Ro been? How much time has been wasted that could have been spent helping?

::Tone — Statement/Defensive: Violence is noticed. It is the quickest way to change.::

"We want to help," Ro speaks before Audra can, but glances to the side to see Audra's lips pressed into a thin line. Breath held, waiting for Audra to object, but she does not.

Xal rotates without moving, encompassing both Audra and Ro with eyeless attention.

::Tone — Formal/Request: Will you leave the Zone with me. To meet with my friend in the government.::

"Is that wise?" Audra glances at Ro.

"I think we should do it."

Audra hesitates, frowning, then shrugs, moving toward the door. Ro hurries to catch up. The air sings between them — Ro, a string pulled taut, thrumming a note of excitement, Audra simply tight, her note as yet unplayed.

"You don't have to do this." Ro's voice is low so Xal, following behind, won't hear.

Audra shakes her head, but doesn't answer. She keeps her hands in her pockets, gaze fixed on the wet stones.

"Hey!" The shout draws Ro up short, bringing the realization they've crossed out of the Zone.

Xal crowds behind them, all three looking toward a knot of men and women emerging from the bar across the street.

"You can't be here." One of the men points at Xal.

To Ro's surprise, Xal slides past them, gathering limbs together the way a human would draw themselves up to stand tall.

::Tone — Fear/Pride: It does not break any laws.::

Of course not; the rules are all unwritten, enforced by silent consent, by looking the other way. Ro's fingers clench – a body caught between fight and flight, heart pounding.

"Fucking Immie! Get back in the Zone." Another man joins the first, the rest of the group bunching closer.

"We should go back," Audra says.

"No." Ro turns deliberately, walking away from the group, further away from the Zone.

Xal and Audra follow, the weight of hostile gazes tracking them. Fear and hope mix in equal parts. Xal is right – if they spark enough conflicts, people can't continue to look the other way. A bottle explodes, glass spraying at their feet.

"Keep walking," Ro murmurs, picking up the pace.

A second bottle flies, higher this time, bouncing off Ro's shoulder before hitting the ground.

"I'm calling the cops." Audra pulls out her phone.

Pounding footsteps, then one of the men grabs Ro's shoulder. Instinct brings Ro's hands up to break the contact with a shove. The man reels on slick, neon-stained pavement and loses his balance, landing hard. One of the women in the group laughs, nervous, unsteady.

Another projectile glances off Ro's cheek, stinging. Ro touches the spot and fingers come away wet with blood. Audra whispers into her phone, voice low and urgent. Xal moves again, a solid mass between Ro and Audra and the group of men and women. The man Ro accidentally knocked down gets to his feet, his face red.

For a moment, no one moves. The red-faced man's fingers curl, his jaw clenched. Ro sees the moment of decision, but isn't fast enough to shout a warning.

It doesn't matter. Xal is there, then not. The man's blow never lands and he stumbles, but keeps his feet this time. One of the women casts about for something to use as a weapon.

"We have to get out of here," Audra says.

Xal holds a line between the two groups of humans. More people emerge from the bar, some merely curious, others spoiling for a fight.

"We're about to have a full-blown mob on our hands." Audra plucks at Ro's sleeve, not touching flesh.

This time, Ro doesn't see the moment of decision, or even where the punch comes from. Fist connects with jaw, and Ro hits the ground. Shouts, feet scuffling. Someone yells. Ro looks up in time to see Xal lift one of the men, tossing him away. Xal's colors and movements speak anger and distress.

A siren cuts through the night, freezing everyone in place. As the cop cars stop, bodies scatter. Ro stands. Audra and Xal move closer, the three of them alone making no attempt to flee as the cops climb from their cars.

⚔

"It might be a while, are you sure you wouldn't..." The officer assigned to babysit them glances nervously between Audra and Ro, trying to pretend he doesn't see Xal at all.

They're in an empty interrogation room, out of the way. They've given their statements, declined to press charges, and been assured no charges are being leveled against them, though the cop delivering the news didn't look happy about it. He'd looked even less happy when Ro requested sanctuary, using the police station as a safe space to meet with Xal's friend. Ro credits Audra with charming him into reluctantly agreeing.

"No. We're fine right here." Audra smiles sweetly, seeming to enjoy the way Xal's presence makes the cops uncomfortable, now that the immediate danger has passed.

The officer withdraws, and Audra pours two cups of coffee from the carafe he leaves behind. In the corner, Xal ripples in silence. Ro's cheek is sore, but the blood has dried and there will be no lasting damage.

But the bruise goes deeper than Ro's skin. Something has changed, but not changed enough. There has to be more; Ro feels it, the seed of an idea starting to grow. Talking to Xal's friend is a first step, but they have to push harder if they want real change.

"I want to go to the Immie homeworld," Ro says, voicing the growing notion in a remarkably even tone. Xal and Audra register surprise — human and inhuman.

"There should be ambassadors on both sides working toward change. You're right, Xal, violence gets attention, but we can do better than that."

As the words stop, Ro's cheeks burn. Said aloud, it sounds ridiculous.

::Tone — Statement/Uncertain: It might be arranged. Humans have never been, but it is not impossible.::

Xal unfolds from the corner, moving closer to the table in the center of the room. Audra puts her hand on the table, near but not touching Ro.

"Ro?"

Ro turns.

"If Xal can arrange it, if it's possible, I have to go. I'm sorry."

Audra's hand moves, not withdrawing, fingers curling in on themselves, a knot of confusion and pain.

"I'm sorry," Ro says again. And again, words are inadequate. For just a moment, Ro considers bridging the gap, touching the back of Audra's hand, but it wouldn't be the same. They shared a moment with Xal, but there's still too much space between them. Necessary space, space Ro cannot bridge.

"I thought..." Audra looks down, studying the table's faux-wood grain. "Maybe because of what happened..."

The lines of her body pull inward. It hurts Ro to look at her, but their truths are too different. Audra must know that.

"I can't change who I am." Ro doesn't look away from Audra, hoping she'll understand.

One of Audra's shoulders lifts and falls again. It might be agreement, dismissal, or shrugging off an absent touch.

"If I go, what will you do?" Ro asks.

"I don't know." Audra traces circles on the fake wood; Ro can almost feel it through the tips of Audra's fingers. "We'll see what happens with Xal's friend. Maybe I'll join the cause. Maybe I won't. I'll keep working, and life will go on."

Audra looks up, and her expression does something complicated. Her eyes are bright, but the light in them reminds Ro of reflections glinting off broken glass.

"My life doesn't begin and end with you, you know." The edge of a smile touches Audra's mouth. "I do have other friends. Family."

The smile becomes a grin. "I like you, Ro. We're friends. I'll miss you, but you're not breaking my heart."

Ro's pulse trips. Audra sounds sincere, Ro believes her, but at the same time Ro doesn't have enough experience to differentiate the temporary sting of rejection from something deeper. Maybe if Ro leaves and comes back, things will be better. Maybe they can learn a mode of friendship — better, deeper — one that doesn't cause either of them pain.

Audra's fingers uncurl. She presses her palm flat against the wood.

"Are you…" Ro hesitates, uncertain how to end the sentence: *Are you sure?* or *Are you okay?*

Xal shifts closer, body forming a complicated pattern. The colors chasing across Xal's skin are sunlight, leaves, and the sensation of flying, not falling. Xal unfurls a limb, brushing the back of Audra's hand with the briefest of touches. The air smells of tangerines and Audra's eyes widen, as if Xal whispered something just for her.

Audra draws her hand away from the table, pressing it to her heart. Ro feels it, the steady thump of blood and life and warmth inside Audra's skin.

On the table, the ghost outline of Audra's hand remains. Footsteps approach
the door, but Ro's attention remains fixed on the table. The fading shape, the
memory of touch, outlines possibility. It is everything.

THE PORNOGRAPHER'S ASSISTANT

The door cracks open, a rust scream. Light enters the bunker. A spill of sand…
grain ticks over grain, inaudible to human ears, and chases footsteps echoing
on the metallic floor.

Has he returned? The Master?

No. I know — human lives are moth-wing brief, and just as delicate. And
it's been years — not sleeping, not dreaming, but…waiting. Longer than a
human lifespan by far.

But who else would come, after so long? Who else would dig through ages
of sand piled against the bunker door? No one knew where we fled, save the
Master.

And now, hands turn the wheel, and it shrieks, the only sound after ages
of *tick, tick, tick* — grains falling against rust, and counting off the years of our
exile. My exile. The Master's ended long ago.

But I remain.

A breath, sharp-drawn, chases footsteps and tumbled grains of sand, the second sound against the silence in all these years. My eyes, never closed, *open*.

✖

Anique's breath catches, heart slamming the roof of her mouth.

There's someone in the tomb, someone sitting at what can only be the Great Pornographer's desk. She backs away, one step, sweat prickling beneath her clothes. Irrational as it is, her first thought is that it must be the Pornographer's desiccated corpse. *Pernaud's Tomb* — the name was meant to be a joke.

She should flee. She knows she should. But she's come so far, searched so long. And this is the bunker where Pernaud lived out his exile. It has to be. A find like this is every archeologist's dream. But more than that, it's *her* dream, the very core of her, a splinter lodged at the heart of her being.

Hands shaking, she lifts the goggles from her eyes. After the terrible wash of sun, burning the wastes pure white, the dark is a relief. Still, she blinks. And forces her pulse to calm. She reverses her flight, and steps forward. Sand trickles in at her heels.

"Hello?" Even whispered, her voice is too loud, crashing against the silence.

Slowly her eyes adjust; the figure resolves. Not a corpse, but metal in the shape of a human being. An automaton.

"Oh." Anique's breath catches again, a different speeding of her pulse this time.

As if afraid of waking a sleeper, she approaches the Pornographer's desk.

The automaton's face is thin-beaten silver, hung upon gears and delicate wires forming the rough shape of a skull. From the skull trails a spine, each vertebra perfectly formed. From the spine, shoulder blades spread outward like wings, and a pelvis flares at the base. Legs, arms, collarbone, knees — a perfect fleshless skeleton. Except for the hands. Like the face, they are plated in thin sheets of metal, bright as starlight. The metal is jointed, and the fingers curl around a pen, a feathered quill, which is poised over a roll of vellum.

The automaton's lips look as though they might part at any moment. Dark eyes shine like spilled ink, like black glass, fixed on the last word written on the page. Anique leans close, wonder-caught. Her breath fogs the silver cheek. Unable to help herself, she touches fingertips to metal skin. Light fills the pooled black. Even though they were not closed, Anique senses the eyes open.

✖

Fingertips touch. Perfect whorls imprint in a thin layer of breath. Exhaled condensation gathers beneath her hand; tiny pearls of moisture lining up in the ridges of her skin, a constellation, a galaxy, spiraling out in the echoed shape of her fingerprints.

I have no breath to gasp, no way to let her know I am alive but to turn. Slowly, so as not to startle her, I move my head. She startles nonetheless, tripping over her heels and hitting the ground, eyes wide.

"My apologies." My voice catches, a faint click and whir in the time-stiffened gears. "I did not mean to frighten you."

"I didn't mean to… I'm sorry. I was looking for…" The woman scrambles to her feet, but remains rooted where she stands.

The flight impulse tenses her muscles, bunching them beneath her skin, but she doesn't flee. Arrested by fascination at my strangeness, perhaps?

I assess. She is short, her body swathed in traveling clothes. An inventory — heavy boots, laced high; cargo pants, many pocketed; a cotton shirt buttoned tight against her throat; goggles pushed up into wind-spiked hair, red as flame. Straps cross her body left and right; a satchel and a canteen hang against either hip.

Despite the space between us, I feel the tension pouring from her in waves. She is afraid in a way I have never known fear.

My sight is not sight; it is a sensation far more complex, far more complete. Looking at her, I feel the sweat beaded on her skin. I feel the quickness of her breath, and the tremble-beat of blood at wrist and throat. There is something else, too.

Metal. There is metal beneath her skin.

It hums. Resonance reaches across the space between us. Reaching for me. It sings.

I have no heart to beat, just as I have no breath to speed.

"I was looking for Pernaud's Tomb."

I do not miss the reverence with which she speaks the Master's name.

The woman's skin warms, a subtle thing, blood spreading to her cheeks as if embarrassed by her admission. So: in her eyes, I am not a thing before which she can mindlessly speak with no fear of reprisal. She perceives me as she would any sentient thing.

Her image fixes in my eyes thus: she stands uncertain, poised for flight. Can she see herself — a ghost drifting in my eyes' endless black? I want to show her what I see — an echo where she is safe. There is no need to flee.

"The Master has not been here in a very long time."

Bolted to the chair, to the table, to the ground, I cannot rise or approach her. I cannot reciprocate the touch lingering on my cheek like a scar where her fingers rested for an instant. But I will remember her, always. Just as I remember the Master's hand, heavy and sad on my shoulder. So marked, I can never forget.

"The master?" The woman blinks confusion. "I don't understand."

"I am the Pornographer's Assistant. Pernaud was my Master." Will the truth keep her here, or will disappointment decide her flight?

Her eyes widen further, catching light. They are green. She steps closer, still skittish, but her gaze moves to the vellum. Though it is long since my pen last moved, I hear the scratch of the nib over a surface thin as skin; it haunts the silence.

The woman's lips move, reading over my shoulder. This time the blood spreads beyond her cheeks, down her neck, and further — a quickening throughout her body. She shifts, pressing her legs close together for a moment before remembering herself.

"His assistant...you recorded Pernaud's words? You were his scribe?" Her breath's pace matches that of her blood.

"He spoke. I wrote." My answer is not a lie.

The woman reaches out, the gesture as unconscious as her fingers on my cheek. Her nails are ragged, torn short. Blood traces the curve of her left thumb. Her skin is chapped, cracked around her knuckles. She touches an edge of the vellum, shy.

I have no heart to beat, no breath to catch. I ache nonetheless.

The woman looks up, and fear leaves her eyes. She will not run. She removes the canteen and her satchel, setting both on the floor. She takes in the bunker — the single cot, the shelves, long-since emptied.

"I've read all of Pernaud's books." Her voice is soft. "People kept smuggling them into the city, even after his exile."

A brief smile touches her lips, then she looks abashed.

"Of course, you know that." Her gaze, skittish, touches me again. "People still read them today. He's still famous."

The air in the bunker scarcely stirs. Even out of the blaze of sun, visible beyond the open door, the space is warm. Dream-caught, the woman undoes the top few buttons of her sweat-and-travel-stained shirt, exposing the arch of her throat. Shadows pool in the hollow just above her collarbone.

"I can't believe he really wrote here," she says.

"He spoke. I wrote." I repeat the words, filled with the sudden, inexplicable need for her to understand.

I should not feel hubris; I should not desire to have even one person in the whole, vast universe know. But I do.

The woman's head snaps up. Her lips part. Doubt blooms in her eyes. A nervous gesture — she runs her fingers along her collarbone. "I ... I don't understand."

But I think she does.

✖

Anique's pulse beats in her wrists and throat. Her blood, her heart, her breath — all are too loud in the silence. She's been searching for so long. Even before she started looking for the tomb, she's been searching. Wanting. And now?

Her heart stutters; she is afraid. Hope is such a fragile thing. Does she dare close it in her hand? No. She should push it down, crush it deep into the dark corners of her mind. If she never lets her desire see light, it need never be real. If she never admits it, even to herself, she need never have her heart broken.

Her eyes close, and she sees Pernaud's words written on her eyelids. They are soaked through her being, cut through her skin, deep as bone. She opens her eyes.

From the memory of crisp-printed text in her smuggled editions, her gaze travels to the flowing script beneath the automaton's pen. The ink shimmers, more than black. It contains hints of peacock blue, bruise purple, emerald green. It is every color, and no color, all at once. Traced on the vellum, the hand loops, curves, flows to capture the essence of the word written. In the automaton's hands, the words she supposed to be Pernaud's *come alive*.

Watching her, light slides across the automaton's eyes.

And it is beautiful.

Shaped bones, thin beaten flesh, fingers curled around the quill pen. Anique holds her breath, wanting, and not wanting to hear how the silver lips will answer her. Her fingers rise and curl, too, echoing the silver ones, and digging into the skin over her collarbone. Teeth catch lip; she bites down, tasting salt and sand.

"The Master…" The automaton falters.

Anique doesn't miss the catch, the hitch in the gears. There is doubt in the strange, flat tone.

"The Master could not read, or write. He told stories. I wrote…" The automaton stops; pain flickers in its inhuman eyes.

"Oh." She lets out a breath, every breath.

And the release goes all the way through her body, shivering just beneath her skin. Her sweat cools, gooseflesh puckers tight.

"You wrote all his stories. You wrote everything, and he never knew?"

"Yes," the automaton says. "His stories were…inelegant. I improved them."

Silver fingers tighten on the pen. From the automaton's curled hand, Anique traces the line of its arm, the curve of its spine visible through its silver ribs behind the tangle of wires. It is bolted to the chair; the chair is joined to the desk. The Pornographer's Assistant can never stand, never move from the chair that was carried from the city in Pernaud's great flight.

"Oh." The sound escapes her lips again. Her heart breaks on it. "Oh."

She closes her eyes; a glimmer of moisture beads her lashes, never falling.

∾

The metal beneath her skin sings. I feel it. Words crowd her tongue; I watch her struggle with them.

She is so frightened, so alone. She is in so much pain.

Her voice comes at last, a tremor in the silence. With her eyes closed, it seems easier for her to speak. What does she see, behind the blood-screen of her lids? Is there a safe space, ink black, glass smooth, lit with a thousand stars?

"I...I was in an accident. The car...the road was slick...and it broke through the barrier. Everything was weightless. Then I fell."

She pauses, breath hitching, and I fear she won't continue. After a moment, she does.

"Sometimes I wake up in the middle of the night, and I think there's broken glass in my hair. I can't move because I'm terrified the splinters will lodge in my skin.

"My bones...everything shattered. My heart stopped. My lungs collapsed. I shouldn't have survived. I didn't *live*, so I shouldn't have survived. But doctors rebuilt me. They put metal under my skin – pins, plates, joints. No one asked me what I wanted. They cut me open again and again, and stitched me back together and acted as though I should be grateful because they saved my life."

She opens her eyes. They shine, but no tears fall. She undoes the rest of the buttons holding her shirt closed, and sheds it, a second skin. Her boots are next, then socks, pants, everything, until she stands naked save for the fine network of scars, imperceptible to the human eye.

But I see them. And I understand.

Naked, she seems less frightened. There is nothing left to hide. She takes a breath; it lifts her small, near-flat breasts. Her nipples are dark, and crinkled hard.

Her voice steady now, she offers one last confession.

"After the accident, or maybe always, I was different. I don't like boys. I don't like girls. But Pernaud's books made me feel less alone."

I have no heart to break for her. But I wish I did.

There is longing in the metal under her skin. It shivers, full of unspoken pain.

"I..." My gears snag. I cannot close my eyes. "I cannot touch you. I can only write."

Will she feel my sorrow, my ache, twin to hers? I try to hold her in my eyes, drifting, reflected in the blackness. I understand. My words hang in the air between us.

"Yes." Her answer is breathless. "Write. Please."

⚞

And Anique feels it. She feels the quill move across her flesh as it moves across the page, inscribing Pernaud's words — the automaton's words. The nib, cutting sharp, draws blood, lays bare her bones. They sing.

A faint vibration, a resonant hum sounds from the metal inside her. It's like standing beneath a web of power lines; the sensation raises the tiny hairs on her skin.

It's like standing in the heart of a storm. She feels it in the space between her bones.

The first word is *lips*, and they chase across her skin. Warmth radiates out, spreading from her ribs to caress her belly, tracing the curve of her spine. The touch, feather-light, puckers her flesh. *Breath* chases lips, brushing her cheek, caressing the line of her jaw. *Touch* finds her mouth with one finger.

She parts her lips, hungry. And *touch* follows the arch of her throat as she tips her head back; it pauses in the hollow above her collarbone. Shadow-light, it becomes a palm, fingers splayed to cup first one breast, and then a second hand, another *touch,* takes the other. The words are physical. They spark light from her bones. She quivers, bowstring taut.

A nib, drawn feather light, teases circles around her nipples, traces her ribs, and continues down.

Her legs can't hold her anymore. Anique sinks to her knees, back arched. The pen moves, scratches vellum and skin. From the automaton's pen, the word *tongue* is born, all loops and swirls, and it moves across her belly. *Tongue* dips into her navel, describes the curve of her hipbones.

And she is falling, weighted and weightless. The car is spinning, end over end, raining glittering shards of glass, but this time she is not afraid.

Electricity arcs beneath her skin.

Inside and outside, she responds — legs part, lips part, she gasps.

And she kicks out hard, legs pumping, swinging out into sunlight beneath the leaf shadows of a tree. Ropes burn her palms, as she clings to them. It is before the accident, when she was only herself, when she could fly. Her heart spins through the space between her bones. She is weightless, and gravity pulls her down, sucking at her, claiming her. And she is falling, and falling, and falling.

But she is not afraid.

Even kneeling is too much. Anique slides, skin slick with sweat, until she lies on her back. Her legs spread wide, feet planted on the floor. The automaton's pen directs her now, and she surrenders to it as she never has — never could — to any human touch. She lifts her lips to a lover who isn't there, a lover who is everywhere.

The words slide down her belly, taste the soft flesh of thighs. *Teeth* nip gently, followed by *finger*, and again *tongue*. The words are both and neither, teasing her. The word *wet* slides between her legs, and she is. *Fingers* and *tongue* trace her clit, an aching circle, and slide inside her, deep, deeper, all the way through.

The words swell inside her, opening her wider, wanting and giving, hungering and sating. They demand everything of her, and she gives. *Gasp* parts her lips, and turns into *moan*.

She is shot through with light. Body arcing in response. Her spine, electric. Her skin, a shiver of notes only she can hear. The pen moves, and the vellum scrolls out, spills from the desk and pools around her. She gathers it, and it runs over her breasts, between her legs, filling all the places where she is hollow.

And she has never been this wet.

And her nipples have never been so hard.

And she has never wanted anything more.

A cry fills her throat, stealing breath.

When it comes, when she comes, it strips her raw.

And she is flying forever, and falling forever — caught at the top of the arc, suspended, perfect. And she will never, ever come down.

※

The woman lies almost still, her only movement tiny aftershocks running across her skin. She breathes out, releasing air that has tightened her chest for years. Moisture leaks from between closed lids, and she turns her face away.

My pen falls still. I watch her, not sleeping, not dreaming, just breathing for a while.

The vellum slicks to her skin, binding her. My words hold her, keeping her safe.

An eternity passes. Sand ticks against the metal walls. When she opens her eyes, they are bright and dry. She stands, legs trembling. She looks at me, and for a moment, I hang suspended in her eyes. A silver ghost, a fleshless skeleton, drifting in all that green. In her gaze, I am so much more. She sees me. She understands.

For a moment, I want to ask her to stay. For a moment, we were one. But the moment is past. She will move on, and I will remain. I will remember.

She bends, gathers her clothes and holds them to her chest. Regret flickers in her eyes. Teeth touch lips, bite soft, as if to hold back words. Before they can escape, she turns away.

I wish I could close my eyes, but I cannot.

At the door, over her shoulder, she whispers, "Thank you."

FOR THE REMOVAL OF UNWANTED GUESTS

The witch arrived at precisely 11:59 p.m., just as September ticked over to October, on the day after Michael Remmington moved into the house on Washington Street. She knocked at exactly midnight.

The house was all boxes, and Michael all ache from moving them. He'd been sitting on an air mattress — the bed wouldn't be delivered for another week — staring at a crossword puzzle at least five years old. He'd found it in the back of the closet, yellow as bone, and peeled it from the floor — an unwitting gift from the previous tenant.

Michael opened the door, only questioning the wisdom of it after it was done. It was midnight in a strange neighborhood; he wore a bathrobe and slippers, and he'd left his phone upstairs. If it turned out to be an axe murderer at the door, he wouldn't even be able to call 911.

"Hello," the witch said. "I'm moving in."

A suitcase sat on her left, and a black cat on her right. The cat's tail coiled around its neatly placed feet. It blinked at Michael, its gaze as impassive as the witch's.

Michael couldn't say how he knew she was a witch, but he did, deep down in his bones. The truth of it sat at his core, as inevitable as moonrise, or spaghetti for dinner on Tuesdays.

"Okay," he said, which was not what he'd meant to say at all.

But he'd already stepped back, and the witch had already picked up her bag and crossed the threshold.

"I mean — What?"

The cat dragged a silken tail across Michael's shins, following the witch. It felt like a mark of approval. A chill wind chased the cat, swirling fallen leaves; Michael closed the door. The witch set her bag down, turning a slow circle while remaining in place.

"This house should have a witch." When she stopped, she faced him.

Her eyes were green, like pine boughs in winter, or the shadows between them.

"A witch needs to live here," she said, sniffing the air. "Can't you feel it?"

Michael sniffed, smelling only the witch herself. She smelled of cinnamon and fresh-cut cedar. She didn't look like a witch, except that she did. Not that Michael knew what witches looked like. People, he guessed. Mostly.

She wore black, a loose-fitting sweater over a long skirt that seemed to have layers. It reminded him of petals, like a flower, hung upside down. Her shoes clicked when she walked.

Michael couldn't begin to guess the witch's age. When he closed just his left eye, she might be around forty, but when switched and closed just his right eye, she seemed closer to fifty. Either way, her skin was smooth, except for a few crow's feet around her eyes, and a few lines at the corners of her mouth. Her hair hung half-way down her back, dark brown like thick molasses, threaded with strands of honey, rather than gray, and she wore a lot of jewelry — most of it chunky, most of it silver.

"Okay," he said again, then, "why?" after he thought about it.

"The windows are in upside down." The witch pointed.

Michael couldn't see anything unusual, but considered he wouldn't know an upside down window from a right-side-up one.

"The board for that step," the witch indicated a tread halfway up the staircase, "comes from a pirate ship that wrecked off the coast of Cape Cod, near Wellfleet."

She paced three steps forward. The floorboards clonked hollow under her shoes.

"There's a black cat buried in the leftmost corner of the basement. Sorry." She addressed the last to the cat at her feet, not Michael.

"So, a witch should live here. I'll take the attic."

"But it's my house," Michael said. "I have papers and everything. You can't just…"

The witch lifted her suitcase: a small thing, battered at the edges, and held closed with two brass catches. She gathered her skirt, and Michael found himself following her up the stairs.

"I haven't even unpacked yet," Michael said.

"I'll help you in the morning. I get up at seven. Tea with honey." She rounded on him so suddenly Michael nearly tripped on his heels.

They'd come to the foot of the second set of stairs, leading to the attic. Close up, the witch's eyes were flecked with gold, like bits of mica in stone. Michael stepped back a pace, but was annoyed when he did. He could follow her up the stairs if he wanted. Couldn't he?

"Hoop," she said.

"What?"

"It's the answer to 47 across." She flicked the crossword puzzle, and Michael realized he still held the yellowed paper in his hand.

"All around, Robin's backward friend. Four letters. It's Pooh spelled backward. As in Winnie the. Sixteen down is Marilyn Monroe. That should give you enough to get started."

"Oh." Michael didn't know what else to say.

"You'll find the mugs in the third box from the left in the kitchen. For the tea. I'll see you in the morning." Halfway up the steps, she paused, and turned again. Her eyes were luminous in the dark.

"You'll want to shut the windows. It's going to rain."

Michael stared until the door at the top of the stairs closed. He listened to the witch's shoes clomp over the floorboards, and wondered where she would sleep. There was nothing in the attic except dust and dead spiders. Maybe she'd hang herself from the ceiling like a bat. Maybe witches didn't sleep at all.

"Okay. Goodnight. I guess," he said to the silence.

Michael went back to his room. He closed the door, and after a moment's consideration, closed the window, too. The witch's cat had taken up residence in the middle of his pillow. It opened one eye, defying Michael to displace it. He sat gingerly and when the cat didn't leave, he risked petting it. The cat rewarded him with a faint purr.

As if on cue, rain tapped light fingers against the glass. The house creaked, settling its bones around them. No, not around them, around the witch. A few moments later, the downpour began in earnest.

The witch came down the stairs precisely at seven, the cat at her heels. She seemed to be wearing the same clothes as the night before, only in the dust-laden light slanting through the kitchen windows they looked deep green, or blue, rather than black. Michael wondered if he simply hadn't noticed the subtleties of shading last night. He handed the witch a mug of tea.

She breathed in steam, beringed hands wrapped around the mug, which he'd found exactly where she said it would be. He'd found the tea and kettle there, too, and other kitchen things, which remained in the box, largely untouched. Michael sipped from a mug that had been chipped in the moving process; to his annoyance, he'd saved the good mug for the witch.

"You can't stay here," Michael said.

He'd rehearsed the words in the predawn light, lying in bed before coming downstairs to make the witch her tea. In his mind, the witch had accepted them, and everything had been perfectly reasonable. Normal. In the bright sunlight, with the witch looking at him over her mug, he wavered.

"Look, you don't even know anything about me. I could be an axe murderer!"

"Are you?"

"Well, no, but..."

The witch's cat leapt onto the counter, a stream of black ink defying gravity. It twitched its tail, smug. Michael wanted to ask how long the witch planned to stay, and what her name was. Would she split the mortgage payment? Did she have a job? Did she expect him to take turns cleaning out the kitty litter? But the witch's even gaze dismissed all his questions before he could voice them. Maybe a witch *should* live here.

If last night was any indication, the witch mostly kept to herself. He'd certainly slept much better, as in sleeping at all, once she'd arrived. It was as if the house had been holding its breath, waiting for her, and when it finally relaxed, he could, too.

"Is there a problem, Michael Remmington?" the witch asked.

The question came so suddenly, Michael choked on his tea. He was certain he'd never told her his name. This morning, her eyes were amber. She no longer smelled of cinnamon, but of salt; it made him think of storms and shipwrecks.

"No. Yes. I mean... Look, I don't want a roommate. Or a cat. I just want to live a normal, quiet, happy life. In *my* house." He left unspoken the word *alone*.

The witch narrowed her eyes, as if she'd heard the part he hadn't said. The cat pushed its head against Michael's hand. Instead of shooing it away, he scratched it behind the ears. This time, there was no mistaking the purr.

A stray leaf, snatched by the wind, smacked into the window, making Michael jump. He had no reason to feel guilty. His name was on all the legal documents for the house. The witch had crashed into his life, invited herself in. He didn't owe her a thing.

"Look…" Michael said.

"Thank you for the tea." The witch set her cup down.

Her eyes had shifted color again, taking on the hue of burnt wood. Michael could almost smell smoke in the air.

"Give me your hand." The witch held out her own hand, palm up. Her bracelets rattled.

She looked younger this morning, no more than thirty-five, at a guess, but Michael was tired of guessing.

"What? Why?"

"So I can be sure you're not an axe murderer," the witch said. Her smile suggested she might be laughing at him.

He gave the witch his hand. She traced the lines, and her eyes turned pale violet, inexplicably making Michael think of dragons. The witch pursed her lips. She said, "Hmmm." He couldn't tell whether it was a good thing, or a bad thing.

A line of concentration appeared about a third of the way across the witch's lip, like an old scar. Like a sudden flash of lightning in the dark, Michael knew things about her — all true down in his bones.

The witch had drowned in 1717, and burned to death in 1691. In the 1800s, she'd died with a rope around her neck. In 1957, she'd been murdered — a kitchen knife to the gut and blunt-force trauma to the head combined.

Michael sucked in a sharp breath.

"It's all true," the witch said, without looking up.

Could she feel him in her head? Or was it like a broadcast, and he just happened to be tuned into her frequency?

"Sorry."

"I don't mind," she said, and then, "I'll be staying until at least Halloween."

"What happens on Halloween?"

She let go of Michael's hand, blinking eyes gone the color of pumpkins. There was a flicker of disappointment in her gaze, as though she couldn't understand why he regularly failed to keep up. The connection broke, taking the witch's deaths, spooling away from her, with it. Which was just as well, because Michael knew somehow they'd been headed for a knife made of stone, and a blood-covered altar, and he suspected there were things in that death in particular he didn't want to see.

"That's up to you." The disappointment in the witch's eyes turned to something else, something deeper and sadder that made Michael's skin crawl.

An apology rose, and he clamped it down. Nothing about the witch made sense. He pressed his lips tight. He couldn't be sure, but he thought he heard her sigh. It reminded him of leaves pulled from branches by the October wind, of shortening days, and snow piling up behind the clouds.

"What do you want?"

Michael didn't realize he'd spoken aloud until the witch smiled, brief as a moth's wing. But the sadness hadn't left her eyes. She held up a hand and ticked off points.

"I want to live in this house. I want tea every morning at seven, with toast on Wednesdays. I want not to die until I'm good and ready." She lowered her hand. "The rest I'm still figuring out."

Ink threaded the gold of her eyes; Michael fought the urge to shiver.

He wished the witch would stop looking at him. But when her gaze moved away, going to the window, he felt lost and unanchored.

The witch's eyes were green again. They reminded him of a toad he'd caught by accident in third grade. He'd given it to his teacher, who'd explained patiently that toads were much happier living outside than in classrooms, and would he please release it back into the wild.

"You should unpack now," the witch said.

Her voice was very quiet, but it still made Michael flinch. He stared at her for a moment before realizing the words were a dismissal. Since he couldn't think of a good retort, he obeyed.

✁

Michael didn't know where the witch went during the day, and he didn't ask. He could picture her flying around the neighborhood on a broom, or transforming into a flock of birds. He could just as easily see her curling up in the attic reading books on economic theory.

He still didn't know her name. He didn't know anything about her really, and sometimes he amused himself by making up little stories about what she was doing at the exact moment it occurred to him to wonder — horseback riding, bowling, waltzing with the Zombie King of Austria on a floor made of crystal teeth. It annoyed him when he caught himself doing this. He constantly had to remind himself that the witch was an unwelcome intruder in his house. He couldn't let himself get used to her. He couldn't let her settle in and simply take over his life. Things just didn't work that way in the real world.

In college, he'd tried to picture what his life would be like after graduation. He'd long since given up on the high school fantasies of being a rock star, or an astronaut. He was tone deaf, and he'd barely passed intro to calculus. He didn't know exactly *what* he wanted to do with his life, but nowhere had his life plans included living with a witch. Magic was for fairy tales. Real life was bills and deadlines, not spells and potions.

Yet the witch stayed, and life went on as though she'd always been there, an inevitable fact as much as the bills and deadlines. He gave the witch's cat the name Spencer, one of several dozen secret names he imagined the cat had accumulated over its lifetimes, as cats do. Michael only ever saw the witch at seven in the morning, and then again after dusk, as though she ceased to exist in between, which he knew was as just as likely or improbable as every other scenario he'd dreamed for her.

On a Thursday afternoon, Michael found himself at the foot of the attic stairs, listening intently. He didn't know what he was listening for, but it never came, so he climbed the stairs. The witch's door stood open. It was just past three.

Afternoon sunlight, already burning to deep gold, slanted through a window set angle-wise in the slope of the roof. What the light illuminated was certainly nothing that had been in the attic before. Either the witch had snuck things in without making a sound, or magicked them into being from dust bunnies and dead spiders.

A rocking chair sat tucked under the angle of the roof, next to a white-painted dresser holding a single, season-incongruous daffodil in a slender vase. A braided rug lay on the floor between the dresser and the bed, and the bed was covered with a neat, white duvet. There was a dress-form in one corner, a carousel horse in the other, an empty birdcage hanging from the ceiling, a cello leaning against one wall, and seven identical pairs of shoes lined up beneath the second window. A sea chest footed the bed, and Spencer sat on it, tail twitching impatiently in response to Michael's wonder.

From the cat's perspective, Michael imagined, it was all so obvious. A chandelier hung, unlit, near the birdcage. The crystals caught the afternoon light, casting rainbows, and tinkled softly. The only thing Michael didn't see in the room was the witch's suitcase.

If he came back tomorrow, he truth-in-his-bones-knew the room would be different — there would be an easel, a fish tank, a music box, an accordion, and a plethora of bookshelves. Spencer jumped lightly from the chest, and wound around Michael's ankles. Where the cat had been sitting there was a leather bound book, swollen slightly, as though the pages had been wet and dried in crinkled waves.

The cat slid past Michael, leaving him alone in a room that suddenly seemed to contain less air than it had a moment before. He shouldn't, he knew he shouldn't, and he still watched himself reach out, his hand hovering just above the leather cover. His fingers touched down. He'd been expecting an electric shock, but nothing happened. The cover was soft, like worn velvet; the book was just a book.

He let out a breath. Still knowing he shouldn't, he flicked the cover aside. The book fell open near the middle, as though its spine had been broken there again and again. The pages were handwritten, the script thin and spidery, the ink brown.

For the Removal of Unwanted Guests
Midnight frost, one cup, melted
Trametes Versicolor, one handful
One each: tail feather of raven, crow, and owl
Six windfall apples
Soil from beneath a ripe pumpkin
Candy Corn, the proper kind

Michael's breath caught. If he didn't know better, he might think the witch had left the spell, the recipe, whatever it was, there for him to find. It was a trick, a trap, it had to be. He glanced around, expecting to find the witch in the doorway, her eyes the color of steel. But he was alone. And that was almost worse somehow.

With his pulse racing, Michael slipped his phone out of his pocket, and snapped a picture of the page. Then he slammed the book closed, turned, and fled down the stairs.

❧

On Sunday, he went apple picking. The place he chose also had pick-your-own pumpkins, which made at least two items on list from the witch's book easy. On the way home, he planned to stop at the store and buy candy corn. That was half the items right there. And that frightened him.

Driving home, jumpy and unsettled, Michael couldn't keep his eyes off the rearview mirror. He expected the witch to come bearing down on him at any moment, all blood and fire and vengeance. He pictured her in a storm cloud, lightning in her hair, her eyes the color of rain. He almost went off the road twice, and when he finally pulled into the driveway and killed the engine, his hands were shaking so badly he could barely remove the keys from the ignition.

What was he doing? The witch wasn't bothering him; he barely ever saw her. Why should he want to get rid of her? And what made him think a spell from a water-logged book would banish her? Fight fire with fire, and magic with magic.

Even if he could gather all the items, what was he supposed to do with them? Brew them up in the witch's tea like a potion, and trick her into drinking it? And if he did, what then? What if he chased her out and she died again? She had drowned and burned and hanged already. All she wanted was tea, to live in his house quietly, and not to die again. Was that so wrong?

He carried the items upstairs, and hid them under his bed. His heart wouldn't stop racing, and he couldn't get his breathing under control.

When he came back downstairs, he found the witch organizing the utensils in the kitchen drawers. Under the butter-warm light, her black clothes looked like an incredibly deep, dark red. The honey strands in her hair stood out. He couldn't even imagine what color her eyes must be. Spencer brushed against Michael's leg, and he nearly screamed.

After a moment, he scooped up the cat. Spencer purred, rubbing Michael's neck with its head.

"You're lucky," the witch said without turning. "She never lets anyone pick her up."

So, Spencer was a she.

"She's the one that found this place, you know." The witch's tone was conversational, but there was a hint of melancholy underneath it, wistful. "I could smell it, but I couldn't pinpoint it. She led me right here. She's got a better nose."

"Where…were you before?"

The witch paused, the knives, forks, and spoons stilling in her hands. Michael wasn't sure he wanted the answer.

"A long way away." The witch's shoulders stiffened.

Her words smelled of bonfires. They felt like dirt, filling his mouth. They tasted like Halloween.

His mind clicking over to her frequency again, Michael saw the witch walking barefoot along the side of a road, headlights sweeping over her through a heavy rain. Broken glass from a car accident cut her soles, but she didn't seem to care. She either walked to, or from, her most recent death, and it clung to her like a shadow. Whatever her death had been, or would be, it wasn't pleasant. Not that any death was ever pleasant, Michael supposed, except for perhaps dying quietly in your sleep.

"Witches don't die that way," the witch said, so softly he could barely hear her. He flinched, and Spencer squirmed out of his arms.

He should go upstairs right now and throw away the apples, the dirt, and the candy corn, pretend he'd never seen the list or been in the witch's room.

But if he did that, he'd be admitting she could stay. Even if he never said it out loud, he'd be inviting her into his life, and nothing would ever be normal again. Magic would be real, and witches, too. A woman could drown and hang and burn and still be in his kitchen organizing his spoons.

Cutlery rattled softly in the witch's hands. Michael stared at her back. If she turned around, the witch's eyes would be the color of smoke, the ghost of a thousand violent deaths drifting in the black at center of them. Could he live with all that death crowded behind her eyes? Could he live with all her impossibility? Michael was glad she kept her back to him. While the witch counted spoons, he turned silently, and slipped from the room.

✂

It snowed the day before Halloween. The last time Michael remembered that happening, he'd been about nine years old. His parents had bundled him off on a Boy Scout trip, up in the mountains. It snowed on October 30, and the Scout leaders cut the trip short after one night because it was too cold. They all came back on the bus with flakes still falling, and white dusting the ground. Michael's mother made him go trick-or-treating in a bulky snowsuit, so no one could tell he was supposed to be Spider-Man that year.

Michael stood in the open front door, coffee in hand, Spencer at his feet, watching the flakes fall. Carved pumpkins all along the street wore caps of white lace. It was peaceful, beautiful even, but Michael couldn't shake his deep unease.

He'd spent yesterday at a nature preserve, where he'd found the mushrooms and the feathers from the witch's list. At least half an hour of the excursion had been Michael sitting in the car with the heater going full blast, comparing mushrooms and feathers to Google image searches on his phone.

He still hadn't decided what he was going to do. He told himself to think of it as insurance. Just because he gathered the ingredients didn't mean he had to use them.

"You're letting out all the warm air." The witch's voice snapped Michael's spine straight, and he wheeled guiltily, accidentally stepping on Spencer's tail.

The cat yowled, and shot away; the witch glared. Her eyes reminded him of sea-wet stones, slammed by endless waves.

"It's my heating bill." The words came more sharply than he intended.

The witch pressed her lips into an even thinner line, breathing through her nose. She'd snapped at him last night, too when he'd suggested tacos for dinner. Spencer had hissed indiscriminately, taking in both their bristled postures without choosing sides, and stalked out the door when Michael had opened it to gather the mail.

Did she know he'd found the book? And if she did, why didn't she come out and say something, or cast a hex on him? Or whatever it was witches did when they were angry. She could turn him into a toad, and the house would be all hers. She wouldn't even have to share. Maybe it was the same for witches as vampires, and he had to invite her in, or she couldn't stay. He had no idea what the rules were, if there were any.

The witch shifted without moving, strain showing in her clenched jaw. Now, more than sea-wet stones, her eyes reminded him of lightning trapped beneath a skin of dark clouds.

There was only one day until Halloween. The witch had said she'd stay until Halloween at least, and the rest was up to him. Did that mean he was supposed to make the potion? That he was destined to betray her?

"Why me?" Michael asked.

He hadn't meant to speak at all. The witch's eyes turned the color of certain snakes Michael had seen on a nature show — the kind that hid in the sand, and uncoiled all at once to strike.

"Because this house needs a witch." The witch returned words like a slap.

"And I thought you needed one, too. But maybe I was wrong."

Even though she hadn't moved, she'd folded the space between them somehow. They were face to face, the witch leaning into him, her nose pointed at him accusation-wise.

"All I want is to live a normal life. Is that too much to ask?" Michael stepped back. Coffee slopped over the edges of his mug, barely missing the witch's toes.

"Yes." The door banged shut behind Michael, punctuating the word. Startled, Michael dropped his mug; shards of ceramic skittered across the floor.

The witch made an impatient gesture with her hand, and the ceramic shards flew across the hall and into the kitchen, pelting the sink like hail.

"Life isn't fair. Nobody gets to choose whether they have a normal happy one or not. If they did, do you think anyone would get sick, or have their hearts broken? Would anyone die? It doesn't work that way."

The witch's deaths were in her eyes again. And her eyes themselves flickered from moonlight, to toadstools, to tsunamis and flames. The heat of them, the cold of them, the shock of them drove him back another step. Michael opened his mouth, but the witch spun on her heel, and banged up the stairs.

The floorboards shuddered when she slammed her door, and plaster dust filtered down from the ceiling. Michael blinked, the grit catching in his eyes.

Something in him tightened, twisting. Her life wasn't fair, but her anger wasn't either. All he'd done was move into a house with upside-down windows and a staircase made of shipwrecks. And he could hardly be blamed for that.

"Damn it."

Michael's slippers smacked at his bare feet as he climbed the stairs. Inside his bathrobe, sweat gathered at the base of his spine. He knocked on the witch's door, and it swung open.

"I'm sorry," he said to an empty room.

Michael gaped. The bed, the dresser, the chandelier — all gone. And the witch, too. A tired looking cobweb hung where the birdcage had been, stirring on a breath of wind. Curtain-less windows let in gray light, showing the desiccated bodies of arachnids in the corners. Dust puffed, gritty beneath his feet.

The sheer emptiness of the room shot through him, a current driven like a spike from his soles all the way up his spine. It was the worst kind of absence and it sent him running down the stairs in unreasoned terror. The witch was so thoroughly gone, she might never have existed.

✖

The house bowed under the insubstantial weight of snow. No, it *mourned*. Down in its bones, the house was melancholy over the loss of the witch. Like a haunting, there were sounds and scents just on the edge of perception. Turning a corner, he would catch a whiff of the sea. He didn't dare touch the walls, knowing they'd weep salt-dampness against his skin. An unplayed note on a harpsichord sighed and shivered its way from the roof down to the basement where a black cat lay buried in the leftmost corner.

He needed to get the witch back.

Michael set out an hour before midnight with a measuring cup, his hands jammed in his pockets. Halloween stood on the other side of the clock's tick, all gathered up with fallen leaves and bats' wings and clouds across the moon. The snow had stopped, but the cold had deepened. The whole year waited to pivot on this point; the world was thin. It wasn't just the house — this night needed a witch, too.

A black cat streaked across his path. It might have been Spencer, or a random stray, he couldn't tell. The cat didn't pause. Michael glanced furtively in either direction. When he was certain he was alone, he used the razor blade he'd tucked into his jacket to shave the frost from his neighbor's pumpkin.

He felt like a fool. It was Devil's Night. The cops would be on high alert. What would they think of a man with a razor — even if it was only a Bic disposable — lurking outside his neighbor's houses, paying far too much attention to their pumpkins?

But he didn't have a choice. He would make the potion, and drink it himself. He was the unwanted guest that needed banishing. Then the witch would come back home, and everything would be the way it was supposed to be. It wasn't rational, but nothing about the witch was. Deep down on his bones, he knew the truth of it. He had to bring her back, because if he didn't... Because if he didn't, there wouldn't be a witch here.

The logic was as faulty as the logic of witches in general. And so it stood to reason his plan would work. It had to.

He moved to the next house, the next pumpkin. When he reached the end of the block, the cup was a quarter full. By the time he'd gone another block, the measuring cup was half full.

His life had been normal and boring until the witch had shown up. Then she had to go smell like smoke, and the sea, and cinnamon, and make him see that life was terrible, and unfair. And it was beautiful, too.

Because the house settled around the witch, and the clomp-clomp of her footsteps over the floorboards comforted him. He slept better with her in the house, and Spencer curled on his chest kept the nightmares at bay. And because the witch kept coming back, no matter how horrible her deaths. The force of life itself, or her will to try again, to live on her own terms, wouldn't let her give up. It was undeniable, and inexorable. Like moonrise, and spaghetti on Tuesdays. Like witches and black cats. And that was something. *That* was magic.

The cup was full. Michael held it up, watching frost melt in the moonlight. Maybe, just this once, life could play along and pretend to be fair after all. If witches were real, wasn't anything possible?

✖

On Halloween, Michael brewed the ingredients from the witch's list like tea. He poured them into a jam jar, and let them cool. The resulting liquid was reddish gold, the color of museum amber.

Michael held the jar. He expected it to hum with power, but it only sloshed as he turned it from side to side. The contents left legs on the glass, like good alcohol. He wanted to say he was sorry. He wanted her to come back, and tell him her name. He wanted her to explain herself, and he wanted the chance to do the same. And he missed Spencer.

Michael sniffed the potion. After all the things the witch smelled of, smoke and the ocean, wet rope, and crashed cars, the liquid in the jam jar smelled of nothing. Not the candy corn, or the soft, half-rotten apples. He screwed the lid on, and slipped the jar into his pocket.

Even though it was just past noon, Michael Remmington decided it was high time he got well and totally drunk.

Sometime after sun down, it began to rain.

Would there be any trick-or-treaters in this downpour? Instead of Spider-Man, they'd all be dressed as kid-in-raincoat. He snickered, but really, it was depressing. He pulled out the jam jar, watching the way the light slid through the liquid as he turned it round and round. He needed to find the witch. She needed to see him drink the potion. She needed to know he was sorry.

He pushed the chair away from the table. The front door was miles away, but he made it somehow, and stepped out into the pouring rain.

A jack-o'-lantern carved from a pumpkin he didn't remember buying sat at the bottom of the porch steps. The lid had been knocked askew, and rain had drowned the candle. Along the street, other houses were similarly struggling.

"Crappy Halloween," he said to no one.

He couldn't even call the witch's name. Liquid sloshed uncomfortably in his stomach and his pocket — the alcohol and the witch's brew. A few brave parents with umbrellas ushered kids from house to house. No one looked happy.

Michael made his way toward the main road and the hum of cars. He could picture the witch walking past the library, and the grocery store; she'd come to the end of the sidewalk, but keep going. She wouldn't be barefoot, but her suitcase would be clutched in her hand, and she wouldn't have an umbrella. Spencer, wet and miserable, would be close at her heels.

He spotted her up ahead.

Michael stopped, blinking water out of his eyes. The witch looked just as he'd pictured her, which made him suspect wishful thinking. Or maybe the alcohol had gotten the better of him. He broke into a run.

A sudden gust of wind pulled leaves from the trees, and slicked them over the sidewalk. Water blew sideways. Michael slipped, nearly turning his ankle.

"Hey!" The downpour stole his voice.

The witch didn't turn. Even over the rain, he could hear the steady clunk of her heels. She clutched her suitcase in both hands, and her black skirt clung to her legs, ink bleeding into her skin, bleeding into the sidewalk, bleeding into the dark.

If she reached the end of the sidewalk, she would be lost. Michael felt it as down-in-his-bones-true. Whatever rules governed witches made it so; those rules governed him now, too.

He kept going, half running and half limping. He reached for her shoulder. The witch whirled on him and shouted something, but it was torn away by the wind.

Tendrils of wet hair clung to the witch's cheeks. She swung the suitcase like a weapon, and Michael ducked. He slipped again, scraping his palm.

The witch stepped off the sidewalk.

His heart lurched.

A black shape streaked past him. Spencer.

Headlights swept around a curve in the road, bearing down on the witch. Michael shot up, rain-blind, drunk.

He might have shouted as he plunged off the sidewalk, chasing the witch, chasing the cat. The witch turned, mouth open, but he couldn't hear her. Headlights washed her out, and made her eyes the same color as the storm.

They collided in midair.

She pushed him out of the way, or he pushed her. Or they pushed each other. Brakes squealed, and over the noise, a sound like wings and all of October taking flight filled the air. Against all reason, he heard the jam jar as it slipped from his pocket and became tiny splinters of glass and a magic potion washed away by the rain.

A slew of water hit him in the face. Michael threw up an arm to shield his eyes, and the bumper of an ancient '67 Oldsmobile stopped inches from his leg.

"Jesus, are you okay?" The woman, soaked the instant she stepped from the car, left the Olds askew in the center of the road, door hanging open.

Something nudged Michael's leg. He looked down. Spencer twined around his ankles, dragging her sodden tail over Michael's pant leg. The witch was nowhere to be seen.

"My cat," Michael said.

He bent and scooped Spencer into his arms. The wet bundle of fur purred louder than he'd ever heard her purr before.

"What?"

"She's okay," he said.

The woman stared. After a moment she nodded, looking more frightened than concerned. She climbed back into her car and shut the door. Michael held the cat, listening to her purr, listening to the woman's engine purr. The rain slackened, still slanting through the headlights cutting the night. He realized he was standing in the middle of the road and limped back to the sidewalk. The woman, ghosted behind the car's windows, shook her head in confusion as she pulled away.

A shape lay on the far side of the road, which might be the witch's suitcase.

He couldn't be sure. But he didn't see the witch. The car hadn't hit her, or him, or Spencer. He squeezed the cat harder until she squirmed in protest; he unburied his face from her fur.

"Come on, let's go home."

The witch would be waiting for them with a cup of tea. Or she wouldn't. But it was possible. And she hadn't died. Just this once, life had decided to be fair. The witch could go on living on her own terms. Anything was possible on Halloween.

"Thank you," Michael said to the night and the turning year.

Behind the rain and the dense clouds, he could sense the sliver of a crescent moon, waiting to break free. It felt like a smile.

A MOUSE RAN UP THE CLOCK

Simon watched the mouse scale the clock's side, whiskers thrumming. The clock struck, and the mouse quivered in time. Its paws lost their hold, and the mouse fell, its legs beating the air as Simon bent to retrieve it.

Carefully he laid the creature on its back atop the counter. He could feel the flutter-beat of a heart through the skin, and above it the gentle ticking of a different kind of mechanism. He soaked the corner of a cloth in chloroform and held it near the mouse's mouth and nose until the shivering stopped. Then he picked up a scalpel and tweezers, peering through his glasses, and opened the creature up.

The mouse's insides whirred, and the same honey-colored light that had lit its ascent winked off golden gears. Simon made a few minute adjustments — tightening here, and re-setting a balance there, and then he righted the mouse. Waking, the animal blinked and smoothed its paws over its whiskers before running for a hole in the baseboard.

The bell hanging over the shop door chimed and Simon looked up. Hastily he pulled the watch, which he should have finished that morning, towards him and feigned absorption in his work. Hard boots clicked over the wooden floor, and the man's shadow filled Simon's peripheral vision, blocking the light. The man cleared his throat and Simon looked up. His heart went into his throat.

"Herr Shulewitz? Simon Shulewitz?"

"Yes?"

Simon could barely swallow. He fought to keep his hands from trembling as he set the watch down and straightened his shoulders, trying to meet the *Staatspolizei* man's eye. The officer held his peaked cap under one arm. The rest of his uniform was in perfect order — pressed and clean with sharp lines and not a speck of dust. The row of medals across his breast would have been blinding if the sun hadn't been behind him.

"Herr Shulewitz." Here the man attempted something like a smile, but it pulled the deep scars around his mouth into ghastly lines and Simon fought the urge to shudder. "Are you aware that you have a vermin problem?"

"Sir?" Simon gripped the counter until his knuckles were white to keep himself from visibly shaking.

"Vermin, Herr Shulewitz. Mice."

The officer drew a plain white handkerchief, folded over to hide what was inside, out of his pocket and lay it on the counter between them. Simon's heart beat high in his throat as the officer reached out one gloved hand and nudged the folds of cloth aside.

One of his mice, looking as though it had been crushed flat by a boot, so gears mingled with blood and fur, lay within. Simon could not help his hand flying to his mouth. The *Staatspolizei* officer smiled.

"A very curious creature, don't you think, Herr Shulewitz?"

"I…" Simon faltered. Tears burned behind his eyes, threatening to fall and make his fear visible. He tried not to think of shattered shop windows and cries in the night, neighbors who disappeared never to be seen or heard from again. It was easy to deny as long as darkness covered it, but now it was broad daylight and the officer was standing right in front of him. Simon darted a quick glance behind the officer. Were his neighbors drawing their curtains, bringing false night and pretending they didn't see?

"A very curious creature indeed, one with a great many uses, don't you think?"

It took Simon a moment to register that the officer was still speaking, still studying him with strange, bright eyes, and still smiling his terrible slashed smile.

"I believe, Herr Shulewitz, that the emperor would be very interested in such a creature, and the man who created it. And if the emperor is interested, then I am interested."

The officer reached out, his leather-clad grip surprisingly strong on Simon's upper arm. "Pack what clothing you need. You are in the service of the empire now."

It was not a question.

✖

Unfamiliar landscape slid by outside the train window — a blur of green and brown. Simon had never been farther than a few miles outside his hometown before. Across from him in the private compartment, Herr Kaltenbrunner, as the officer had eventually introduced himself, was still looking at the clockwork mouse. When Simon had asked where he was being taken, Kaltenbrunner had smiled his terrible smile and replied, "Lodz, Herr *Tinker*."

Simon had heard of Lodz, a shadowy city far distant, which he pictured as gray and full of rain.

"Truly remarkable!" Kaltenbrunner exclaimed, turning the mouse over again to examine the gears within.

"Machinery melded with living flesh. Truly you are a visionary. Think, just think, of how such a thing might be employed — scoop out the eyes and put in eyes of glass instead and there you have it, the perfect spy! It goes tiny and unnoticed through every house at night, seeing who has been naughty, and who has been very, very bad."

"It won't work," Simon answered, distracted.

He was still gazing out the window. For the moment he had forgotten to be afraid, and he continued to forget as he divided his mind between the outside world and the thing Kaltenbrunner was proposing.

"A mouse needs a brain to live. You can augment what is there, but you can't take too much out. A device to watch behind glass eyes is simply unfeasible."

"Ah, but it *is* feasible, Herr Tinker, if you know the right methods to employ."

Simon dragged his gaze away from the glass and blinked. Kaltenbrunner had once more tucked the mouse carefully away. There was something in the officer's eyes, in his smile, that made it seem as though all the heat had suddenly drained out of the car.

"The emperor has many interests. Clockwork is only one of them."

Simon opened his mouth, but Kaltenbrunner laid a finger across his lips, his eyes shining.

"You will see soon enough, Herr Tinker."

The train seemed to pick up speed then, as though through Simon's alarm, hurrying them across the country side towards the city full of imagined rain.

✄

When they arrived in Lodz, Simon saw little besides the platform and the plain brick walls of the station. Almost immediately upon disembarking,

Kaltenbrunner slipped a black cloth over Simon's eyes and tied it tight, binding his hands as well before bundling him into the back of a car. When they stopped again, Kaltenbrunner took his arm. Simon was half-dragged from the car. He heard voices as they passed through some sort of gate, and Kaltenbrunner led him blind through the streets on the other side. He stumbled once, but Kaltenbrunner hauled him up.

Around him, the streets were full of noise. Simon could hear footsteps shuffling over broken stones. Did nobody notice him being led away? Or did they simply not care? Simon pictured the men and women, heads bowed, hats pulled low, eyes downcast and perpetually shadowed.

"Almost there now." The officer spoke close to Simon's ear; Simon felt hot breath, scented with brandy.

All around them rose the stench of the bodies too closely packed, and waste, both animal and human. Wherever Kaltenbrunner led him stank of tallow, and oil, garbage and blood. Even blind, Simon felt the closeness as they pushed through narrow streets until they stepped through another gateway, and they were suddenly alone.

The air felt damp on his face, and he longed to pull the blindfold away. The rope binding his wrists cut into his skin. Beyond the cloth, the light lessened. The surface underfoot changed, and Simon knew they had stepped inside. Echoes of their footfalls bounced back to them, and Simon lost count as they twisted through corridors until at last he heard a door being opened.

Kaltenbrunner half-pushed him through, and all at once the blindfold and rope binding were both pulled roughly away. Simon blinked. They were in a vast space with a high ceiling of corrugated metal. Workbenches spread with objects Simon couldn't even begin to name were scattered across the floor among other debris, so it looked like a scrapyard brought inside. Dim, gray light filtered through glass panels and lit the floor in strange pale patches, broken by beams and pillars, which kept the structure upright and cast long shadows on the floor.

At first Simon thought they were alone, but a sound among the scattered chaos made him turn. A man who had been seated at a workbench rose and came towards them. Like Simon, he was young, but with darker hair, an added brightness to his eyes, and a kind of fierceness in his smile.

"Hello, you must be Simon. Our good friend Ernst here told me he was going to fetch you."

Simon stared. He could clearly see the yellow star sewed to the man's sleeve. His face was too thin by far, and there was no question he was a prisoner, yet he stood here shaking Simon's hand and calling the *Staatspolizei* captain by his first name.

"Who..." Simon managed, but he could get no further.

"Your new partner, Herr Tinker, Itzak Chaim Bielski."

✳

Even when the door had clanged shut, and Kaltenbrunner had left them alone, Simon continued to stare.

"Let's have a look at your little toy, shall we?"

Itzak crossed to one of the many work tables, kicking clutter out of the way as he went. Still feeling as though he was blind, Simon stumbled after him. Only at the table did Simon see that Itzak now held the white handkerchief. He had not even seen Kaltenbrunner give it to him. Itzak spread the cloth and his expression wrinkled into one of faint disgust.

"He didn't leave us much to work with, did he? Still, I'm sure in all this mess we'll be able trap ourselves a replacement. What did you use?"

"What? Oh, crumbs, whatever I had, in a box lined with rags soaked in chloroform. I rigged the box to spring closed once they were inside."

Simon couldn't help grinning a little, coming out of his distraction. He had been staring around at the wondrous room and the first spark of curiosity was beginning to grow into something like excitement. There were tools and parts here he would never have been able to get back home — a veritable treasure trove of riches.

"Crumbs. I think I can manage that."

Itzak lifted a sheet of metal to show a half-eaten crust of bread underneath. "Here." He tossed the bread to Simon. "You start on building that box, and I'll see if I can't find us some chloroform."

Simon allowed himself to become lost in the work — forgetting everything but the delicate movements of his hands as he spring-loaded the trap and lined it with the rags Itzak had found.

"I think I've seen some coming in over there." Itzak pointed, and Simon carried the loaded trap over and set it down where indicated.

"And now we wait." Itzak crossed his arms over his chest and leaned back. "So where did they bring you in from?"

"Near Tuchola."

As the words passed his lips, it was as though Simon had been struck. Work had been a good substitute for shock, but now that one had worn off, the full weight of this situation came crashing down around him. Everything he knew, everything he loved, had been left behind. He was simply gone, plucked out of his life as if he had never been.

"You're shaking. You look like you could use a smoke."

"I don't smoke," Simon murmured.

"Then I'll do for both of us."

Simon looked down at his hands, pinned in the pale light from overhead and trembling like moths. A million questions tripped on his tongue and pressed behind his teeth. He could scarcely find the breath to ask the first of them, but somehow he managed.

"What am I doing here?"

There was a faint snapping sound from the corner where they had set the trap; the spring releasing and the door falling into place. Simon couldn't help jumping at the sound. Suddenly it was hard to breathe.

"That."

Itzak pointed, and then brushed past Simon as he went to retrieve the trap. He grinned around his cigarette when he straightened, trailing smoke back to the workbench to hang like ghosts in his wake. Simon watched as Itzak released the door and tipped the sleeping mouse onto the table.

"There you are. Go to it."

"I don't understand."

"Work your magic." Itzak waved his hands. "Though I'm afraid you're going to have to go a little farther than usual and take the brain and eyes out as well."

"Kill it?"

Simon started back.

"Only temporarily."

Itzak grinned, and there was something in it — in his teeth and his eyes — that reminded Simon of Kaltenbrunner. Not cruelty, exactly, not joy in pain, but a kind of wildness. Something dangerous.

As if in a dream, he moved to the workbench and sat down.

Simon found his hands were surprisingly steady when he set to work. A kind of numbness had taken hold. It was as though he was looking out through someone else's eyes, watching someone else's hands as they worked. Itzak peered over Simon's shoulder with curiosity.

"You're in my light," Simon muttered, not looking up.

"Sorry."

He heard Itzak chuckle and then shift to lean against one of the other benches. Smoke drifted around them as Simon picked up the blade and began to cut.

"Why me? Or why just me?"

He spoke quickly, and what he hoped was casually, forcing himself to concentrate on the mouse. His heart was beating as fast as the creature's should have been.

"It wasn't just you. I guess Ernst didn't tell you? They raided the whole city, really smashed it up. Or at least that was the plan. It wasn't just your town either."

"What?"

Simon whirled around and immediately sucked in a sharp breath of pain. The scalpel slipped and cut his palm, and a bright red line of blood appeared.

"Easy, there."

Itzak handed Simon a cloth, and Simon pressed it to the wound.

"I suggest you hurry up. We're losing light, and besides you don't want that thing to stiffen up." Itzak pointed to the mouse. "Herr Kaltenbrunner is a great man for results."

For the first time Simon heard a note of bitterness creep into Itzak's voice. A smile that was not quite a smile twisted the edges of the other's lips, but before Simon could meet his eyes, Itzak turned away. Reluctantly, Simon turned back to his work.

"There."

Simon breathed out at last. He had the mouse almost hollowed out, lying on its back with the gears in place. The creature was utterly still.

"But I don't see what good it will do."

"Ah." Itzak's eyes shone. "Just you watch. Now it's my turn."

Simon stood back, moving cautiously behind Itzak and peering over his shoulder. The light was almost gone and shadows pooled around them. Simon leaned forward to see better, and he could hear a grin in Itzak's tone.

"You're in my light."

Simon withdrew further into the shadows, watching as Itzak spread pale long-fingered hands. For the first time, he noticed how delicate they were, and how scars crossed the knuckles and ran up to disappear beneath Itzak's loose sleeves. He shivered. Kaltenbrunner was a man for results indeed.

Itzak hunched over the mouse on the table, muttering something unintelligible. At first Simon thought the other man was talking to him, and he made to step forward. But it was as though something pushed him back, some intangible force that made the air heavy so it seemed to thicken around Itzak — thicken and grow darker.

Beneath the untidy mop of Itzak's hair, his brow grew paler and broke out in little beads of sweat. His eyes rolled back, flickering in his head, and for a moment Simon was afraid the man was having a seizure. All at once, Itzak's head snapped back and he opened eyes of pure white. Simon gasped. Then Itzak's head lolled forward, drained, and he grinned.

"There."

He stood shakily, and stepped aside as Simon drew closer. At first nothing had changed except that the mouse had been turned right side up again. Then the creature on the table twitched. There was a click and a whir, and its eyes flew open. Simon gasped again. The eyes were blood red, despite the clear glass he'd installed. Simon watched in amazement as the mouse scurried nimbly off the table.

"Look here."

Itzak drew something out of his pocket, and held it out for Simon to see. It was a plain mirror, reflecting the ceiling. As Simon watched the glass clouded and changed, and then the warehouse jittered into view. The angle was all wrong, leaving Simon dizzy. It was as though he scurried along the floor, seeing through the mouse's eyes.

He glanced up. Itzak was still pale, and there were new shadows around his eyes, showing a clear strain.

"How?"

"As I'm sure our good friend Ernst told you, the emperor has many interests — the occult among them."

✕

"I never thought it would work, not something this large."

Simon grinned as he wiped blood from his hands with a rag

"And now we're producing one a week!"

Itzak laid his hand on the horse's quivering flank. His hair hung in a sweaty tangle, hiding his eyes, but behind it Simon sensed strain. He had never fully realized the toll their work took on his partner. He had been too wrapped up in his own excitement — their successes together, a fusion of metal and magic beyond his wildest dreams.

"Are you all right?"

Simon slid a cigarette from its carton and passed it to Itzak who took it in trembling fingers. It took Itzak three tries to light it.

"You need some fresh air. Do you think Kaltenbrunner might let us out for just a little while?"

Simon glanced around the workspace that had essentially been his home since he had arrived in Lodz. It struck him that he had lost track of time, and he had no idea how long he had been here. The quality of light falling through the windows above wasn't enough to show the change in seasons, just enough to light their work and dazzle off the crystals and gears and scrying mirrors that littered every surface.

"Sure, why not?"

Itzak's lips peeled back from his teeth in a smile that left Simon thinking of a skull.

"Isn't he afraid we'd try to escape?"

"Would you?" Itzak raised an eyebrow. "Besides, where would we go? Lodz is a closed city, or didn't you know that?"

Simon shook his head, but he remembered where the car had stopped, and the gate they'd entered through.

"Sounds like *you* need some fresh air." Itzak took his arm and pulled Simon towards the door, banging on the metal with the flat of his hand.

"Hey! This one is finished, and my friend and I need a walk."

After a moment the door slid open, and the guard on the other side regarded them with a look of disdain. Without a word he jerked his head, indicating the corridor beyond him, which Simon had never actually seen.

"Just like that? It's that easy?"

He stared in wonder as Itzak led him to an outer door where another guard let them out. Burnt-white sunlight greeted them as they stepped out into an enclosed yard of stone. Simon blinked and held his hand up to shade his eyes.

Itzak led him towards a high wall topped with razor wire where a third guard looked them over once, and then undid a heavy lock and opened the gate. On the other side Simon turned and gawked back at the building they had come from. It was a sprawl of featureless stone and metal, squatting ugly over a courtyard of flat gray. The first thing that struck him was that there wasn't a tree in sight.

"They're really just going to let us walk around?"

"Oh, they'll set someone to tail us, I'm sure. And they'll use our own little toys against us too, I'd imagine."

Itzak pointed upwards as a bird shot overhead, twittering. Simon shivered. Was it just his imagination or had the bird's eyes been mirrors, and had its wings clicked and whirred? He pushed the thought from his mind as they made their way into the narrow streets. The ground sloped downwards, and because of the slight hill Simon could see what Itzak had meant before — the city was surrounded by a massive wall.

The smells that had greeted him on his first day assaulted him again now, but somehow worse. Piles of garbage filled the sidewalks, and men and women with hollow eyes moved around them. Simon caught his breath. Some were wearing no more than rags, and beneath the rags they were bone thin — and each one among them wore a yellow star sewn to their clothing.

A sound made Simon turn. They had come to a crossroads where four of the narrow streets spilled into a kind of town square. In the middle was a dry fountain, stained brown where water had once run. In front of the fountain stood one of his and Itzak's creations.

The horse let out a terrible scream — no natural sound — and its metallic hooves glinted cruelly in the light as it reared and struck the air. In spots, the creature's glossy black flanks had been peeled back to show silver gears and pistons, which lent the horse an unnatural strength. Astride the creature, and gripping its mane, was a black-clad *Staatspolizei* officer, brandishing a riding crop.

The officer was shouting at a terrified crowd. Simon was jostled forward and then he saw the source of the panic. A woman with a shawl pulled close around her thin shoulders cowered back against the dry fountain, clutching a bundle against her chest. Only when the bundle let out a plaintive wail did Simon realize it was a child.

"Stop!"

He heard someone yell, and a man darted forward, pulling the terrified woman back. The horse's hooves landed, and sparks struck from the stone. The officer wheeled around.

"You!"

The man who had rescued the woman froze, and then slowly turned. The officer nudged the horse forward, staring down with burning eyes. Then without another word he brought the crop down hard across the man's face. The man crumpled. The crowd fell silent, huddled in mute horror as the officer jumped down from his mount and went to the man. The officer's boots clicked on the stone, the same bright metal as his horse's hooves, and there was a sick sound as his foot connected with the man's ribs.

The fallen man jerked, and he coughed blood onto the stone. The officer struck him once more, and then turned swiftly and remounted, riding away. For a moment longer the crowd remained frozen, then a woman dashed forward and knelt at the man's side.

"Somebody, help him!"

"Annah?"

Simon blinked and stepped forward. The woman looked up, and their eyes met over the body of the man. Her family had run a shop near his and lived above it as he had lived above his, but her face seemed so incongruous here. She regarded him with wide eyes out of a face far thinner than he remembered. Her cheeks were hollow and smudged with dirt. His gaze flickered down to the hurt man.

"My uncle."

There was a bitter edge to her voice, and she did not take her eyes off Simon as she tried to get her hands under the fallen man's shoulders and lift him. Simon crouched and reached to help her, but she jerked back, glaring at him.

"Don't touch him."

"I'm sorry, I just wanted to help."

"You've done enough already." Her lips curled in a sneer, which did nothing to hide the core of hurt behind her words. Simon blinked again. Was she afraid of him?

"Annah, please."

He reached out a hand towards her, trying to put kindness and reassurance in his eyes. He saw himself reflected in her dark gaze, and all he saw was a traitor. He tried to conjure words of comfort to assure her he was just like her, but the words stuck in his throat, tasting like a lie. He had enough to eat; he had a roof over his head. Simon let his hand fall.

As if she read all this in his eyes, she pulled back her sleeve so Simon could see the scars lining her arms. Her eyes remained locked on his as she let the fabric fall. Her voice was very soft when she spoke again.

"In case you're wondering, they're all over my body."

"Why?" Simon swallowed hard, and his voice trembled. He was afraid of the answer. A vague memory drifted to the surface of his mind, a memory of Annah's father giving him a hard candy and waving Simon's payment away when he and Annah had both been young and it was Simon's father who ran the watch shop.

"Because I stole an extra ration of bread to feed a sick man who was dying, and your toy spies caught me."

"I didn't know..."

"Of course you didn't!"

The anger had returned to her voice, and it struck him like a physical blow stealing his breath and all the words he might have spoken in return. He felt dizzy and sick all over again. A hand touched his elbow, and Simon turned. Itzak stood behind him, looking grim.

"We'd better go."

Simon straightened. Annah's gaze followed him, still crouched over her uncle who lay broken on the stone. Her dark, shadow-haunted expression stayed with him even as he let Itzak lead him away.

⬥

"I didn't know."

Simon's head rested in his hands. He sat at one of the workbenches, and Itzak leaned against another, watching him.

"What did you think we were doing here?"

Itzak's voice was very soft. Smoke curled around him, trapped in the light, and Simon thought of Annah's face, tortured and thin.

"I didn't think. I just got so caught up in everything...things I never thought were possible. I never stopped to *think!*"

Simon's hands shook as he ran them through his hair. "What do we do?"

He glanced up, eyes wild. Itzak's expression was hard to read behind the veil of smoke.

Before either of them could speak again, the door of their workspace was hauled open with a sound of tortured metal, and both men flinched. Kaltenbrunner stood framed in the doorway, grinning at them. If anything the scars on his face seemed to have deepened, forming a patchwork of stitched skin that made Simon think of a mask; utterly inhuman. The *Staatspolizei* captain's eyes shone, and Simon felt cold settle in the pit of his stomach like a ball of ice.

Kaltenbrunner's steps echoed hollowly as he crossed towards Itzak and Simon. He held a roll of papers under one arm, and he laid them on the table, but he did not smooth them flat.

"I hear there was an altercation in town earlier today." He spoke casually, but his eyes continued to gleam.

"I was relieved to hear that neither of you were *involved*. The emperor would hate to lose two such valuable minds."

He smirked visibly now, scars tightening across his skin, and Simon felt his fists close into balls at his side. For one mad moment, he wanted to launch himself at the *Staatspolizei* man, but Itzak caught his eye and the other shook his head. Then, just as easily as if he was slipping on a mask of his own, Itzak grinned and stepped forward, touching Kaltenbrunner's shoulder as if they were old friends.

"What have you got there, Ernst?"

He gestured to the papers rolled on the table. Kaltenbrunner's eyes narrowed for a moment, and then he smiled.

"New orders from the emperor. Plans."

Unceremoniously he swept a number of Simon's tools aside and spread the papers, smoothing them down. Both Itzak and Simon stepped forward to look over Kaltenbrunner's shoulder.

The diagram showed a roughly spherical shape, which seemed to contain other smaller spheres within — a construction of interlocking metal and gears, delicately wrought. Simon frowned, pulling the diagram closer. Kaltenbrunner watched them, something both amused and almost hungry in his gaze.

"I shall leave you to it, then."

For a moment Simon thought the captain was about to sketch a mocking bow. Instead he turned sharply on his heels and moved for the door. The smile did not leave his lips, and it lingered in Simon's mind, chilling him, even when the door was closed and they were alone.

There had been something in Kaltenbrunner's eyes, in his smile, something that nagged at Simon like a persistent itch on the wrong side of his skin. He turned to Itzak, his mouth open to ask the other's opinion, but Itzak's expression stopped Simon's words in his throat.

Shadows carved Itzak's features and his shoulders slumped in defeat. Something in his haunted eyes reminded Simon of Annah, crouched over her uncle. It was an expression he had never seen in Itzak's eyes before, and it left him more than cold.

"What's wrong?"

Simon found his voice at last, and glanced back at the plans Kaltenbrunner had left. He studied the diagram again, frowning, and again the nagging sensation came to haunt him. Then at last it clicked in his mind.

"It's all copper and wire. There's no heart, no substance, it's just an empty shell. There's nothing inside."

"Not yet."

Itzak's voice was a raw whisper, and Simon turned to him, alarmed. There was a strange look in Itzak's eyes, at once bright and full of shadows.

"I don't understand."

Itzak shook his head, and then smiled a humorless smile. "Then consider yourself lucky."

Simon started at him, uncomprehending, but his partner said no more.

⚹

Something tugged at the edges of Simon's consciousness, pulling him up from dreams where wheels with bright sharp teeth spun ceaselessly and crushed faceless people beneath them. Shadows transformed the scrap metal and junk into blurred and unfamiliar shapes of darkness. The scrying mirrors and crystals were blind eyes, watching him.

He sat up, looking for the thing that had woken him. A fire-shaded point of light burned in the darkness. An intake of breath, and the light illuminated a face. Smoke curled away from Itzak's cigarette, and Simon moved towards him.

Itzak's lips moved, but Simon could hear no sound. The other seemed unaware, or uncaring, of Simon's presence. Now that he was right beside him, Simon could hear the murmured words and he jumped. Itzak seemed to address him, but without once glancing his way.

"I could do it. I could make the thing work. Kaltenbrunner knows it, and he knows that I know. He knows I'll be tempted to try, just to show it can be done."

"What?"

Simon strained forward. Itzak's head snapped up, startling him. The other's eyes burned as bright as the cigarette in his hand. After a moment, Itzak smiled, showing the shadows and the strain.

"We're very alike, you and I."

His voice was soft again, and he took another deep breath. Smoke curled around them.

"We're fascinated not only by the working of things, but by the possibility of them. If we suspect something can be done, we want to try. We push ourselves just a little bit farther each time, to see if it really will work. Given space and means, we will push to the exclusion of all else."

"What are you talking about, Itzak?"

Simon's voice trembled. He was frightened, but he was no longer sure whether it was for, or of, the man in front of him. Tonight, of all nights, Itzak seemed entirely *other*, alien and strange. Itzak's features were pale, almost translucent, and that same wildness, that same danger Simon had seen the first time they had met, shone brightly in his eyes.

"I have an idea." Itzak's voice was barely audible, and something in it made Simon want to shiver. "Do you trust me?"

Itzak's gaze found Simon in the dark and pinned him. Simon forced himself to look at the myriad things he saw in Itzak's eyes — hurt, fear, and yes, passion too. But it was all part of what made Itzak what he was, and Simon found himself nodding.

"Good, because I can't do this alone."

≫

The night was cloudless and moonlight spilled through the glass to touch Simon as he crouched over Itzak on the floor. Above them, the golem loomed, wrapped in shadow and watching over them with unseeing eyes. Simon held a knife, but his hand shook so hard he couldn't keep it still.

"I can't do this." He spoke through clenched teeth.

Itzak moved his head to either side, checking the bonds on his wrists, and then turned back to face Simon.

"Yes, you can. You have to."

The moonlight showed Itzak's skin, and it was terribly white. His chest was bared, showing the scars running over his ribcage and legs and arms, disappearing around to his back, which was pressed against the cold floor.

"What if it doesn't work?"

"It will!"

Itzak's voice was fierce, and it startled Simon so he almost dropped the blade. Itzak's eyes pinned him, burning and frightened all at once. Simon's heart beat in his throat; he swallowed hard around the lump it made. Of the two of them, he had no right to be afraid.

"I'm sorry," Simon murmured.

Itzak nodded, his lips pressed into a thin line. "It's okay. You have to hurry though. Just do it, quickly. Don't even think about it."

Something like a grin twisted Itzak's lips, and Simon shook his head, feeling tears coming to his eyes. "I never have." He took a deep steadying breath, and plunged the knife in.

There was more blood than Simon could have imagined. Despite what he knew intellectually, it still surprised him — the red spilling over his hands and leaving them slick.

Simon gagged, nearly sick as he reached into the cavity, lifting Itzak's heart in his hands. He was sharply aware of his own heart, its beat twin to the one he held. Through it all Itzak's eyes remained on him, bright and wild, and the other continued to breathe in shallow panting breaths. Simon could almost see the net of will Itzak used to hold himself together.

Simon felt a moment of panic, freezing him. He held Itzak's heart in his hands, and impossibly, it still beat. He knew what he was meant to do, but he couldn't get his limbs to obey him. Mice and horses were one thing, but a man, his friend…

Simon shook himself. He had promised. And if he didn't act, Itzak's life would be wasted for nothing. Trembling, he moved to the golem and opened the plate covering its chest. Everything was laid out as he and Itzak had planned and built it, using the parts intended for the emperor's Grand Bomb. It gleamed coldly in the light. Simon took a deep breath and forced doubt away. He let his hands take over, and did what Itzak had advised – he didn't even think about it.

As though from a great distance Simon watched his hands moving in a red-white blur. Metal was joined to muscle as if it was the most natural thing in the world. Moonlight caught the characters on the golem's forehead, and they winked back at Simon. Beneath them, the creature's face was lifeless and still.

He stepped back. His hands were still red, but they were no longer shaking. A strange calm filled him as he regarded the golem. He took one last steadying breath then raised his blood-stained hand and brushed it gently across the golem's brow.

Itzak gasped behind him. Simon turned in time to see his friend's body go rigid, straining terribly upwards as if he was trying to pull free of his bonds. A hole gaped where his chest had been, and crimson ribbons ran over the white of Itzak's skin. Then, as though a string had been cut, Itzak slumped back and was still.

The golem opened its eyes.

They were not Itzak's eyes. They were strange things of mirror and glass, and though blind, they saw. The golem trembled, and then took a lurching step forward. There was a scream of tortured metal – a scream that might also have been a cry of pain.

Simon felt a pang of fear, mixed with guilt. Now the wildness of Itzak's shape matched the wildness Simon had seen so often in his eyes; there was nothing left to hold the pain and darkness at bay. And the shape Itzak wore now had been built for only one thing. But it had been Itzak's choice. It was the only way.

He stood back as the golem ripped open the workroom door.

For a long time, Simon merely cowered in the shadows, listening. The first cry cut through him like a knife; he felt it in his very bones. He was sure he would never move again. They would find him one day — bones amongst the twisted metal and gears. A terrible crashing sound followed the first cry, then a dull roar.

The sound unfroze him. Simon jumped up, running without thinking. He pelted through the corridors, pushing past shouting officers. Panic was a tangible thing, thickly filling the air. The golem tore the *Staatspolizei* headquarters apart piece by piece. Heat rushed towards Simon as something caught flame.

A door leading off to the side of the corridor opened, and Simon stopped. Flames framed a man, making him a shape of blackness, torn from the light. Simon stared and the man turned slightly, just enough so that the light was no longer behind him, falling on his face instead.

Firelight played in the deep lines of Kaltenbrunner's scars. His eyes shone. Simon had expected rage, but there was none. The hunger and the amusement were gone as well. What Simon saw in that gaze was far more terrible still. All around them, *Staatspolizei* officers dragged up from their sleep screamed and died and burned as Kaltenbrunner's eyes locked on Simon's.

In this moment, Herr Tinker, you and I are not so different after all.

Even though he didn't speak the words aloud, Simon heard them crystal clear. The faintest of smiles touched the mask of Kaltenbrunner's face — a smile that was not a smile at all. Then, as others ran from the chaos and the flame, Kaltenbrunner turned back to the burning room and closed the door.

No guard stood at the door leading into the courtyard, and none by the gate, but the lock was still in place. Simon tore his shirt off and climbed. At the top of the fence, he wrapped the torn fabric around the razor wire, leaving it behind as he dropped to the other side.

Breath burned in his lungs, and his legs ached as he pounded through the narrow streets. Someone shouted, and it took Simon a moment to realize it was him. He was laughing too, and there were tears in his eyes. Smoke, heavy with ash, drifted down from the direction he had come.

"Out! Out! Everybody out! We have to leave, now."

He banged on doors, on windows and walls, any surface he could get his hands on. A wild, uncontrolled panic boiled through him as he moved through the streets. Doors behind him opened; frightened faces peered out. He could see it in their eyes, like Annah, they didn't trust him. He didn't blame them.

But they noticed the fire up on the hill, and their distrust was immediately forgotten.

"Leave your things. Take a little food, only what you can easily carry. Come on!"

Simon rushed forward; exhilaration, shot through with panic, carried him. His eyes lit on a woman standing in a doorway, watching him. Annah's eyes were frightened, but her expression was hard. She held her arms crossed over her chest, watching him with suspicion.

"Annah!"

Simon rushed forward and caught her hands. This time she did not pull away. She glanced past him to the flames, and they reflected in her eyes.

"Hurry, we have to leave, now."

He was fully aware of the metallic sound that had been on the edge of his hearing for some time now. It was coming closer. Annah darted another glance over his shoulder. Her eyes widened, and she nodded silently. All around them bodies pressed close, wild in their panic. People ran for the walls.

"We have to go." Simon gripped Annah's hands, and at last he felt her fingers soften beneath his.

Annah turned and called into the room behind her. Her uncle and two small children emerged, looking fragile and frightened. Simon lifted one of the children into his arms, glancing back just long enough to see that Annah followed him.

Simon's heart pounded in his throat as he ran. People scrambled up the walls, *Staatspolizei* officers among them. Those too weak to climb were being left behind, stepped on in the panic to escape. Someone above him, whose face he couldn't see, reached down thin arms and Simon handed the child up into them. Then he too began to climb.

At the top of the wall he paused. One leg hung down inside the ghetto and the other out. The warehouse burned with angry red flames that clawed at the black sky. What moon there had been was now obscured by smoke. Backlit against the flames on the hill, small figures ran in a chaos of fear. Among them, one large figure, a blot of shadow against the night, swung massive arms. Even from this distance, Simon heard the golem's tortured metallic scream. He couldn't help thinking of the heart beating within that metal chest.

"What *is* that thing?" Annah had climbed up on the wall beside him.

Simon turned. Annah's eyes met his. A hot wind full of ash lifted the hair around her face. Once more he saw the thinness, the bruises, and the unmoving shadows. Simon turned back to look at the golem one last time.

"A friend."

EVIDENCE OF THINGS UNSEEN

Interview #1 — November 14, 2011

"He called it a period of grace. Everyone gets one. It's a transition period. A way to ease the pain."

The camera catches her mid-conversation, as if she would have been speaking regardless of whether anyone was watching. She might not even know the camera is there. Except you know she does.

The shot angles over her left shoulder, showing an over-full ashtray, but not her face. It shows hands — nails ragged and bitten — one finger tap-tapping ash, not nervous, but compulsive nonetheless. The camera shows glossy black hair, cut so straight it looks like a wig, and a shoulder, bare but for the narrow strap of a white tank top.

She keeps talking, the camera rolls on. You watch.

"Nothing is forever, that's what he always said. The world is in a constant state of flux — no sharp breaks. Everything liminal, in-between. That's the way he lived his life. If he left, he could come back. And he always did."

She breathes out, a long sound filled with smoke. The camera flattens the breath, and stills everything else in the room. Tap-tap, more ash falls against thick glass, a drift building and threatening to overflow.

"That's what the period of grace was for — forgiveness. Our whole lives were one long goodbye. He always said he was going away for good, but he never did. He always came back. I think he was afraid to leave."

One hand turns the ashtray, glass scraping over-loud against the wood.

"Sometimes, when he was in one of his moods, he'd yell and accuse me of drawing him back against his will. After, he would cry and thank me. I think he needed me to save him. He wasn't always in his right mind; he needed me to make it okay.

"Nothing has changed."

She's alone in the room. She insisted, wouldn't talk if anyone else was there. But she'd let you watch. Through a two-way mirror, through a camera, speaking through the intercom if you needed to ask her a question — as long as a barrier existed between you, she would talk.

The microphone catches every nuance of her exhaled breath, every movement of her fingers tapping ash, her body, shifting against the chair. The resulting recording is good, but it doesn't quite catch the voice speaking off screen. The sound comes through, static-shot, low. It might be your voice, you can't tell. It sounds strange, and you don't remember what you asked her or when. The microphone is good, but not that good; it doesn't catch the question, only her answer.

"No, it didn't work that way. He wasn't always in control. It wasn't his fault."

A pause, and if sound fills the silence, the camera doesn't catch that either.

"I forgave him."

On the screen, the room is black and white. Ghost-gray. Pearl. Charcoal.

The space is crowded with shadows. If you stare hard enough, long enough — and you always do — they pull away from the edges of the screen and close in. They shrink the world, narrowing it to a tunnel you could reach through to brush a hand against her skin. Tap-tap — the cigarette against a beveled edge of glass. The ashtray is always full; her cigarette never burns down.

"He made me watch," she says.

The words stand alone, unprompted, and bring no response from the static-choked intercom.

Against the silence, your heart pounds. It's not standard procedure to ignore a witness' statement, especially when they volunteer information.

But you did. You do.

You lean forward. A shadow passes across her shoulder — a hand just out of view, about to touch, but never lowered into the frame. She rubs that shoulder. Coincidence? The strap of the tank top shifts a fraction. Nudged by her fingertips?

The angle doesn't show it, but you can imagine: if the camera shifted to the left, you'd see the hard press of her nipples against the fabric of her shirt, defiant. She wants you to know how little stands between you and her skin.

You've watched the tape a dozen times, maybe more. You squirm every time. You know you should look away, but you don't. You never do.

The intercom crackles, the voice again — yours? The reaction is immediate, and it makes you jump every time.

The woman turns and looks straight at the camera. She looks straight at you. Not you then, but you here and now. Her eyes are black-black, ink pooled on white flesh.

"I didn't kill him," she says. "But he made me watch him die."

Video Evidence #1 — Date Unknown

"Watch the tape."

She stands at your right shoulder, close enough to touch, but careful not to. Close enough for you to feel the way her skin doesn't brush yours; close enough that your flesh prickles, electric, but you can't tell whether the hairs on her arm rise. She leaves the distance to imagination and possibility, never closing the gap. She wants you to know she's in control.

"Watch."

She points. You catch a hint of sour sweat and stale cigarettes, as if she hasn't showered in days. The scent shouldn't turn you on…

You think about saying, "I don't want to see this," and you don't say anything at all.

The edge of her smile catches the corner of your eye. That smile, even if it's imagined, binds you. It stitches your lips closed, keeps you silent and lets you hold your ground. It gives you permission; it makes whatever happens next okay.

You watch.

Together.

The camera angles high over her left shoulder. She is alone in the room.

Shadows gather at the edges of the screen, leaving spaces full of doubt. The image is grainy, the color somewhere between night-vision green and faded black and white. Light pools around her, either from the camera, or maybe from her skin — luminous and self-illuminating.

Where the light ends, faint markings circle her, chalk on bare wood.

She kneels on the boards, back to the camera's lens, legs tucked beneath her, leaving just the tips of her toes peeking out beneath the curve of her ass. She's wearing the same white tank top — fabric so thin you could see right through it if only she'd turn around. There's nothing underneath. You're sure.

Your breath quickens, watching the screen. The edge of her smile snags at you. There and gone so quickly you might have imagined it. But you didn't. She wants you to know.

She's wearing black silk panties. Her legs are bare.

Her hands are tied behind her back.

A blindfold covers her eyes.

"It isn't about control."

She speaks so close that you can't tell whether her voice is coming from behind you or behind the screen. You flinch, caught leaning forward, yearning toward the flickering image trapped beneath the glass. But even that movement doesn't bring you any closer to touching. She keeps the space between you careful, full of promise that will never be realized.

You swallow guilt. But she wants you to watch, otherwise why would she show you these things? And you want her to watch you, watching her, an endless, recursive loop. You want her to know. But at the same time, you want to be alone in the room with the glow, with the screen, safe and dirty and small.

You shouldn't want these things. Any of them. But you do.

And you can't look away.

"It isn't about power. It's about freedom, absolution, forgiveness. It's permission to let go."

On the screen, she shifts. She's alone, but the camera catches a sound the way her smile catches your breath. It's a voice, guttural and so low you can't possibly have heard it. It has to be in your mind.

"You want this."

Or that's what you think it says. You don't dare ask her to verify. She doesn't volunteer the information.

You can't see her face, but you imagine her lips parting. You imagine them bitten, cracked, warmed with hot breath.

The camera shows her muscles tensing, her shoulders flexing and pressing the sharp edge of her bones against fabric and skin. She pulls against the bonds, but not as though she wants to break free.

She breathes out, and the breath is a word.

"Yes."

She's alone in the room. You're almost sure. She has to be.

"It's about safety," she says.

You're dizzy. Her voice disorients, her image lures. The way her skin glows leaves you feeling as though you're falling, called then and there to be with her, trapped in the past. Or is it the present? The eternal now?

Time doesn't work right in that house.

She told you that, once. Or you think she did.

Everything is in between. A constant state of grace. Of letting go.

Her voice – here and now? There? Or only in your head?

"Once you consent to be bound, you have to accept whatever happens next. You give permission, and receive it at the same time. Your hands are literally tied, and in the instant they are, you've already accepted everything that will be done to you. Whatever comes next is beyond your control, and you're forgiven for it, whatever it might be. It's already happened, and you can't change it."

The camera watches as she tilts her head back, and you watch, filtered through its eye. Everything that happens is beyond your control. That makes it okay.

The arch of her throat is revealed, her face showing at last. Her lips part. She swallows hard.

If you could just see…if the angle of the camera would only show…

You imagine her nipples are hard.

She moves her legs, bringing her knees closer to the circle holding her in.

"I made my body a prison for him," she says. "I bound him, took things beyond his control. I made it okay. I forgave him."

On the screen, she arches her back. The movement lifts her small breasts, presses them hard against the thin fabric of her shirt. It's enough to show…

She bites her lip, holds it between white teeth. She squirms, straining against the bonds. But not struggling to get free. Her breath comes faster. There's a low sound in the room — with her, or coming from her — guttural, trapped, afraid. It is the sound of weeping, if weeping were no longer reserved for humans.

She lets out a low moan. That sound, you're certain, is all her, and there's no mistaking it for anything other than what it is.

Your breath quickens. You lean forward. You know you shouldn't, but you do.

She's watching you; watching you watching her. If you turned, would you catch her smile?

You should get up. You should leave the room, go splash water on your face. You don't. Her presence behind your right shoulder is a physical weight, restraining you, holding you down.

She makes you watch.

On the screen, her head snaps forward. The movement is so sudden, so violent, you're certain it must have broken her neck. Only she's here beside you, isn't she? So you know she can't be dead. She trembles; every bone, every vertebra presses hard against her skin.

"There is freedom in being bound. It's permission, because once you're tied, once you consent, everything that happens after is okay."

On screen, her body bucks, her breath catches, and you hear it as sharp and as close as if it's right next to your ear.

You know you should look away. But you don't. You never do.

She makes you watch as one by one the bruises appear.

She's alone in the room.

It's an impossible thing, but you've seen it with your own eyes a dozen times. Like petals the color of plums, like smoke and ash, or smudges of shadow, they bloom from the white spaces of her flesh.

Each bruise elicits a sound. A low whimper. A tiny gasp. They are not sounds of pain.

She trembles, bound and kneeling on the floor. The bruises appear on her shoulders, on her neck, on her thighs. Like marks left by a lover's teeth. Like fists, beating at her skin from the inside.

Her breath quickens there and then, here and now. What's happening on the screen isn't for you. It never will be. But it doesn't matter. Your breath matches hers. It's not for you, but she makes you watch anyway.

Together.

You watch her come.

✳

Video Evidence #2 — Date Unknown

She leads you to the house, but not inside.

You stand in front of the porch, looking up at the implacable façade. Paint worn, window-eyes blind — the place might have been empty for years.

You can't remember how long you've known her. When this whole thing began. You should have better case notes, not just scattered pieces of evidence.

She smiles. A cold wind chases leaves drained of every color but dead across the porch's bare wooden boards. They catch in drifts around the base of a dozen — or more? — television sets stacked in a rough pyramid. They're the old-fashioned kind — bulky backs and convex screens, the images yearning outward, teasing the promise of a connection that will never close.

"I don't understand," you say.

"Halloween decorations." She shrugs.

She picks a fleck of ash from her bottom lip.

"Watch the screens," she says, pointing.

And you do.

But out of the corner of your eye, you watch her. You know you shouldn't, but you do.

Her hands are buried deep into the pockets of her coat. Her collar is turned up against the wind. You can't be sure, but you suspect that under her coat she's wearing that white tank top, so thin her nipples must ache with the cold. Even wrapped in fabric, she looks translucent. If she'd only turn, you'd see the sky right through her skin.

You shove your hands deep in your pockets, too, but it has nothing to do with the cold.

"I don't understand what I'm looking at," you say, focusing on the screens. You try to sound impatient, not nervous, not afraid.

"It's the house. The feed is real time."

Her voice is flat. You can't look at her anymore — the set of her shoulders, hunched forward like a vulture, tells you as much, along with the intentness of her stare. She wants you to watch.

"I live here with Ray." Not lived, *live*. This is the first time she's spoken his name.

Every screen shows a different room. Each room is empty. You're almost sure.

"A closed-circuit television?" you ask.

"Something like that."

Gray light flickers across a dozen convex surfaces. No television is set quite flush with any other. The angles are all cockeyed, unsettling. Yet everything is held in perfect balance. Nothing is out of place.

In the upper left corner, of the upper leftmost screen, something moves.

"Did you see?" she asks.

You don't have the breath left to answer her.

The image shifts, jumping to the next screen, and your gaze follows. Blood beats too close to the surface of your skin. Your mouth goes dry.

The house is empty. It has to be.

The furniture on every screen is old, worn down. Some rooms are completely empty. The floorboards are bare.

She watches the screens, and you watch her. She leans forward, lip caught between teeth, fighting against the quickness of breath. You know the look. Neither one of you can look away.

You turn back to the televisions. Movement. A shadow stretching from the corner of the screen, unnaturally thin. Static. Liquid. Like nothing you've ever seen before. It slides from one screen to the next. Jumps. Quick cut.

Just beside your right shoulder she leans forward, eyes bright.

A fall of snow. One of the screens goes dark before flickering back to life. You see what you shouldn't see, what can't possibly be there. A man — starved thin — stands naked in an empty room. He stretches his arms wide, and grins. His teeth are a razor slash splitting open his face.

He looks right at you when he smiles.

Not the camera. *You.*

Scars trace his ribs, faint, but still visible. They wrap his arms like pale thread and march down his thighs. No part of his skin remains untouched, unkissed by a blade.

There is no sound, but his lips move. If you had to guess — and you do — you'd guess he says "Watch this."

Or maybe he says, "Want this."

It's over so quickly you can almost pretend you didn't see anything at all.

Except you did. He wants you to watch. He wants you to know.

His hands are empty, then the right holds a blade. The straight razor moves, deep on the left, wavering to the right. The gashed line appears as though by magic, opening his throat like his smile opens his face. Ragged. A dark spray. The scarecrow man bleeds out and the razor falls to the floor.

The screen flickers. Jumps. A fall of snow.

It's over so quickly you couldn't have seen what you know you saw.

The room is empty. Or it should be. Shadows pull in to the center, forming a solid mass in the instant before the image goes dark. You can almost pretend it's only a trick of the light. The shadows don't, *can't*, form the shape of a woman, kneeling before the scarecrow man. Hands bound. Watching. Her shoulders hitching with the force of silent tears.

✖

Interview #2 — Somewhere between November 21 and December 3, 2011
"He called it a period of grace. He was always talking about it. He said he could come back from anything. Anyone could. It wasn't just him. Anyone can be forgiven."

Tap-tap. Her finger knocks ash into the glass tray. You feel like you've seen this all before, an endless loop, an endless repetition, a ghost trapped behind the screen. The camera watches over her left shoulder. She rubs her skin, and in the wake of her hand, a faint smudge appears, like a bruise, just starting to fade.

Seven days. Or at least you think it's been seven days. You can't remember why you waited so long to talk to her again, or why you even called her in. She isn't a suspect. She never was. You had no cause to hold her. But you can't leave it alone. No matter how many times you've been told you're not on the case, there is no case, no woman, no house. Forget it and leave it alone.

You can't let go.

She's alone in the room, you're sure of it, and this time there's no crackle of static from the intercom. It's just the camera, and her body, sitting rigid in the chair. It's just the press of her bones against her skin, the thinness of her shirt. It's just her finger on the cigarette, and the specter of her smoke, filling the room.

It's just you, alone, leaning forward to catch her words through the video screen.

"It's not about forgiveness, it's about freedom. When you're bound, you have no more responsibility. Anything that happens after that, you can't control."

You can't see her face, but you imagine she smiles. You lean forward, wanting so badly to believe in her words. You almost touch the screen, even knowing she's beyond your reach, knowing you can't change what happens, only watch it unfold.

A jacket hangs from the back of her chair. She reaches into the pocket, tap-tapping the cigarette with her other hand, and lays something on the table. The camera, angled over her shoulder, shows a silver disc in a plastic sleeve. There's a word written in black marker on the sleeve, and she positions it just so, knowing the camera is watching. She wants you to see.

The word is *Restraint*.

"It's permission to accept what happens next, and be forgiven."

Tap-tap. She crushes the cigarette, and turns to face the camera. Her eyes are black-black, and she does not smile.

"It's already happened. You can only watch. You're helpless, but you're free. And that makes it okay."

※

Video Evidence #3 — Restraint — October 17, 2011

She left the disc for you on the table in the interrogation room. She wanted you to watch. And you do.

A time stamp in the bottom corner marks the date, and the time counts down, or counts up. Counts towards *something*, always falling from here to there and forever caught in-between. If you can believe anything she says the video was shot before Ray died. If Ray exists. If any of this is real.

You haven't seen her in days. But you imagine her standing just beyond your shoulder, not touching your skin, her breath almost stirring the tiny hairs of your ear. Watching as you watch her on the screen.

The image is black and white. The camera is set high, somewhere above her left shoulder. She's tied to a bed, both wrists bound to brass rails with black silken cord.

The camera shows the taut line of her belly, the space where her white tank top rides up and the fabric doesn't quite meet the black silk of her underwear. You can't see her face, but you're certain it's her.

Her nipples press against the thinness of her shirt, just like you knew they would.

She moves her legs, rubbing one foot against the other, impatient. She pulls against the bonds.

She isn't alone in the room.

At the foot of the bed, where the camera is focused, there are shadows. They crowd, obscuring, so you can't see what you think you see, and you can't be sure. Someone is sitting on a chair, watching her, knees apart, hands dangling loose between them. One hand holds something bright.

She makes a low sound, not fear, not pleasure, not pain, not anything you can define. She strains against her bonds, and finally, she speaks a single word.

"Please."

"Not yet." The voice is so low it might not be there at all. "I want you to watch."

"Please." The word again. "Let me..."

"No." The voice almost isn't there; it cuts her off so you'll never know what she might have said next.

She doesn't want you to know.

The sound again, low in the back of her throat. Frustration. It's barely human, an animal whine full of need. The shadows at the end of the bed shift, and you can only imagine what she sees — bound and unable to act.

Her legs move, restless, impatient. You can only imagine what she wants to do, the reason for the sound. But you don't know. You lean forward, breath quick, watching skin strain against rope.

No one is forcing you this time, but you can't stop watching. You know you shouldn't. But she's given you permission.

Everything that happens from here on out isn't your fault. It's already happened. You can't change it. And that makes it okay.

The shadows at the end of the bed shift. She whines again. But she can only watch. And watch. Watch her watching him, an endless loop, an endless regression, all trapped together in the spaces in-between.

It's dark, and you can't be sure what you see, but you watch as the shadows at the end of the bed seem to raise an arm, and something bright glints against the darkness, cutting deep.

✄

Video Evidence #4 — Want — January 21, 2012

There's one more video. She must have left it. For you. It *has* to be for you.

You went back to the house, one last time, alone. The disc was on the porch where the televisions used to be. The word on the envelope in black permanent marker is *Want*. You've watched it a dozen, a hundred, a thousand times. And you swear it's different every time.

The camera is close in. You can't see her face, but it's her. It has to be her. The white tank top is the same — so thin you can almost see her skin. She's wearing the same black panties. Her nipples press hard against her shirt. The camera, fixed, shows her body between neck and mid-thigh, but not her face, so you'll never know for sure. But you'd know her voice anywhere, spoken close, as if against your ear. Raising hairs, prickling skin — so breath-hot it has to be there, has to be real.

You press play for the dozenth-hundredth time.

The light is wrong — cast by the static-glow of too many television screens, all stacked one atop the other, all showing empty rooms.

At first, there is only breath. Her breath, raising goose-bumps on your skin. It has to be her, because those are her blunt, ragged nails tracing the fabric of her shirt, lifting it, stopping just short of the curve of her small breasts.

She speaks — a calling, a binding. It isn't for you. But you want it to be.

"I want you," she says, though you can't see her face. "I want you so badly I can feel it in my bones, in my blood, in every part of me. And I want you to want me, too. I want you to want me so bad you can't think of anything else. I want to become your entire world."

Her hands lift her shirt higher, teasing. Her words don't make any sense; they're not for you. But you don't care. An eternity passes before she catches the edges of the fabric, pulling the shirt over a head the camera doesn't see, revealing small breasts, nipples puckered hard in the wrong-colored, staticky light.

"I know you like to watch. So watch me. Watch me, and know how much I want you. Even though you can't touch me. Not yet."

Your breath catches. You swear, on the hundredth, or the thousandth view that she reaches out a hand and presses it flat against the glass — not the camera lens, but the screen.

So close you could touch her.

You want so badly for it to be true.

But it isn't for you. It can't be. Except it has to be, because Ray — if he ever existed — is dead. And the date in the corner of the screen says it's been weeks since she disappeared. This can't be her, calling him home, binding him in her flesh, holding him against his will, and forgiving him. Time *can't* work that way.

You don't want it to.

You are lost, too. She must see that. And you want so badly for her to call you home. To forgive you.

She cups her breasts, small as they are, before sliding her hands over her belly, down to her hips to tease the edges of her panties. She slips her fingers beneath the waistband, and lower, where the fabric meets the soft flesh of her inner thigh. The camera doesn't show her face, but you swear she smiles.

Slow then, agonizingly slow, she peels the silk away, stripping, but not completely, letting the material rest around her thighs. You can't help but think of rope, silken and black. Binding. You squirm, knowing you shouldn't watch. But you can't look away. You never could.

You can't change anything that's happened. Or will happen. So that makes it okay.

"I want you to want me so badly that you can't resist. I want you to *come*."

Her hand slides between her legs, brushing soft and slow at first, then stroking faster, more insistent. Her rhythm quickens with your breath. The silk strains around her parted legs.

The image shifts, flickers. The light turns strange. Stranger. At the edges of the screen. A shadow resolves, a face — half seen — just over her shoulder. It smiles.

"I want you inside me. I want to hold you, even when you don't want to be held."

The frame judders. Her hand, between her legs, doubles, until it isn't her hand anymore. Someone else strokes her, sliding a finger between her lips, parting her so the camera almost, but not quite, sees. The fingers extend, tendrils of shadow leaking away from themselves. One slips inside her.

You can't see her face, but you imagine she bites her lip. Her legs part wider, straining silk to the limit. When her breath hitches this time, it is real. That animal sound, the low growl echoing the image of her bound on the bed and aching toward a figure, half-seen. It is not fear. It never was.

"And I want you to know I forgive you."

The screen flickers. Shattered light reflects on her body, on her hand as her fingers/not her fingers move between her legs, as her hips buck towards the camera, rocking beneath the touch.

A tendril of shadow slides around her throat. Her head tilts back. A bruise that it not a bruise appears against the whiteness of her shoulder. She gasps.

And sometimes, only sometimes, on the dozenth-hundredth viewing, the tendrils of shadows draw her arms behind her back, binding them, so you *know* it can't be her hand between her legs. Those ribbons of darkness, ethereal and insubstantial, circle her hardened nipples, teasing, pinching. They are hands, lips, tongues, and none of those things at all.

Crack. A sound like a whip, and welts appear on her skin.

Her head snaps forward, and she smiles, razor-blade sharp.

You think she says, "Want me." But you can't be sure.

She shudders. Hands that are not hands, and certainly not her hands, cup her breasts. Shadows become solid. One strand of darkness curls upward to trace the fullness of a mouth you can't see. You imagine parted lips; beneath the hot impact of her breath the tendril of darkness shudders. You imagine gooseflesh rising on insubstantial skin. You understand.

How much of this is real?

The screen flickers again, and you can almost her feel her tongue, wet and warm, on the shadow tendril, drawing it in, swallowing it whole.

Her nipples, hard, hard, hard, are darker than they were ever meant to be. Who is restrained; who restrains? Who binds, and who is bound? Who is in control?

Almost substantial, something, some*one*, traces the line of her belly, tastes the slick wetness between her legs. Again, she makes a little sound, but it is not surrender. It is victory. The darkness thickens, penetrating and not penetrating. Called. Absorbed. Summoned. Her head snaps back.

"Yes." A whisper, only half heard.

The shadow envelops her.

"Yes."

And she takes it all in.

The shadow fills her, pulsing between her legs.

Her hand moves, but it is not her hand.

She soaks darkness into her being. She takes it inside of her in every way, and at the end, there is a scream — not hers. The thing surrounds her, loving her, fucking her. Then it is gone.

It is her.

And she comes.

The screen goes dark.

But it isn't always the same.

Sometimes, you see what you can't possibly see. More than a shadow stands behind her. And for just an instant, its arms spread wide, skeletal-razor grin stretched across sunken cheeks, something bright held in its hand. Its eyes are fixed on you. Watching.

SISTERS OF THE BLESSED DIVING ORDER OF SAINT PETER AND SAINT ANDREW

Lucy came to the Blessed Diving Order of Saint Peter and Saint Andrew in the usual way: her parents abandoned her as a babe in a little woven basket on the shore. Her first lullaby was the hush of waves rolling smoothed stone over stone and stringing tangled seaweed around her cradle. But with seaweed and stone, the waves brought something far more unusual as well. Drawn from the depths by the uncanny ability to sense an unwanted child crying, they brought a nun.

Sister Francine of the Eternal Abalone emerged dripping onto the sand. The first part of her to appear was the rounded curve of her copper diving helm. As she broke the surface, the tubes hooked to her oxygen tank hissed. Her breath clouded the glass of her faceplate as she leaned over Lucy in her basket and cooed.

"Who's a darling little girl? Who's a little darling abandoned by Mummy and Daddy? You are! Yes, you are!"

With one finger covered in a thick rubber glove, Sister Francine touched the tip of Lucy's nose. The baby gurgled and kicked her chubby little legs happily. Her eyes were as blue as the sea.

Sister Francine carefully fitted a tiny diving helmet — kept by the order for just such occasions — over Lucy's head, and wrapped her in a thermal, waterproof blankie. Then she turned with the babe in her arms, clumping heavily in her massive boots, and submerged, her bright copper helmet sinking like a setting sun.

Upon her arrival at the drowned chapel of Our Lady of the Waters, Lucy was given a new name. She was christened in salt water as Sister Amelia of the Holy Conch. Still, in later years, when she learned to think of herself as an independent being, she thought of herself as Lucy. It was the name left pinned to her chest by her absentee parents, and she kept it carefully sealed in a clear but impermeable bag, taking it out to look at it when no one else was around.

"A new name is a new life," Sister Francine had explained to her once when Lucy asked. They were sitting on the chapel roof, watching schools of bright fish graze among the carefully tended kelp gardens.

"It's like being born anew. Whatever troubled you in your life before the waves can't touch you anymore. It's a second chance. It's freedom."

There was a faraway look in Sister Francine's sea-gray eyes, which were like the waves just after a storm, as she explained this. The expression was one of wistful sadness, or regret for something long since passed. At the time Lucy had not thought to ask about it, and in later years it seemed too late. But she always regretted not asking.

Despite Sister Francine's explanation, Lucy liked having two names. To her mind it meant she had the freedom to choose exactly who she wanted to be when the time came to decide such things.

✖

As Lucy grew under the order's care, she learned. The first thing she learned was how the Blessed Diving Order of Saint Peter and Saint Andrew had come to be formed. It was a vague, somewhat mystical tale, involving a boatload of nuns bound for the new world, a deep-sea-diving expedition on a mission to explore the waters off the coast of Greece for the lost city of Atlantis, and a terrible collision mid-sea during an epic storm.

The second thing Lucy learned was how to care for the drowned chapel. As a junior sister, it was her duty to replace chipped shells in the mosaics depicting, variously, the sainted lives of Peter and Andrew, the parable of the loaves and the fishes, and Christ walking on the waves.

She polished the pearls in the eyes of the Drowned Virgin until they glowed with an eerie, beautiful light, and she kept algae from growing in the baptismal font. She tended the bright garden of anemones and kelp surrounding the chapel, and cared for the long, green-white bones of ships and unnamed sailors in the graveyard.

She sang the strange, warbling masses that echoed through the waters, which in times past had been taken for the song of mermaids. And when she was finished with her chores, Lucy swam up onto the chapel roof, and fed the fish that flocked like pigeons to roost in its walls. In these moments of stillness and solitude, Lucy learned the greatest lesson that the Sisters of the Blessed Diving Order had to teach her — how to listen to the waves.

By the current, Lucy could tell the mood of the sky. She could guess the color of the sunset and the direction of the wind, or know when a storm was brewing. When she was thus listening one day, Lucy heard the waves groan.

Cocking her head inside her copper helmet, full-sized now, Lucy listened as something shifted in its sleep. The dreaming rumble was followed, after a moment, by the oddest and most beautiful sound she had ever heard. It was singing, but a song far more lovely than even whale song, or the entire choir of the drowned chapel singing Ave Maria in perfect unison.

The brightly colored fish that had been nibbling at the tips of her gloved fingers darted away. The light filtering through the blue-green waves overhead darkened, and for a moment the ocean was hushed, almost still.

Lucy braced one hand against the bell tower and peered out through the sea. Through the newly dark waves she could see nothing. A shiver of fear traced her spine, and a sharp intake of breath, followed by a quick exhale, fogged her faceplate. Very slowly she pushed away from the bell tower and let herself drift down through the waves.

The song was softer now, but she could still trace it — a tangible vibration, shivering through the water. It was coming from the boneyard where the drowned ships creaked and sighed behind their beards of barnacles and seaweed — grumpy old men disturbed in their dreams. As she drew closer, the waves groaned again and a hollowed ship that was all but rotted away rocked upon the ocean floor. There was something trapped underneath.

The thing was roughly human and almost luminous in the slanting shafts of light piercing the murky fathoms of water. Tatters of flesh hung from long, wave-polished bones and eyes the very color of the oceans' deepest depths gazed up at her. The mouth was open and he was singing.

Lucy gasped, and swam towards him, crouching beside him where he was pinned beneath the remains of the ship. She could see the dead man's face more clearly now. There was a longing in his sunken expression, a lost quality to the dimmed lights of his eyes. A curious fish, one of those that Lucy had so recently been feeding, darted close and nipped experimentally at the dead man's arm, and Lucy saw a chunk of flesh rip away.

"What are you?" Lucy whispered.

The man turned his watery eyes upon her and answered simply. "I am dead."

"Oh." Lucy rocked back on her heels a bit and considered.

"Does it hurt?" she asked after a moment.

"I want to go home."

There was an ache in the dead man's voice that wasn't exactly fear, but more like a memory of longing. Lucy considered the ship pinning him down. Even hollowed by years of waves its bulk was too much for her to shift alone.

"Will you wait here for me? I'll be right back."

The dead man nodded, though in truth he had little choice. She kicked off, and her long, powerful legs carried her back to the drowned chapel. She touched down lightly, and white sand rose up around her in a shimmering cloud.

Once more she swam up to the bell tower, and peered in through one of the many ragged holes in the roof. The waves had lightened again, but the sun was setting so burnished gold shafts gleamed through the sea-colored glass in the chapel's windows. Sister Francine, who was now Mother Superior of the order, was humming to herself as she prepared the sacraments for evening mass.

Lucy drifted in through one of the drowned chapel's empty windows.

"Mother Superior?"

Sister Francine turned. Blue and green light dappled her copper helm, and she smiled behind her faceplate.

"Yes, my child?"

"I've come to ask a favor."

Lucy bowed her head and folded her hands, trying to look demure and modest. But she couldn't help peeking up at the Mother Superior to gauge her reaction.

"There's a man..."

"Oh?" Sister Francine arched an eyebrow, a gently mocking smile ready to play at the corners of her mouth.

"A dead man," Lucy continued, and behind her faceplate the Mother Superior sucked in a sharp breath.

"He needs our help," Lucy finished, raising her head to plead silently with her eyes.

"Sister Amelia." The Mother Superior's tone was warning, but if she noticed Lucy flinch at the name, she was kind enough not to draw attention to it.

"The dead are unclean things. We have no business with them." She set her mouth in a line to match the firmness in her voice, her arms crossed before her, already bracing herself for Lucy's retaliation.

"He isn't unclean! He's lonely, he wants to go home."

"The dead aren't lonely, they are simply dead. Once they have passed through the veil, there is nothing more that they need from us, or we from them."

Through Sister Francine's faceplate, Lucy could see two spots of color — bright as coral — blooming high on the Mother Superior's cheeks.

"He's hurting," Lucy plead.

"And what would you have us do about that?"

"I thought…I thought maybe you could give him a new name, christen him the way you did me."

Lucy looked up, hopefully. The coral blush was gone, and now Sister Francine's face was very pale. Her eyes shone, and her mouth was set in a grim line.

"The dead are not baptized, they are shriven. What you're suggesting is not only unclean, it's unholy!"

Sister Francine trembled a little inside her heavy diving suit. Lucy had never seen the Mother Superior so upset before, but she couldn't help herself. The dead man's song, the longing in his eyes, had worked its way inside her bones, and she plowed on.

"But, Mother Superior, he was singing!"

Sister Francine threw her hands up, whether in exasperation or silent prayer, Lucy couldn't tell.

"Of course the dead sing, child! Do you think we're all deaf except for you?

It doesn't change anything. There's nothing we can do."

"But it isn't right. We can't just…"

Sister Francine held her hand up to stall Lucy's words. Her sour expression and the quirk of her mouth suggested that she knew the truth of Lucy's words, but that any reasonable person should know better than to parade such truths around in polite company.

"Hush, child!"

Lucy bowed her head again, looking properly abashed. Over the Mother Superior's shoulder the polished pearl eyes of the drowned virgin shone serenely. The faint smile on her marble lips suggested a secret, maddeningly out of Lucy's reach. Lucy forced herself to take a deep breath, and keep her voice calm.

"Mother Superior, isn't it the duty of the Sisters of the Blessed Diving Order of Saint Peter and Saint Andrew to help and give succor to *all* those stranded by the sea?"

Lucy raised her head, sea-blue eyes meeting Sister Francine's sea-gray ones. After a moment Sister Francine sighed, a frown tugging her lips downward as though she had tasted something bitter.

"Listen to me very carefully, child. The good book promises salvation for *all* christened souls, and we must trust in that. Only children and ships can be christened, not dead men, do you understand me?"

Sister Francine's eyes shone like the pearls of the drowned virgin. Lucy stared at her, trying to fathom the meaning behind her words. She was about to speak again, when Sister Francine spun in place, an oddly graceful movement.

"It is a lesson you must learn well, child," she called over her shoulder and then, with a swift kick, she disappeared through a window.

Lucy stared after the Mother Superior, through the broken window where she had disappeared. After a moment Lucy kicked off as well, and swam through the darkening waves back to the boneyard. Above the waves the sun was sinking further, tinting the water a deep gold, warped by the ebbing tide. Lucy swam under a mirror of beveled glass like polished bronze, and all around her rainbow-hued fish darted close to tease her fingers, though she barely noticed them.

✂

She touched down again by the hollowed wreck of the ship, and the dead man turned his face towards her. She wondered what it must have been like for him to wake up under the waves. Were his last memories of the touch of wind on his cheek, the sunset playing in his hair, and the roll of the deck beneath his feet? All those things that she herself had never felt...

A sudden ache, a sudden longing, rose in her — quick as a swell. More than ever now, she wanted to help the dead man. Carefully she took his fragile fingers in hers, feeling the bones shift beneath his soft, waterlogged flesh.

"I'm sorry," she murmured. "I thought I could help you, but I guess I can't."

The dead man said nothing, and Lucy let herself sink until she was sitting on the ocean floor beside him, her legs crossed and his hand still held in hers.

The waves shifted, like a cool breeze that might have stirred her hair up on land. Beside her the hollow bones of the ship swayed and groaned, and beneath them the dead man's bones lengthened in the waves. Absently, Lucy reached out with her free hand, picking at the frayed and splintered edges of the ship's hull, peeling large strips away and worrying the boards back and forth until whole chunks of the ship came away in her hand.

"Of course!" she exclaimed, and the dead man looked at her with startled, lantern-like eyes. She wondered if he was seeing horizon and shore instead of the endless blue-green around them, whether he felt a breeze rather than the current moving against his drowned flesh.

"It's so simple!" Lucy grinned.

She jumped up and spun a little pirouette in the waves. The water was almost completely dark now that the sun had set. Even so there was luminescence all around from glowing seaweed and phosphorescent eels, moving like slow bolts of lightning, and darting fish like lost stars.

"Don't worry," Lucy assured the dead man. "I know exactly what to do."

"I want to go home." The dead man's voice was very soft, as though he had barely heard her words. There was a plaintiveness to his tone, and now Lucy was certain he was remembering the stars beyond the water's beveled-glass sky, and aching after them.

The dead man's hair lifted in the current, stirring against the mossy algae clinging to the bones of the ship. Through one side of his ruined face, Lucy could see his skull; it was the same color as the ship's hull.

Lucy grasped the weed-slick wood with her bulky-fingered gloves. It was soft and rotten, and she was surprised at how easily the plank came away in her hands. She continued stripping the flesh from the bones of the ship, and as she worked the dead man began to sing.

It was more than a sound. It enveloped Lucy and cradled her, as familiar as the waves that had borne her up all her life. She drifted in the dead man's song, and it was an echo in her bones — a sweet, aching longing that spoke of all the things she had never known and whispered of their wonders. Inside her helmet, Lucy caught her breath, and her faceplate fogged with tears.

When she had a sizable pile of timber beside her, Lucy turned to the dead man.

"Do you think you can wiggle free?" Her voice was husky with the tears, but she smiled through them, tasting the salt that was like her native home.

The dead man nodded, and she grasped his arm, ignoring the softness of his flesh. After a moment of gentle tugging he was free. He drifted before her, anchored to the ocean floor by her touch. The lost look had not left his eyes, and she could see the hurt in the low-banked fires of his gaze. The years of salt and waves drifting through him had hollowed him out, but left enough of his humanity that he could still dream of what had come before. How long, she wondered, had he been dreaming?

Lucy took a deep breath and forced herself to meet the dead man's eyes.

"Do you trust me?"

"I want to go home." The dead man nodded, as though that was all the answer he had or all that was needed.

"Okay."

Lucy braced herself, and reached for the dead man's arm. She held it so it was stretched straight in front of him, worked her fingers under a loose chunk of flesh, and pulled. It was like peeling the boards from the ship. His skin was rotten and soft and came away easily in her hands.

The dead man did not flinch, and that was almost harder to bear. Lucy felt her eyes well up with tears again, until she could barely see through the smudged blur of her faceplate. But she forced herself to keep looking at him. And once more, the dead man began to sing. It was a lullaby, like the first she had ever heard as a babe abandoned by the shore.

As the dead man sang, Lucy continued methodically stripping his flesh from his bones, casting it into the waves so the fish could feed. When she was done the man stood before her — all naked salt-bleached white, gleaming in the light of the distant moon. There was an aching beauty to his vulnerability, and Lucy almost lost her nerve. But she took a deep breath and, as gently as she could, Lucy began to take apart the dead man's bones.

His eyes, as luminous as any of the star-bright fishes, tracked her with a kind of detached curiosity. Even stripped bare, he continued to sing. Even when she wrenched his skull from the remains of his spine and laid it on the cold ocean floor, impossibly, he continued to sing.

When she had a pile of clean, white bones beside the pile of wood, she started to fit them together, interweaving them with long strands of seaweed until a small vessel began to take shape. The waves were dark and Lucy was exhausted when she at last fit the dead man's skull to the prow. With her hands on either side of his bleached skull, Lucy looked into his glowing eyes.

"Are there others like you? Other dead men who sing beneath the waves?"

Very slowly, on his curving prow-neck of wood and bone, the dead man nodded.

"Okay."

Lucy nodded in turn, her jaw set into a firm line. There was a nervous fluttering like a school of fish swimming in the pit of her stomach, but in an instant she had made up her mind. She knew who she wanted to be.

✄

Through the dark waters, Lucy swam, pulling the boat of wood and bone behind her. When the final mass of the day was at an end, Lucy slipped into the chapel and led Sister Francine of the Eternal Abalone out to admire her handiwork. Lucy held her breath as the Mother Superior studied the little rowboat.

Sister Francine's lips twitched, caught halfway between a smile and a frown.

"And just what do you plan to do with this boat, child?"

"Increase our ministry!" Lucy answered evenly. It was not a lie.

"You propose to become a missionary, then?" Sister Francine arched a brow, her expression wry.

"If you'll allow it, Mother Superior." Lucy bowed her head demurely, and hid her smile.

Sister Francine shook her head, a gesture that was both exasperated and amused.

"Very well. May the Drowned Virgin watch over you and guide you, child."

When Lucy looked up, Sister Francine was smiling.

"One more favor, if I may, Mother Superior." Lucy looked at Sister Francine hopefully.

"Yes?"

"May I gather the order to help christen my ship?"

Sister Francine sighed and shook her head again, but her lips quirked upwards at the corner. With a smile Lucy swam up to the bell tower, and rocked the great lichen-crusted bell. It was heavy and hard to move underwater, but the clapper in the sleeve echoed through the waves and called the sisters back to the chapel yard.

There, among the bright anemones and the gently waving kelp, Sister Francine blessed the ship of wood and bone and gave both it and the dead man a new name. Lucy could feel the other sisters around her. On one side, she was flanked by Sister Genevieve of the Holy Kelp, and on the other, Sister Iris of the Unwavering Coral Reef. Their voices were strong in the water, and they gave Lucy strength, too. As the order prayed, Lucy raised her head and snuck a glance at the Mother Superior. Behind her faceplate there was a twinkle in Sister Francine's eyes — a spark that might have been pride.

At dawn the next morning, Lucy pulled the little boat up to the surface and righted it upon the waves. As she surfaced, her copper helm was a gleaming twin to the rising sun. Lucy pulled herself on board, and then looked back down through the waves.

The beveled view was strange, like seeing the world upside down. Drifting in the current, the Sisters of the Blessed Diving Order waved, and just beyond them she saw Sister Francine, hanging back a little, but still smiling. The Mother Superior raised her hand, and Lucy raised hers in turn.

The waves lapped gently against the hull of wood and bone, and though it had been hastily built the sea bore it up and it did not leak. Cautiously Lucy reached up and undid the seals on her helmet. There was a hiss of air as she twisted it and lifted it free. The breeze kissed her cheeks with the new sun, and both light and wind played in her long red-gold hair.

Lucy leaned forward, and rested her hand on the dead man's skull. She let her touch linger a moment, and then she took up the oars. The dead man was silent in the prow, his bony face turned into the wind, but faintly she could hear a song much like his shivering through the waves. There was much work to be done. Lucy turned *The Fisher of Men* towards the sound, and began to row.

THE KISSING BOOTH GIRL

An impact woke Beni from a dream of gears and a face like burnished gold in the setting sun. She sat up, nearly hitting her head on the bunk above hers.

"Shit."

Mouse snorted in his sleep, rolling over. She'd seen him sleep through the worst thunderstorms, but how the hell could he sleep through this? The ground trembled as Beni swung her legs out from under the covers, an aftershock traveling up from the soles of her feet.

She snatched her trousers and work shirt from the pile at the foot of her bed, never mind they were streaked with the previous day's dust and sweat. She hopped barefoot into the trousers, then she was out the door, running.

Her first thought was of one of the rides gone up in flames, or something terrible happening to an animal from the Mechanical Menagerie. But whatever had happened seemed to have happened just beyond the midway and the trailers where the performers and workers slept. A glow like nothing Beni had ever seen backlit a knot of people, turning them to silhouettes against the lightening sky. The stars were still out, but they were pale, half swallowed in pearly-gray light.

"What's going on?" Beni buttoned her shirt as she reached the edge of the crowd.

"Something fell from the sky," Mattie, who ran the ring toss game, said. His red hair stood out at all angles, and sleep gummed the corner of his eyes.

Beni had visions of a month's worth of work undone. "What was it? It didn't hit any of the rides, did it?"

"I dunno." Mattie grinned, gap-toothed; the constellation of freckles across his cheeks stretched to fit his smile. "Let's go see."

He took off, and Beni followed, weaving through the crowd of performers and workers roused from sleep. A constant hum vibrated in her back teeth; she clenched her jaw against the sensation.

"Stand back, everyone, back." Phineas Akers, the owner of the World's Last Steam Circus and Wondrous Mechanical Traveling Show, spread his arms, still muscled from his days as a performer, and used his body like a cattle scoop against the growing crowd.

"You." Akers singled Beni out, though she was far from the only one craning her neck to get a look. "Back to bed. Don't let me catch you sleeping on the job tomorrow."

For the sin — in Akers's eyes — of her sex and her brown skin, the carnival's owner was constantly looking for any excuse to berate her, or give her more than her share of work and less than her share of food. He threatened to fire her at least once a week, and he'd never have taken her on in the first place if not for Lotts. Beni's mentor had designed all the Steam Circus's rides and attractions, and he still ran the crew that kept them going, even if his role was diminished these days. He'd made it clear when he signed on with Akers that he and Beni came as a package deal.

A sharp reply leapt to Beni's tongue, but the force of the crowd moved her back. Hank and Fen, Akers's muscle-men, were out now, shooing away onlookers. Winnie, the World's Strongest Man, had been enlisted, too. Beni watched him kneel to lift something from the ground.

No, not some*thing*, some*one* — a girl with skin that wasn't just pale, but as white as the chalk the aerialists used on their hands; she was the source of the glow The girl opened her eyes, and despite the gathered crowd, looked right at Beni... Beni froze.

Winnie turned, and the bulk of his body hid the girl from sight. Beni blinked, free from the intensity of the girl's gaze. But an afterimage remained, the girl — luminous as a fallen star — repeated in a dozen flickering iterations each time her lids closed.

✖

Beni sheltered in Gertie's shadow, and pressed a sweating soda bottle to her brow. If the mechanical elephant hadn't spent all day baking in the brutal sun, she would have risked leaning against Gertie's massive leg. Beni's work shirt lay crumpled on the ground beside her. Let Mr. Akers fire her; she would strip her flesh from her bones if she could, just to get relief from the heat.

A shadow fell across her. Mattie kicked the scuffed sole of Beni's left boot, looking smug.

"I'm on break." The last thing she was in the mood for was Mattie's damned freckle-faced grin.

"You're missing it."

"Missing what?" Beni shielded her eyes against the glare.

"The thing that fell from the sky. They're setting it up on the midway now. It's the new attraction."

Not it, *her*, Beni thought, but she didn't say it aloud. She'd almost convinced herself she'd dreamed it. It had been nearly a week, and in the intervening time,

Akers had kept her so busy she'd fallen exhausted into her bunk every night. There had been no time to sneak out and see whether a girl had really fallen from the sky, or whether she'd imagined it.

"Come on." Mattie reached down, and Beni let him haul her to her feet.

Mattie let out a whoop, pelting down the midway, stirring dust in his wake. "Let's go!"

A crowd had already gathered around the newest booth. Beni could smell the paint, still fresh, hastily slapped onto the plywood. Jimmie Seeds, the Steam Circus's best barker, threw open the booth's shutters with a flourish.

"Ladies and Gentlemen: I give you the Kissing Booth Girl! Lips that beguile. Oh, I promise, the nearest thing to nuzzling an angel can be yours — today! — for a shiny round Seated Liberty I know you carry in your very pockets as I speak."

Beni sank her teeth into her lower lip to keep from letting out an astonished whistle. Even in broad daylight, the girl shone. The whole thing seemed even more like a dream now. The girl who had fallen from the sky sat perched on a stool in the deep-cool shadows of a midway booth.

Without meaning to, Beni took a step forward, stretching on her toes to get a better look. The girl's hair reminded Beni of ropes of pearls, a series of complicated knots woven around the top of her head dripping down to her shoulders. She wore a sleeveless dress, just a shade darker than her pale skin. Her arms ended in unmarred stumps just below her shoulders. She resembled those pictures Lotts had showed her of the marble statues in Rome. Art intended for the pedestal, to be admired, never to be touched.

A row of people two deep stood between Beni and the Kissing Booth Girl, but the girl's gaze slipped past them. Her eyes an impossibly bright blue. Like her skin wasn't *just* pale, her eyes weren't *just* blue either. She wasn't like Mattie, or Lotts, or any other white person Beni had ever seen. She was uncanny. Her gaze lifted a moment to lock on Beni, just like it had when Winnie had first picked her up from where she'd crashed into the ground. Then the girl flashed a smile, and Beni had the brief impression of many teeth. The Steam Circus had a real live shark as an attraction for a while, but the mechanical tail to replace one hacked off by hunters eventually poisoned the water in the tank with oil. That ever-grinning fish had taken off Muddy Cowler's hand in the brief time it had been with them. Muddy hadn't lasted long after that either.

And now she wondered if Muddy's stomach had flipped so at seeing the smile before the bite. Warmth spread through her that had nothing to do with the beating sun. Fear and a thrill of excitement all at once, and it made her want to squirm out from under that gaze.

She became ashamed of the grease worked deep into her skin, her shorn-close hair, dewed with sweat, and the fact she was wearing nothing but her grimy undershirt. She hitched up the straps of her coveralls, crossing her arms over her chest.

"I'll take a go." A man stepped forward.

Beni didn't recognize him — a paying customer then. He dug in the pocket of his clean linen pants, and flipped a quarter to Jimmie Seeds, who caught it in the air.

"Now, sir, hold on just a minute." Jimmie vanished the coin neatly before putting a hand against the man's chest. "There are a few especial rules, you see. Our Celeste is very particular about who she kisses. You pay to start, but you got to give a little something extra."

The crowd tensed. "What kind of scam is this?" the man asked as he reached for Jimmie's shirt. Jimmie evaded the man's grasp like a weaving prizefighter. He winked at the crowd.

"Celeste is no ordinary girl. And the World's Last Steam Circus and Wondrous Mechanical Traveling Show is no ordinary carnival. A kiss from *our* Kissing Booth Girl — well, it's wishing on a falling star. You might get your heart's desire, but you gotta win her over first. We all know you have to *impress* a lady."

A rough-looking man in the crowd grabbed his crotch. "Hey, I got something to impress her right here!"

Jimmie Seeds ignored him, eyes fixed on the mark in front of him. Beni had seen it a hundred times before — the sincere look Jimmie got when calculating the best way to take someone for everything they were worth.

"Do you think you have what it takes, sir?" Jimmie asked the man who hadalready paid, with his best I'm-rooting-for-you-pal expression.

Beni held her breath. No one in the crowd spoke. The quality of sunlight shifted, going lemon-gray, like the build-up before a storm. The man licked his lips, and leaned forward, putting his lips against Celeste's ear.

Celeste's quiescent expression remained unchanged. The entire Wondrous Traveling Show stood still for a moment, and Beni's pulse with it. The Kissing Booth Girl shook her head. The man flinched. He started to turn away, but at the last moment, he wheeled and reached into the booth, grabbing Celeste by the back of the neck.

The Kissing Booth Girl's stool rocked precariously. The man crushed his lips against hers. Almost immediately, he let out a muffled cry and leapt back, clutching his face. Blood seeped between his fingers.

"You bitch!" The words emerged crimson-flecked.

He lunged, but Jimmie was there, smooth as ever, a bulwark preventing so much as a finger from reaching Celeste. Despite his slender build, Jimmie Seeds could be strong as a bull. He winked over the man's shoulder, and addressed the crowd as though letting them in on a great secret.

"Steal a kiss from an angel and there's hell to pay." He pushed the shutters closed. "Come back and try your luck tomorrow!" Jimmie hustled the cursing, wounded man away, probably to someplace where there'd be more liquor than liniment.

Once the crowd dispersed, Beni approached the shutters and lifted one. Celeste did not acknowledge her. The Kissing Booth Girl was once again serene — an elegant queen on a simple throne, not a girl on a stool in a plywood shack. A queen with a smear of red slicking her lips and chin.

"Oh, boy! Did you see that?" Mattie popped up in front of Beni, blocking her view, and she realized she'd been staring. She let the shutter fall closed, focusing on the ring-toss boy.

"Wow. I've never seen anything like that before. She almost bit his lips off. Do you think it's true?"

"What?" Beni shook her head, feeling lightning-struck. Mattie's rapid-fire speech, ricocheting from thought to thought, was harder to follow than usual.

"The thing about the wishes?"

"I don't know. I guess." Beni glanced over Mattie's shoulder. Was it her imagination, or did a faint glow seep around the edges of the shutters, coming from Celeste, sitting perfectly still in the dark? Despite the heat, the skin at the base of Beni's spine prickled.

"Yeah? I mean, why not." Mattie ran a hand through his hair. "We got everything, right? Magic just finds its way here. Remember the frog that told fortunes? And the Vanishing Lobster Boy who forgot how to reappear one day? Why not a falling star? We're the World's Last Steam Circus!" Mattie copied Jimmie Seeds' stance, puffing out his chest. Beni knew he had designs on rising from ring-toss boy to barker someday.

"Our Magical Mechanical Menagerie will sweep you away to other worlds! Our — "

"Not if I can't get it fixed, first." Beni held up a hand, cutting Mattie off.

Disappointment bloomed in his eyes, but his mood changed just as quick. "You gonna give it a try?"

"What?" Beni's mouth went dry.

Mattie jerked a thumb over his shoulder and made a kiss-kiss sound with his mouth. "You do like girls, don't ya? Plus, you get a wish. Not a bad bargain."

Mattie grinned sly, and Beni's stomach dropped, her cheeks warming.

Could Celeste hear them through the booth's thin wood?

She took Mattie's shoulders, hustling him away further down the midway. "What are you talking about?"

Mattie's freckles stretched further with his grin, and he punched Beni in the arm. "I seen the way you look at the Girly Girls in Madame Osprey's Aviary Show. I won't tell if you don't want."

"I — " But before Beni could finish, Mattie let out a whoop, and took off, arms spread wide, thundering down the midway.

Beni stared after him. If Celeste was a fallen star, then Mattie was something inhuman, too, a living wind-up toy. If he ever stayed still long enough, she'd check him for a keyhole and springs.

Her gaze drifted back to the Kissing Booth, and the nervous flutter she'd managed to suppress returned.

A kiss and a wish. It was stupid, impossible, but she desperately wanted it to be true.

≫

Beni locked the trailer door, even though Mouse wasn't likely to be back anytime soon. He'd be too busy grubbing under rides for dropped coins, and picking pockets on the midway.

Kneeling, she pulled out the cigar box she kept under her bed, the one that held everything that mattered. It smelled of cedar, and the ghost of tightly wrapped leaves — smoke waiting to be born. The top layer of the box held a packet of postcards from Lotts. He'd traveled the world — chasing Grand Exhibitions and World's Fairs, and visiting all the top Academies — before he'd gotten sick and settled with the Steam Circus.

Beni moved the postcards with a pang of guilt. She hadn't been to visit Lotts in weeks. The sickness had changed him, left him a shadow of the man who'd seen natural talent in her and offered to help her hone it, never giving a damn, or even seeming to notice that her skin wasn't lily white and she wasn't a boy.

Hating herself a little, Beni dug out the square of folded paper wedged at the bottom of the box. Was she only thinking of visiting Lotts now because she needed advice? Selfish.

Beni unfolded the square of paper. The same lightning-to-skin feeling she got looking at the Kissing Booth Girl, Celeste, coursed through her. Elegant, simple charcoal lines swept across the page — her blueprint, her automaton.

Someday, the charcoal lines would become a woman with beaten-copper skin, twisting coils of wire hair, birdcage-delicate ribs, and softly ticking gears. Once built, the Clockwork Woman would be Beni's ticket to the Grand Exhibition, the World's Fair, any Academy she wanted. She'd travel the way Lotts had, exhibiting her marvel. And she'd never have to say yes sir and no sir to the likes of Mr. Akers again.

Beni's fingers traced the lines of her design without quite touching, careful not to smudge them. How long had the paper been folded in the bottom of her cigar box? She could have built the woman by now, or at least tried. But she hadn't because she feared failure.

But if she built just part of the woman, just an arm, wouldn't that be something the Kissing Booth Girl had never seen before? Wouldn't it impress her enough to give Beni a kiss and grant her wish? Beni folded the paper, smoothing the edges.

She closed her eyes, and the flickering afterimage of Celeste painted itself on Beni's lids — Celeste, serene and bloody in the shadows of the kissing booth, with a smile that sparked like flint against Beni's bones. She'd seen what Celeste had done to the man who failed her test. Shouldn't she be more afraid? But the man had tried to force a kiss, and Beni would never do that.

If she was being honest with herself, that was part of it, too. Not just the promise of a wish fulfilled; Beni wanted Celeste to look at her with those more-than-human eyes and judge her worthy. Out of all the men, and maybe some women, who would line up outside the Kissing Booth, Beni wanted Celeste to choose her.

A hollow she thought she'd sealed up with gears and grease, with following the Steam Circus from town to town, opened up inside Beni with such force it took her breath away. Katarina had chosen, and Beni hadn't been her choice.

Don't you have a dream, Beni? Something you want more than anything? Something you'd give up everything for the chance to chase?

Katarina, straddling two worlds, with skin just light enough and a voice sweet enough, that the world let her pass. Katarina with eyes the color of a mossy pond, lit by sunshine. Katarina, who'd gone chasing her dream and left Beni behind.

A memory of sitting on the waterfront, the lights of Jackson Square behind them, filled the trailer with the green scent of water. Beni remembered watching golden lanterns sway on the steamboats cruising along the river as music wailed, slow and hot, sultry as the night.

"Are you a virgin?" Katarina had asked her.

She leaned close, mischief glinting in her eyes. Beni's tongue turned to lead, and her cheeks warmed.

"There was a boy..."

She'd never talked about sex with anyone before. Certainly not anyone as worldly as Katarina, whose parents took her to fancy-dress parties, and let her taste alcohol. Katarina had snuck a bottle of syrupy-sweet pear brandy from the latest party, a masquerade, and brought it to the waterfront to share with Beni.

Katarina still wore her party gown, buttery silk the same color as the light on the water. Beni wanted to run her fingers over it, but didn't dare. A feathered mask, flashing with bits of amber, dangled from Katarina's fingers. She sipped from the bottle, and passed it to Beni.

Beni drank deeper than she meant to, the glass warm and sticky where

Katarina's lips had touched it. She coughed, and Katarina pounded her on the back.

"Did you like it?" she asked.

"The brandy?" Beni wheezed; her eyes watered.

Katarina took the bottle from Beni's fingers, skin brushing skin. "The *boy*. Did you like him? Did you like being with him?"

Katarina's breath smelled of sugar and pears. Beni wasn't sure what Katarina was asking. The question felt like a trap. What answer would stop Katarina from looking at her with such intensity and curiosity?

"It was okay, I guess. I don't know."

"Then you're still a virgin," Katarina said. "You're a virgin until it means something, until it makes you happy. Otherwise, it's just bodies. That doesn't count."

Katarina's lips met Beni's before Beni could say anything else, or make sense of Katarina's words. A shocked moment stretched before she unfroze, and returned the kiss. Katarina's mouth tasted like brandy, like pears, but purer and sweeter and stronger than the drink.

Katarina drew back, her eyes shining with a new light, one that asked permission. It was more hopeful than Beni had ever seen Katarina look before. She was still worldly, but she was human, too, and beautiful. And she'd chosen Beni.

Beni nodded, not trusting herself to speak.

There, by the waterfront, it meant something.

✖

Dust chased Beni's heels all the way to Lotts's trailer. Her folded drawing thickened her back pocket. Music, laughter, and the salty-sweet smells of the midway, washed over her.

Lights shone in Lotts's trailer, but Beni hesitated outside the door. At the creak of a footstep, Beni's heart leapt to her throat, her guilt returning. Lotts opened the inner door, peering through screen.

"Are you going to skulk out there all night, or are you going to come in?"

"I didn't want to bother you." Beni faltered; the short distance from his chair to the door had left Lotts winded.

But the last thing he wanted was pity, she knew that. Lotts ignored her discomfort, waving her inside. Beni sat while Lotts made tea. She didn't dare offer to help.

Beni's mental image of Lotts was a man with the sun inside his skin, letting it shine out in a near-blinding smile. That man had a chest like a barrel, a strong, straight back, and could have lifted her clear over his head if she'd let him. This Lotts ran the faucet with bent fingers. His back curved. His hands trembled lifting the kettle to the stove.

Beni cleared her throat. "We'll have Gertie back in top shape by tomorrow. The whole Menagerie will be running just like you designed it."

Lotts carried two mugs from the small camp stove, handing one to Beni before lowering himself into his beaten chair. His trailer was wide and he lived alone, luxurious, compared to anyone else but Mr. Akers's living conditions.

"We miss you," Beni said.

Her throat closed on the words. They were true, but if she missed him so damn much, why hadn't she been to visit him before now? It wasn't fair. Lotts was the one who had to live with his wasted body, day in and day out. Avoiding him just because it made her uncomfortable was the height of selfishness.

"Nobody needs me getting underfoot."

"You're still the foreman." Beni tried on a grin. "I think this whole thing is a put-on so you can get out of work."

"I wish, Beni-girl, I wish." Lotts settled back in his chair.

Somewhere along the way, Lotts had become a ghost trapped inside a cage of skin and bones.

"What are you doing here, Beni-girl?" The suddenness of the question startled her.

A hint of the old fierceness returned, a flint edge coming into Lotts' gaze.

"And I don't mean here, here," Lotts said, indicating the trailer. "I mean the Steam Circus. You're not a child anymore, Beni. You should be studying at the finest Academy."

Beni's stomach clenched. "I…"

Beni pulled out the sketch, and handed it to Lotts, holding her breath. He studied it a moment, before handing it back.

"Ambitious."

"That's it?" Beni nearly spilled her tea. She'd never shown the sketch to anyone before. Anger mixed with defeat. From Lotts of all people she'd expected a least some word of encouragement.

"Well?" Lotts arched a brow; it seemed an eternity before one corner of his mouth crept upwards. He gestured at the paper in her hand. "You've got everything you need, what more is there to say?"

Beni gaped. The first wave of rage went out of her, replaced by indignation. Lotts held up a hand.

"Beni-girl." He took a deep breath. "The design is good. It'll work. So, again, what are you doing here?"

Beni fought the urge to squirm. There was more iron in Lotts' gaze than she remembered, or maybe it simply hadn't been showing of late. Even with the sickness eating at him, he was still the man she remembered. He held the sun inside his skin, even cloud-dimmed. She knew the answer he wanted, but she couldn't bring herself to say it aloud. And she needed him to tell her that was okay.

"I can't do it," she said.

Lotts' gaze didn't waver. Under his scrutiny, Beni's anger returned. How could he possibly understand?

"It doesn't matter." Beni's voice came out sharper than she intended. "No Academy would accept me anyway."

Not like the music Academy in New York City that had accepted Katarina, Beni told herself, and she held her anger like a shield.

She pointed to a framed picture on the wall, Lotts's graduating class at the Boston Academy. "Academies don't take girls, and they especially don't take black ones." She hated the tremor in her voice, and the stinging in her eyes.

Lotts didn't flinch. Unlike the hard, sharp blue of Celeste's eyes, Lotts's eyes were the open bowl of the sky. He shrugged, meeting her outburst with a mild tone. "So, you'll be the first." Lotts set his mug aside, and leaned forward, hands on his knees. "You're making excuses, Beni-girl."

The words acted like a pin touched to a balloon. She wanted to explode, shout at him that it didn't work that way, he couldn't possibly know. His skin and sex had never kept him out of any place he'd wanted to go, and Lotts had been everywhere. But his words and the steadiness of his gaze held her back. What if they were true? She hadn't even tried.

"I'm an old man, Beni. I don't have time for bullshit." Lotts's gnarled fingers gripped the frayed arms of his chair. "If you want it bad enough, you take it, and you don't let anyone tell you it isn't your right."

Beni looked away. The weight of Lotts's expectation was too much. What right did he have to tell her what the world would allow her to do? The Academies were full of men like Mr. Akers, looking down on her.

Lotts's next words brought another jolt, causing Beni to whip around and stare at him.

"And don't go thinking that this Kissing Girl will solve all your problems."

"How did you — ?"

"I ain't dead, Beni-girl. I still hear things, and I know what they're saying about her. She's a fallen star. She can grant wishes. Don't go pinning your hopes on something you know nothing about. Wishes are dangerous and fickle things."

The image of Celeste's mouth, slicked in blood, sprang to mind. Lotts settled back in his chair, his voice quiet. "And did you ever think about what this Kissing Booth Girl might want herself?"

Any retort rising to Beni's lips died on her tongue. The last of the anger ran out of her, leaving her hollow inside. She hadn't thought of the Kissing Booth Girl at all, not beyond as a means to an end. She'd fallen from the sky. What if she was lost and couldn't get home? Or if she was here on purpose, what would she take from a person in exchange for giving them their heart's desire? Beni's stomach churned, simultaneously cold with fear and hot with shame.

She'd come looking for easy answers, and Lotts had only given her more questions. Beni rose, moving toward the door. She needed to think.

"Your schematics," Lotts said.

Beni looked back. The sketch had drifted to the floor.

"It's a good design, Beni, a solid one. It'll work. Just be sure you're building it for the right reasons."

Words stuck in her throat. Beni folded the sketch, stuffed it back in her pocket, and slipped out the door.

✖

Instead of returning to her trailer, Beni went to the workshop set up near the Menagerie. The sun was down to a thin, fire-colored line at the edge of the sky. Against it, Gertie was a bulk of shadow. When the Menagerie worked right, the animals never lurched or stuttered. Their oiled gears were magic, mimicking life, but moving in ways flesh and blood animals never could.

Beyond the Menagerie, colored lanterns glowed along the midway. A hot-air balloon, ghost-pale and mirroring the rising moon, drifted above the Last

Steam Circus, tethered by a line thin as spider-silk.

A lump clogged Beni's throat. Even if everything Lotts said was true, did she really want to leave all this behind? Beni rested a hand on Gertie's thick leg — cool enough in the twilight she could touch it without burning her skin. What did any Academy have to offer compared to this? A bunch of stuck-up students in stiff collars and starched shirts? People who would look down on her at best, turn to violence at worst. The Steam Circus was magic. Lotts wouldn't have settled for anything else.

Beni tried to picture Lotts, the brash, bold, wind-burned foreman, among those lily-white suits. A grin caught the corners of her mouth. The Boston Academy never saw Lotts coming, she'd bet that much.

And they'd never see her coming, either.

Her pulse kicked. Despite the risk, maybe because of it, getting herself into an Academy was still worth it. Even if she had to work twice as hard for half the recognition, she wanted to be there. She'd go precisely because they didn't want her. She'd go for herself, and for all the other girls out there who might come after her. And if she got there with a little help from a fallen star, what was the harm?

Beni stepped into the workshop. The dim space held the day's heat, warm and musty. It smelled of wood chips, grease, and the memory of metal.

Underneath the work tables were boxes filled with scraps. Beni knelt, sorting out lengths of thin copper tubing, handfuls of springs and gears, and scraps of leather. Rocking back on her heels, she surveyed her finds. Everything she needed was right here. If she worked at night, while the rest of the crew was out spending their day's pay on booze, she could get a rough prototype together.

Akers seemed to have forgotten about her for the moment. If she could keep avoiding him, she could probably avoid any extra work as well. As long as she didn't let her regular workload slip. She wrapped the gears and copper in a spare bit of canvas, and tucked the bundle in the corner behind a collection of unused tent poles. As Beni pulled the door shut behind her, she nearly collided with Mr. Akers.

"Sh — " She almost swore, but Beni managed to clamp down on the word at the last second.

"Abeni." Mr. Akers's voice was honey, taking pleasure in drawing out her full name. "Working late?"

"Just tidying up." Beni bit the inside of her cheek hard, and added, "sir," remembering to look down as she said it, even though it made her skin crawl.

Mr. Akers snorted. When it seemed he wasn't going to say anything else, Beni risked looking up.

"Enjoy your night, sir." Beni's attempt at sincerity slid around in her mouth, and she cursed herself inwardly, hoping Akers didn't hear the edge in her tone.

Akers let her get two steps before he spoke again, his voice casual.

"Abeni? Mr. Seeds was having some trouble with the Gyro Wheel earlier." Akers' eyes held an unpleasant light. "Stop by and see if you can give him a hand before attending to your other duties."

"Yes, sir." Beni kept her head down, her hands stiff and straight at her side. Her fingers wanted to curl into fists. Akers continued to stare at her; Beni could feel herself being weighed in his gaze and she forced herself to look up and meet his eyes.

"Is there anything else, sir?" This time she didn't bother to keep the edge out of her voice, biting off her words.

Mr. Akers caught her arm, his grip reminding her again of his performing days. He leaned close, letting Beni smell the night's first drink on his breath.

"You'd do well to remember, *girl*, if I catch you doing *anything* wrong, it's not just on your head, it's on Lotts's, too. Understand?"

"Yes, sir." This time Beni didn't have to fake looking down. Genuine panic flooded her, and her throat hurt when she swallowed.

Akers released her, stalking away. Beni waited until she couldn't hear his footsteps anymore before looking up. When she was sure there was no chance he would hear her, she said, "Asshole."

✄

The stars were just coming to full above the Last Steam Circus and Wondrous Mechanical Traveling Show. Beni emerged from her trailer, carrying the prototype arm wrapped in canvas. It had taken her twice as long to assemble as she'd hoped. Akers kept finding extra tasks that needed her attention right away, even though most of them turned out to be like him ordering her to go see Jimmie Seeds.

"The Gyro Wheel?" Jimmie had tilted his straw boater at an angle so he could scratch his hair. "It's working perfectly. Don't know why Akers would tell you otherwise."

Beni had seethed. Akers wanted her to waste her time. It didn't make a bit of difference that he knew nothing about the arm, or what he was keeping her from doing with her free time. All that mattered to him was proving he could make her dance like a puppet, and there was nothing Beni could do about it.

Now the arm was complete, but she could barely remember the last time she'd slept. Between building the arm, her regular work, and Mr. Akers' extra tasks, she was exhausted.

Glancing over her shoulder to make sure the way was clear, Beni hurried between darkened trailers, making for the bright midway. Gertie, now fully repaired thanks to Beni and the rest of the crew, trumpeted a brass horn blare. With a hiss of steam, she rose on sturdy hind legs, waving her articulated trunk to thunderous applause.

Despite herself, Beni grinned. When she was in good working order,

Gertie really was a marvel. Most people only saw the bright fittings and the faux-gems worked into Gertie's hide, giving the illusion she was covered in rubies, sapphires, and pearls. Beni saw beneath all that to the gears. She'd never seen a real live elephant, but she couldn't imagine any flesh and blood creature more wonderful than Gertie.

Caught up in the Menagerie's performance, Beni didn't see Akers until he was right in front of her. The carnival owner melted out of the shadows, blocking her path, and Beni's stomach dropped.

"Abeni." Colored glass lanterns painted the Akers red and gold. "I believe you have something that belongs to me."

Akers pointed to the canvas-wrapped bundle, and Beni tightened her grip. "Sir?"

"I don't think I have to tell you, Abeni, all materials in the workshop, scrap or otherwise, are the property of the Steam Circus. Which means they are *my* property."

Beni's mouth went dry. She hugged the bundle closer, the arm's metal rods digging into her chest through the canvas. She wouldn't give it up. Let Akers have her arrested. Akers' next words struck her like a physical blow.

"I wonder what your mentor will have to say about this, hmm? I imagine he'll be disappointed to learn he staked his reputation, and his future with the Steam Circus, on a petty thief."

"Lotts has nothing to do with this!" Beni took a step toward Akers before she realized what she was doing. A hand caught her shoulder, pulling her back. Startled, Beni almost dropped the mechanical arm.

"Lotts is perfectly capable of speaking for himself, thank you very much, and he is not disappointed in the least."

Beni heard the faint catch in Lotts's breath, the evidence of exhaustion, but his shoulders were squared back and his gaze firm.

"Beni has been working on a special project for me. If you'd care to check the books, I think you'll find all the supplies paid for in full."

The hand resting on her shoulder betrayed a faint tremor, but Lotts's expression didn't waver. When he trained his blue eyes on Akers, the Steam Circus's owner flinched.

Akers opened his mouth, and shut it again, the edges curving in a frown. Beni saw him search for words, and find none. He turned on his heel and strode away.

She let out a breath she hadn't been aware of holding. The tremor was worse now, and she caught Lotts's hand, helping him to a nearby bench. He so rarely left his trailer these days. Had he come looking for her?

"Just felt like taking in the sights." There was a faint wheeze in Lotts's voice, even as he grinned. Beni gaped at him. Could he read her mind now, too? Maybe it was like Mattie said, the Steam Circus was magic, and maybe Lotts was a little bit magic, too.

"I thought he was going to fire you," Beni said.

Lotts waved a hand. "He needs me, and he knows it. This whole damn place would fall apart without me. Besides, I knew him back when he was a young pup, and that includes an awareness of certain facts, deeds, and indiscretions he'd rather I didn't know, and certainly would rather I didn't share."

Beni's eyes widened again.

"A story for another day." The blue of Lotts's eyes was bright with mischief now.

"I haven't even thanked you," Beni said, suddenly remembering herself.

Lotts waved her off. "You'll pay me back one day, Beni-girl." A smile quirked the corner of his mouth. "Who do you think will be supporting me in my old age?"

Beni grinned relief. The copper rods of her mechanical arm poked her in the chest through the canvas, and she realized just how hard she was hugging the bundle.

"Well, let's see it." Lotts gestured.

Dutifully, Beni unwrapped the arm; it gleamed, catching glints of sapphire, emerald, ruby, and amber from the midway lights. Lotts's fingers shook as they traced the air above the copper, leather, and wire, almost but not quite touching.

Lotts let his hand fall back to his lap, where the shaking stilled.

"Just like your design." A wistful smile tugged at the corner of Lotts's mouth, one touched with sadness that Beni couldn't fathom. "It's good work, Beni-girl."

"Good enough to impress the Kissing Booth Girl?"

"Good enough to win you your heart's desire without the luck of a fallen star, I would think."

"Oh." Beni didn't know what else to say.

Sudden fear gripped her, leaving her skin clammy and cold. She wanted to believe Lotts, but what if he was wrong? She tucked the cloth around the arm, and Lotts reached out to rest his hand on the back of hers. His skin was hot, his hand light, as though filled with hollow bones.

"Just something to think about, Beni-girl."

Beni hugged the arm to her chest again. "I promise." The words came out husked, and Beni was surprised to find tears prickling the back of her eyes. Half ashamed, and half panicked, Beni turned and fled down the midway.

It wasn't until she'd almost reached the far end, where Celeste's booth stood, that she stopped. A line snaked away from the Kissing Booth. From the open front, Beni could see Celeste's glow.

She ducked to the side, hiding herself behind the tent that housed Madame Osprey's Aerial Aviary. Doubt made her stomach clench. It had all been so clear just an hour ago, and now? Beni sat, folding her knees against her chest, trapping the arm between her body and her bent legs.

How much of her life had been running, making excuses for herself to settle, not to try in case she failed? Katarina hadn't asked her to go to New York, and Beni hadn't asked Katarina to stay. She'd bought a bottle of rotgut, drank half of it trying to work up the courage, but in the end she'd chickened out. She'd thrown the rest of the bottle in the river, and she hadn't even gone to the train station to say goodbye, even though she'd promised Katarina she would.

Beni had convinced herself she was doing the right thing. It was better to let her dreams go than chase after them and watch them crumble. A girl like Katarina couldn't possibly fall in love with someone like Beni. Just like the Academies couldn't possibly admit someone like her, no matter how good she was at building things and making designs.

Lotts was wrong. This was her one shot. Win Celeste's favor, win her heart's desire.

Beni stood, brushing the dust off her clothes. She joined the end of the queue, heart pounding. She stared at the narrow back of the man ahead of her to distract herself. His shirt stuck to his skin. He held his hat in his hands, kneading the brim and shifting from foot to foot.

The line shuffled forward, agonizingly slowly. Then all at once, the man ahead of Beni was approaching Celeste, and Beni's heart leapt into her throat. She willed herself to be more like Mattie, living in the moment, letting go of doubts and fears.

The man with the narrow back showed Celeste something cupped in his palms. Beni couldn't see if from where she stood, but the Kissing Booth Girl shook her head. Had anyone succeeded in winning their heart's desire? She'd been so busy building the arm, she hadn't even thought to ask. Surely Mattie would have told her. What if it was all a glitzy lie, a way to make money, and Beni had been taken in just like any other rube?

The man ahead of her bowed his head, slinking away. Beni stepped forward, her legs stiff. Up close, Celeste's gaze was like the heart of a flame in a gas lantern, shivering blue, gold, and violet. It raised goose-bumps on Beni's skin.

"Hello." Celeste smiled; Beni blinked away the afterimage of her chin slicked with blood.

"Hi." Beni's voice cracked.

Up close, Celeste didn't even look human. Beni gripped the copper and clockwork arm so tight her fingers ached.

"Have you come to win your heart's desire?" Celeste asked. Something about her voice reminded Beni of ringing glass.

Even if she managed to impress Celeste with her mechanical arm, what then? If Celeste really could grant her heart's desire, then Beni would never know if she was good enough to get into the Academy on her own. If she tried and failed, at least she would know where she stood. And she could work harder the next time, or straight out barge into the Academy and dare all those white men to kick her out again.

"I'm more interested in what you want than what I want." The words came out in a rush.

"Oh?" Celeste arched a perfect white eyebrow, her lips quirked in a smile.

Panic gripped Beni. What had she done? One chance to win the Kissing Booth Girl's favor, that's all anyone got.

Beni's gaze traveled over Celeste's sculpted features, her marble skin, the knotted crown of her hair, and the perfect, rounded ends of her arms. She was the loveliest thing Beni had ever seen. She'd fallen from the sky. What would a star want with a clockwork arm? What would she want with any of the trinkets any of the people here could offer her?

"Not many people ask me that," Celeste said. "Maybe I want what you're holding in that cloth bundle."

The flash of that dangerous smile — the one that reminded Beni of the half-mechanical shark — ghosted with blood. She wanted to step back, but Beni found herself moving forward. Somehow, the wrapping had come undone from the arm, and Beni held it out toward the fallen star. Light from the multi-colored lanterns strung around Celeste's booth caught the copper joints, the tiny gears that would move the arm in fluid dance when it was joined to Beni's clockwork woman.

Beni fought to stay focused. She had to keep the arm, build the rest of the woman. Then the Academy couldn't possibly turn her away.

Her head ached. The air around her seemed to hum. This close to Celeste, it was hard to think straight.

"Is that for me?" Celeste's gaze picked at Beni, tugging, willing her to say yes.

A fallen star might not need trinkets, but she needed *something*. Maybe she needed people to wish on her, to hold out their desires like a handful of coins. Beni forced herself to look at Celeste, really look this time. Behind the shivering flame of her eyes, Beni saw the dark between the stars.

Celeste wasn't lost, she hadn't fallen. She had come here on purpose, and she was hunting.

"No." The word quivered at first, Celeste still trying to exert her will. The star's gaze flickered, troubled. She wasn't used to being refused.

"No." Beni repeated the word louder, and this time she put the force of her body behind it as well.

She thought about Akers, every sneer, every useless task. She thought about Katarina leaving her behind. She thought about Lotts, and how she wanted to make him proud. She thought about the mechanical woman she would build one day, and how the arm was just the beginning.

Beni dropped her shoulder and bulled into the side of the Kissing Booth. The plywood tipped and she kept pushing until the whole thing tumbled down. Screams erupted on the midway around her, and Beni ran.

⚒

Beni paced to the edge of the track and peered down its length, checking for the train for the hundredth time. Any moment now a meaty hand would land on her shoulder, the cops come to drag her to jail. Or maybe Akers would come himself. Maybe he wouldn't bother with jail. Maybe he'd have one of his goons push her onto the tracks just as the train arrived.

"When you get to the World's Fair, you send me a postcard, Beni-girl."

Beni whirled. Lotts stood behind her, gripping a cane. She nearly swung the sack she held, carrying all of her belongings, few as they were. After the debacle on the midway, she'd grabbed what she could and run.

"You scared the shit out of me." Beni's shoulders slumped.

"You were going to leave without saying goodbye."

"After what I did, I couldn't exactly stick around."

"The way I heard it, a particularly vicious gust of wind knocked over one of the midway booths." Lotts eyes shone, despite his hunched stance.

Beni's mouth dropped open. Behind her, the train finally chugged into the station, hissing steam.

"What makes you so sure I'll make it to the World's Fair?" Beni gathered herself, shouting to be heard over the train.

"Because I know you, Beni-girl. So I'll be waiting for that postcard."

Beni let her sack drop, wrapping her arms around Lotts and squeezing him hard. She could see the appeal for Celeste, of having someone believe in you. Beni hadn't even needed to wish for it. She'd earned it, just like Lotts had earned her respect. The back of her eyes prickled again, but this time, Beni wasn't ashamed. She stepped back, grinning, and retrieved her sack.

"I promise. And I'll send you a postcard from every place I go after."

"Oh? Where?" Lotts' eyes twinkled — a young man's gaze in an old man's skin.

"Everywhere." Beni grinned. "Cairo, London, Mexico City. There are lots of Fairs, lots of Exhibitions, lots of Academies around the world. I'm going to see them all."

Lotts stuck out his hand. After the hug, it seemed strangely formal, but

Beni understood. He was welcoming her as a colleague, an equal, a future graduate of an Academy, just like him.

She shook his hand, then climbed onto the train. Inside, she paused in the doorway. Lotts raised one hand, keeping the other on his cane. His eyes were damp, too, but he smiled, and she could just hear him over the hiss of the train.

"I just bet you will, Beni-girl. I just bet you will."

FINAL GIRL THEORY

Everyone knows the opening sequence of *Kaleidoscope*. Even if they've never seen any other part of the movie (and they have, even if they won't admit it), they know the opening scene. No matter what anyone tells you, it is the most famous two and a half minutes ever put on film.

The camera is focused on a man's hand. He's holding a small shard of green glass, no bigger than his fingernail. He tilts it, catching the light, which darts like a crazed firefly. Then, so very carefully and with loving slowness, he presses the glass into something soft and white.

The camera is so tight the viewer can't see what he's pushing the glass into (but they suspect). Can you imagine that moment of realization for someone who *doesn't* know? Watch the opening sequence with a *Kaleidoscope* virgin sometime, you'll understand. The man pushes the glass into the soft white, and moves his hand away. A bead of bright red blood appears.

As the blood threads away from the glass, the sound kicks in. Only then do most people notice its absence before and discover how unsettling silence can be. The first sound is a breath. Or is it? Kaleidophiles (yes, they really call themselves that) have worn out old copies of the film playing that split-second transition from silence to sound over and over again. They've stripped their throats raw arguing. *Does* someone catch their breath, and if so, *who?*

There are varying theories, the two most popular being the man with the glass and the director. The third, of course, is that the man with the glass and the director are the same person.

Breath or no breath, the viewer slowly becomes aware they are listening to the sound of muffled sobs. At that moment of realization, as if prompted by it and thus making the viewer complicit right from the start, the camera swings up wildly. We see a woman's wide, rolling eyes, circled with too much make-up. The camera jerk-pans down to her mouth; it's stuffed with a dirty rag.

The soundtrack comes up full force — blaring terrible horns and dissonant chords. The notes jangle one against the next. It isn't music, it's instruments screaming. It's sound felt in your back teeth and at the base of your spine.

The camera zooms out, showing the woman spread-eagle and naked, tied to a massive wheel. Her skin is filled with hundreds of pieces of colored glass — red, blue, yellow, green. Her tormentor steps back; the viewer never sees his face. He rips the gag out, and spins the wheel. Thousands of firefly glints dazzle the camera.

The woman screams. The screen dissolves in a mass of spinning color, and the opening credits roll.

You know what the worst part is? The opening sequence has nothing to do with the rest of the film. It is what it is; it exists purely for its own sake.

But let's go back to the scream. It's important. It starts out high-pitched, classic scream queen, and devolves into something ragged, wet, and bubbling. If there was any nagging doubt left about what kind of movie *Kaleidoscope* really is, it's gone. But it's too late. Remember, the viewer is complicit; they agreed to everything that follows in that split second between silence and sound, between sob and catch of breath. They can't turn back — not that anyone really tries.

Here's another thing about *Kaleidoscope* — no one ever watches it just once; don't let them tell you otherwise.

The opening is followed by eighty-five minutes of color-soaked, blood-drenched action. (Except — if you're paying attention — you know that's a lie.)

The movie is a cult classic. It's shown on football fields, on giant, impromptu screens made of sheets strung between goalposts. It flickers in midnight-double-feature theaters, lurid colors washing over men and women hunched and sweating in the dark, feet stuck to crackling floors, breathing air reeking of stale popcorn. It plays in the background, miniaturized on ghostly television screens, while burn-outs fuck at 3:00 a.m., lit by candles meant to disguise the scent of beer and pot.

Here's the real secret: *Kaleidoscope* isn't a movie, it's an infection, whispered from mouth to mouth in the dark.

Hardcore fans have every line memorized (not that there are many). They know the plot back and forth (though there isn't one of those, either). You see, that's the beauty of *Kaleidoscope*, its terrible genius. It is the most famous eighty-seven and a half minutes ever committed to film (don't ever let anyone tell you otherwise), but it doesn't exist. If you were to creep through the film, frame by frame (and people have) you would know this is true.

Kaleidoscope exists in people's minds. It exists in the brief, flickering space between frames. The *real* movie screen is the inside of their eyelids, the back of their skulls when they close their eyes and try to sleep. When the film rolls, there is action and blood, sex and drugs, and not a little touch of madness, but there are shadows, too. There are things seen from the corner of the eye, and that's where the true movie lies. There, and in the rumors.

Jackson Mortar has heard them all. Crew members died or went missing during the shoot (or there was no crew); a movie house burned to the ground during the first screening (the doors were locked from the inside); fans have been arrested trying to recreate the movie's most famous scenes (the very best never get caught); and, of course, the most persistent rumor of all: everything in the movie — the sex, the drugs, the violence, and yes, even the flickering shadows — is one-hundred-percent real.

※

"You know that scene in the graveyard, with Carrie, when Lance is leading the voodoo ceremony to bring Lucy back from the dead?" Kevin leans across the table, half-eaten burger forgotten in his hand.

Jackson nods. He traces the maze on the kiddie menu, and refuses to look up. Kevin is a fresh convert. Like moths to flame, somehow they always know — when it comes to *Kaleidoscope*, Jackson Mortar is the man. Jackson supposes that makes him part of the mythology, in a way, and he should be proud. But his stomach flips, growling around a knot of cold fries. He pushes the remains of his meal away, rescuing his soda from Kevin's enthusiastic hand-talking.

"And you know how Carrie is writhing on the tomb, and the big snake is crawling all over her body, between her tits and between her legs, like it's *doing* her, and she's moaning and Lance is pouring blood all over her?" Kevin grins, painful-wide; Jackson can hear it, even without looking up.

"Yeah, what about it?"

"Do you think it's real?"

Jackson finally raises his head. Sweat beads Kevin's upper lip; his burger is disintegrating in his hand. A trace of fear ghosts behind the bravado in his eyes.

"Maybe." Jackson keeps his tone neutral.

The glimpse of fear gives him hope for Kevin, but Kevin's smile does him in. Maybe the kid sees more than the sex and drugs and blood, but that's all he *wants* to see. Kevin has seen *Kaleidoscope*, and wishes the movie was otherwise.

That, Jackson cannot abide.

"Listen, I gotta get going." Jackson stands. "I got work to do."

"Oh, okay. Sure." Kevin's expression falls. Another flicker of unease skitters across his face.

Guilt needles Jackson — he can't leave the kid alone like this — but Kevin pastes it over with another goofy, sloppy grin. "Maybe we can catch a midnight screening together sometime?"

Jackson's pity dissolves; he shrugs into his worn, black trench coat, "Yeah, sure. Sometime."

Jackson squeezes out of the booth. Kevin turns back to his cold hamburger. Jackson wonders how the kid stays so skinny. As he pushes through the restaurant door, out into the near-blinding sun, Jackson tries to remember to hate Kevin for the right reasons, not just because he's young and thin.

Jackson steps off the curb, and freezes. Across the street, on the other side of the world and close enough to touch, Carrie Linden walks through a slant of sunlight. She glances behind her, peering over the top of bug-large sunglasses, which almost swallow her face. She hunches into her collar, pulls open the pharmacy door, and darts inside.

A car horn blares. Jackson leaps back, the spell broken. His heart pounds. No one has seen any of the actors from *Kaleidoscope* since the movie was filmed. There are no interviews, no "Where Are They Now?" specials on late-night television. It plays into the mystique, as though *Kaleidoscope* might truly be a mass hallucination thrown up on the silver screen. No one real has ever been associated with the film. The credits list the director as B. Z. Bubb and the writer as Lou Cypher.

It's been nearly forty years since *Kaleidoscope* was filmed, five years before Jackson was born (but long before he was *really* born). But Jackson knows it's her; he would know Carrie Linden anywhere.

Jackson has been in love with Carrie Linden his whole life. (Yes, he considers the first time he saw *Kaleidoscope* as the true moment of his birth.)

When Carrie Linden first appeared on the screen, Jackson forgot how to breathe. The scene is burned into his retinas; it, more than anything else, is his private, skull-thrown midnight show. He sees it on thin, blood-lined lids every time he closes his eyes.

Jackson refrains from telling anyone this unless he knows they'll really understand (and fellow Kaleidophiles always do). The problem — the reason he can't say anything to converts and virgins — is that the first part of Carrie Linden to appear on screen is her ass.

It's during the party scene. She walks across the camera from left to right. Long hair hangs down her back, dirty blonde, wavy, split ends brushing the curve of her buttocks. She wears ropes of glittering beads, but the viewer doesn't know that yet. They are the same beads used to whip Elizabeth in the very next scene, horribly disfiguring her face, but the viewer doesn't know that yet, either.

What the viewer knows is this: Carrie Linden walks across the screen from left to right. She climbs onto the lap of a man at least twice her age. She fucks him as he lifts tiny scoops of cocaine up to her nose, balancing them delicately on the end of an over-long fingernail.

The first time the viewer sees Carrie's face, she is sprawled naked on the couch. The camera pans up from her toes, pausing at her chest. Her breathing is erratic, shallow, then deep, then panicked-fast — a jackrabbit lives under her skin. Her head lolls to one side, her eyes are blissfully (or nightmare-chokedly) closed. A trickle of blood runs from her nose.

While Carrie sleeps, but hopefully doesn't dream, Elizabeth is whipped with Carrie's beads. Elizabeth screams. She's on her knees, and sometimes it looks as though she's stretching her hands out toward Carrie. Some viewers (Kaleidophiles, all) have made the comparison to various religious paintings. Elizabeth's face is a sheet of blood. When she collapses, her torturer steps over her, and drops the bloody beads around Carrie's neck. Almost as an afterthought he sticks his hand between Carrie's legs before wandering away. She doesn't react at all.

Jackson stares at the pharmacy door for so long that the woman he *knows* is Carrie Linden has time to conclude her business and slip out again, still darting glances over her shoulder as she hurries away. Once she's disappeared around the corner, Jackson dashes across the street, ignoring traffic. He yanks open the pharmacy door, and runs panting to the back counter. Luckily, Justin is working. Justin is a *Kaleidoscope* fan, too. (Aren't we all?)

"Hey, buddy. Here to get your prescription filled?" Justin winks.

Jackson ignores him, trying to catch his breath. "The woman who just left, did you see her?"

"Yeah. Dark hair and glasses? Not bad for an older broad." Justin's grin reminds Jackson of Kevin. He wants to reach across the counter and throttle Justin, who is skinny too, but old enough to know better. He's older than Jackson (not counting *Kaleidoscope* years, of course).

"Percocet," Justin says as an afterthought. He has no compunctions about confidentiality. If he didn't know the owner too well, he'd have been fired a long time ago.

"Can you get me her address?" Jackson asks. His mind whirls (like colors dissolving behind a credit roll while a woman screams).

"Sure." Justin shrugs. No questions asked — that's what Jackson likes about him. Justin consults his computer and chicken scrawls an address on the back of an old receipt.

"Thanks, man. I owe you!" Jackson snatches the paper, spins, and sprints for the door.

"Hey, who is she?" Justin calls after him.

"Carrie Linden!" Jackson slams through the door, answering only because he knows Justin won't believe him.

The name written over the address Justin gave him is Karen Finch. The address isn't five blocks from the pharmacy. Jackson runs the whole way, heaving his bulk, dripping sweat, legs burning, breath wheezing. It's worth a heart attack, worth the return of his childhood asthma, worth anything.

The street he arrives on is tree-lined and shadow-dappled. Cars border both sides of the road, dogs bark in backyards, and two houses over a group of children run in shrieking circles on an emerald lawn.

Jackson approaches number forty-seven. He's shaking. His mouth is dry in a way that has nothing to do with his mad, panting run. His heart pounds, louder than the dying echoes of his fist knocking against Carrie Linden's door. What is he doing? He should leave. But *Kaleidoscope* isn't that kind of movie. It isn't a movie at all. It's an infection, deep in Jackson's blood.

The door opens; Jackson stares.

Light frames the woman in a soft-focus glow, falling through a window at the far end of the hall. Her hair is dyed dark, but showing threads of gray (or maybe they're dirty blonde). The ends are split and frayed. She isn't wearing sunglasses, but shadows circle her eyes, seeming just as large. She is thin — not in a pretty way; her cheekbones knife against her skin. But she *is* Carrie Linden, and Jackson forgets how to breathe.

The second most famous scene in *Kaleidoscope* is the carnival scene. It's the one most viewers (not Kaleidophiles, mind you) rewind to watch over and over again. It's spawned numerous chat groups, websites, message boards, and one doctoral thesis, which languishes untouched in a drawer.

The scene goes like this: the characters go to a carnival — Carrie, Lance, Mary, and Josh, even Elizabeth, even though her face is horribly scarred (but not Lucy, because she's dead). The carnival is abandoned, but all the rides are running. The night flickers with halogen-sick lights, illuminating painted signs and gaudy-bright games. The whole scene drifts, strange and unreal.

The gang enters the funhouse. But it's not just a funhouse, it's a haunted house, a hall of mirrors, and tunnel of love all rolled into one. The cars crank along the track, but jerk to a stop in the first room, as if the ride is broken. They proceed through the ride on foot. And this is where the movie gets weird.

It fragments. Time stops. (Do any two viewers see the same scene?) The camera follows scarred Elizabeth; it follows meathead Lance. It follows Carrie Linden. Voices whisper, words play backwards, things slide, half-glimpsed, across the corners of the film, at the very *edges*, spilling off the celluloid and into the dark. (Is it any wonder the movie house burned down?)

The funhouse is filled with painted flats and cheesy rubber monsters loaded on springs. But there are also angles that shouldn't exist, reflections where there should be none.

There are odd, jerky cuts in the film itself, loops, backward stutters, and doubled scenes, as if bits of different films are being run through a projector at the same time. It's impossible.

Everyone is separated, utterly alone. The strange twists of the mirrored corridors keep them apart, even when they are only inches away. And here debates rage, because something happens, but no one is quite sure what.

Maybe Carrie Linden steps through a mirror into the room where Elizabeth is raking bloody nails against the glass, trying to escape. Some viewers claim that it isn't really Carrie, because she stepped through a mirror too. (Inside the funhouse, is anyone who they used to be?) What follows is brutal. With eerie, cold precision Carrie tortures Elizabeth. Accounts vary. Is blood actually drawn, or is the pain more subtle, more insidious than that? (What did *you* see? What do you *think* you saw?)

What makes the violence even more shocking is that up until this point in the film, Carrie has been utterly passive. (Is it possible to watch her push a sliver of mirrored glass through Elizabeth's cheek and not feel it in your own?) Elizabeth's face fills with terror, but oddly, she doesn't seem to notice Carrie at all. Her gaze darts to the mirrors. Her panicked glances skitter into the shadows.

She look straight at the camera, and tears roll silently from her eyes.

Four people leave the funhouse at the end of the scene — Carrie, Josh, Elizabeth and Lance. (Do they?) Mary is never seen again. Her absence is never explained. It's that kind of film.

The crux of the movie hangs here. Kaleidophiles know if they could just unravel this scene, they'd understand everything. (Do they really want to?) When she leaves the funhouse, what is Carrie holding in her hand? Was there really a reflection in the mirror behind Elizabeth's head? When Carrie leans down and puts her mouth against Elizabeth's ear, what does she whisper?

"Can I help you?" The woman's voice snaps Jackson back to himself. His skin flushes hot; panic constricts his throat.

The woman flickers and doubles. Carrie Linden (or Karen Finch) is here and now, but she is there and then too. Jackson shudders.

Something passes through the woman's eyes, a kind of recognition. It's as though all these years Jackson has been watching her, she's been looking right back at him.

"You're Carrie Linden," he says. His voice is thick and far away.

Her expression turns hard. Jackson sees the cold impulse to violence; for a moment, she wants to hurt him. Instead, she steps aside, her voice tight. "You'd better come inside."

Jackson squeezes past her, close enough to touch. He catches her scent — patchouli, stale cigarettes, and even staler coffee. Her posture radiates hatred; her bones are blades, aching towards his skin. When they are face to face, Jackson glimpses the truth in her eyes — she's been expecting this moment. Carrie Linden has been running her whole life, knowing sooner or later someone will catch her.

She shuts the door — a final sound. Jackson's heart skips, jitters erratically, worse than when he ran all the way here. Carrie gestures to a room opening up to the left.

"Sit. I'll make coffee."

She leaves him, disappearing down the narrow hall. Jackson lowers himself onto a futon covered with a tattered blanket. Upended apple crates flank it at either end. A coffee table sits between the futon and a nest-shaped chair. The walls are painted blood-rust red; they are utterly bare.

Carrie returns with mismatched mugs and hands him one. It's spider-webbed with near-invisible cracks, the white ceramic stained beige around the rim. The side of the mug bears an incongruous rainbow, arching away from a fluffy white cloud. Jackson sips, and almost chokes. The coffee is scalding black; she doesn't offer him milk or sugar.

Carrie Linden sits in the nest chair, tucking bare feet beneath her. She wears a chunky sweater coat. It looks hand-knit, and it nearly swallows her. She meets Jackson's gaze, so he can't possibly look away.

"Well, what do you want to know?" Her voice snaps, dry-stick brittle and hard.

Jackson can't speak for his heart lodged in his throat. There's a magic to watching *Kaleidoscope* (unless you watch it alone). The people on screen dying and fucking and screaming and weeping, they're just shadows. It's *okay* to watch; it's safe. None of it is real.

Motes of dust fall through the light around Carrie Linden — tiny, erratic fireflies. The curtains are mostly drawn, but the sun knifes through, leaving the room blood hot.

"All of it," Carries says, when Jackson can't find the words.

"What?" He gapes, mouth wide.

"That's what you're wondering, isn't it? That's what they all want to know. The answer is — all of it. All of it was real."

Jackson flinches as though he's been punched in the gut. (In a way, he has.) Should he feel guiltier about the cracked light in her eyes, or the fact that his stomach dropped when she said "that's what they all want to know"?

He isn't her first.

Carrie Linden's hands wrap around her mug, showing blue veins and fragile bones. Steam rises, curling around her face. When she raises the mug to sip, her sleeve slides back defiantly and unapologetically revealing scars.

"Well?" Carrie's gaze follows the line of Jackson's sight. "Why *did* you come, then?"

She bores into him with piercing-bright eyes, and Jackson realizes — even sitting directly across from her — he can't tell what color they are. They are every color and no color at once, as if her body is just a shell housing the infinite possibilities living inside.

"I wanted to talk about the movie. I thought maybe…" Jackson glances desperately around the bare-walled room — nowhere to run. In his head, he's rehearsed this moment a thousand times. He's *always* known exactly what he'll say to Carrie Linden when he finally meets her, but now it's all gone wrong.

I'm sorry, he wants to say, I shouldn't have come, but the words stick in his throat. His eyes sting. He's failed. In the end, he's no better than Justin, or Kevin. He's not a Kaleidophile, he hasn't transcended the sex and gore — he's just another wannabe.

Unable to look Carrie in the eye, Jackson fumbles a postcard out of his coat pocket. The edges are frayed and velvet-soft through years of wear. It's the original movie poster for *Kaleidoscope*, wrought in miniature. Jackson found it at a garage sale last year, and he's been carrying it around ever since. He passes it to Carrie with shaking hands.

As Carrie looks down to study the card, Jackson finally looks up. Like the movie, Jackson knows the card by heart, but now he sees it through Carrie's eyes; he's never loathed himself more. His eyes burn with the lurid color, the jumbled images piled together and bleeding into one.

The backdrop is a carnival, but it's also a graveyard, or maybe an empty field backed with distant trees. A woman studded with fragments of glass lies spread-eagle on a great wheel. Between her legs, Carrie lies on an altar, covered in writing snakes. Behind Carrie, Elizabeth's blood-sheeted face hangs like a crimson moon. From the black of her wide open eyes, shadowy figures seep out and stain the other images. They hide behind and inside everything, doubling and ghosting and blurring. The card isn't one thing, it's everything.

"I'm sorry." Jackson finally manages the words aloud.

Slowly, Carrie reaches for a pen lying atop of a half-finished crossword puzzle. Her hand moves, more like a spasm than anything voluntary. The nib scratches across the card's back, slicing skin and bone and soul. She lets the card fall onto the table between them, infinitely kind and infinitely cruel. Jackson thinks the tears welling in his eyes are the only things that save him.

"It's okay," she says. Her voice is not quite forgiving. For a moment, Jackson has the mad notion she might fold him in her bony arms and soothe him like a child, as though he's the one that needs, or deserves, comforting.

Instead, Carrie leans forward and opens a drawer in the coffee table, fishing out a pack of cigarettes. Something rattles and slithers against the wood as the drawer slides closed. Jackson catches a glimpse, and catches his breath. Even after forty years he imagines the beads still sticky and warm, still slicked with Elizabeth's blood.

Carrie lights her cigarette, and watches the patterns the smoke makes in the air, in shadows on the wall. They don't quite match.

"I'm the final girl," she says. The softness of her voice makes Jackson jump. He doesn't think she's even speaking to him anymore. She might as well be alone. (She's always been alone.)

"What?" Jackson says, even though he knows exactly what she's talking about. His voice quavers.

"It's fucking bullshit, you know that?" Her voice is just as soft as before if the words are harsher. "I wasn't a helpless fantasy at the beginning; I wasn't an empowered hero at the end. I was just me the whole time. I was just human."

She stands, crushing her cigarette against the cupped palm of her hand without flinching. "You can stay if you want. Or you can go. I don't really care."

And just like that she's gone. Jackson is alone with Carrie Linden's blood-red walls and her battered couch, with her beads hidden in the coffee table drawer, and her autograph on a worn-soft postcard. When she walked onto the screen, Carrie Linden stopped Jackson's heart; walking out of the room, she stops it again.

He sees Carrie Linden doubled, trebled — bony-thin hips hidden beneath a bulky sweater; the curve of her naked ass, teased by long blonde hair as she saunters across the screen; a hunted, haunted woman, glancing behind her as she darts into the drug store.

Jackson has sunk so low, he can't go any lower. (At least that's what he tells himself as he leaves to make it okay.)

At home, Jackson hides the postcard and Carrie Linden's beads at the bottom of his drawer. He covers them with socks and underwear, wadded t-shirts smelling of his sweat and late night popcorn, ripe with fear and desire.

It doesn't matter how rare the postcard is, never mind that it's signed by Carrie Linden; he'll never show it to anyone, or even take it out of the drawer. The beads are another matter.

✖

Everyone knows the opening sequence of *Kaleidoscope*, but it's the closing sequence that plays in most people's minds, projected against the ivory curve of their dreaming skulls, etched onto the thinness of their eyelids. It bathes the late-night stupors of lone losers curled on their couches with the blankets pulled up to their chins against the flickering dark. It haunts midnight movie screens in rooms smelling of sticky-sweet spills and stale salt. It looms large on sheets stretched between goal posts, while orgies wind down on the battered turf below.

It is the third most famous scene in cinema history. (Don't let anyone tell you otherwise.)

Carrie is running. Everybody else is dead — Lance and Lucy, Elizabeth and Josh and Mary, and all the other brief phantoms who never even had names. She is covered in blood. Some of it is hers. She is naked.

Ahead of her is a screen of trees. More than once, Carrie stumbles and falls. When she does, the camera shows the soles of her feet, slick and red. But she keeps getting back up, again and again. The camera judders as it follows her. It draws close, but never quite catches up.

Carrie glances back over her shoulder, eyes staring wide at something the camera never turns to let the viewer see. (Imagination isn't always the worst thing.) Carrie's expression (hunted and haunted) says it all.

There is no soundtrack, no psychedelic colors. The only sound is Carrie's feet slapping over sharp stones and broken bottles and her breath hitching in her throat. She's running for the grass and the impossibly distant trees.

The credits roll.

The screen goes dark.

But Carrie is still there, between the frames, bleeding off the edges, flickering in the shadows. She'll always be right there, forever, running.

THE ASTRONAUT, HER LOVER, THE QUEEN OF FAERIE, AND THEIR CHILD

"Tell it right this time, Mama." Dizzy nestles her head against my shoulder as I tuck the covers tighter around us.

Tell it right, Mama.

Oh, moon-child, I will. The problem is, there's never been only one way to tell the tale. This is a story about Silvie, and truth doesn't stick to her skin. It twists and turns and slides like smoke through my hands.

"I'll try, moon-child." I kiss the top of my daughter's head, burying my nose in her strawberry-shampoo-scented curls.

I'll try.

I've been trying for years, and I'll try again, for Dizzy's sake. I'll unravel the story again, and somewhere among the myriad threads, I'll find a truth I can offer my little girl.

It's hard to know where to begin. I don't want to give my daughter a story of leaving, but every arrival of Silvie's is wrapped up with her going away again.

Tell it right this time, Mama.

Oh, moon-child, I am telling it right. But the story is different every time.

I'll start with a beginning, not *the* beginning, but the first time Silvie came back to me.

Gin wakes to the sound of a stone pinging against her window. Sheets tangle around her legs, but she pushes up the window pane and catches the second stone before it hits the glass.

"Wake up, sleepy head." Silvie stands on the gravel drive, her palm full of more missiles to throw. She lets them pour through her fingers with a rattling sound as Gin leans out into the chill.

"You can't be here." Breath curls from Gin's lips as the words slip free.

It's impossible. Except here she is, standing underneath Gin's window, grinning up at her like nothing happened.

In the moonlight, her scalp is a field of stubble. The last time Gin saw her, Silvie's hair hung halfway down her back. The last time Gin saw her, Silvie didn't even say goodbye. Gin's mother sat her down and tried to explain, but the words made no sense – hospital, and sick, and going away for a while. Those weren't words that applied to Silvie and Gin had stopped listening.

"Are you just going stand there? Come on." Silvie gestures; Gin sees the bandages wrapped around her wrist.

A shock travels up her spine. Her mother's words try to creep around the edges of what Gin knows to be true, and she pushes them away. Of course they're not true, because Silvie is here, isn't she?

"Shh." Gin glances over her shoulder, sure at any moment her parents or sister will come bursting into her room. "Give me a second."

She scrambles into sneakers, jeans, and a hoodie. She's dressed before she's fully decided to go with Silvie, but of course, it isn't a choice, really. Go with Silvie, or get left behind again. Gin tucks the stone Silvie threw at her window into her pocket before climbing onto the roof.

The shingles are slick with frost, but Gin makes the leap to the tree outside her window and shimmies down. Years of doing just this, jumping down to Silvie in the middle of the night, running away for secret adventures while her parents are sleeping, make her feet sure.

"Shouldn't you be in the hospital?" Gin drops down beside Silvie, breathless.

Despite the chill, Silvie is wearing a hospital gown. It gapes in the back where it's tucked into her jeans, and leaves her arms bare.

"Time off for good behavior." Silvie waves her arm like a trophy, showing the plastic admittance bracelet circling her wrist. "Shouldn't you be in college?"

Shouldn't you? Gin wants to retort, but she holds the words back along with all the other questions she's afraid to ask Silvie. *Where have you been? Why did you leave me behind? Why didn't you say goodbye?*

"Come on." Silvie's fingers are suddenly there, cold and hard between Gin's as she tugs on her hand.

"Aren't you..." Gin swallows, her throat tight.

"Aren't I what, Gin?" There's a thinness to Silvie's face; her eyes are too big, full of moonlight shine. Her tone is hard.

More words stick in Gin's throat. *Sick. Suicidal.* She shakes her head. Thinking about where Silvie has been makes Gin's head hurt. She has a vague notion that maybe she has it wrong, maybe she was the one who was sick, not Silvie.

"Cold," Gin says, turning away. Better to focus on the here and now. Silvie is back, they're together, that's what matters.

She lets Silvie lead her to the car she claims is borrowed from her brother, which Gin knows means borrowed without asking. Of course Silvie intends to return it, but Silvie's intentions don't always match reality.

"Where are we going?" Gin reaches to crank the heater as Silvie pulls down the road.

"You'll see."

As she hits the bridge crossing the bay, Silvie opens the glove box. She pulls out a pack of cigarettes and a fifth of vodka. She holds them in her lap, daring Gin to say something.

Gin keeps her mouth shut. A fluttery, panicked sensation keeps trying to take root in her stomach. She focuses on breathing, on the lights sliding past outside the car. Silvie can't vanish mid-bridge; as long as they're driving, they're safe.

But as the car slows, the panicked feeling returns, doubled, and then full-force when Gin sees where they are.

"Muir Woods? Seriously? Are we going to break in? We'll be arrested."

Silvie doesn't answer for a moment, keeping her hands on the wheel, studying her chewed-short nails and her wrists wrapped in bandages.

"I'm sorry I didn't say goodbye properly last time," Silvie says.

It isn't an answer. Unease continues to prickle Gin's spine, a cold creeping steadily beneath her skin.

"What are we really doing here?" She looks at Silvie side-wise.

"You worry too much," Silvie says, climbing out of the car.

Gin scrambles to catch up. There really should be someone to stop them, but time with Silvie follows dream logic. Somehow, they're already past the barricades, in among the trees.

"Oh." Gin lets out a wondering breath, and all at once, she forgets to worry or be afraid.

The woods are different at night. Silence swallows everything and the sky turns a slow wheel above the treetops, only the barest glimmer of stars against the dark. Silvie threads her fingers between Gin's.

"See?" Silvie says. "This is the way it's supposed to be. Just you and me. I'm sorry I didn't say goodbye last time. I'll make it up to you now."

Gin's pulse quickens as Silvie leads her deeper among the trees. With Silvie's palm against hers, she forgets to be cold. Neither of them stumble despite the roots trying to tangle themselves across the path. Then all at once, Silvie stops. The absence of her hand is palpable as she digs in her pocket for the cigarettes and lights one. Gin shivers; she doesn't remember Silvie smoking before she went away.

"There are rules," Silvie says.

She uncaps the vodka and takes a slug, walking carefully, heel to toe in a straight line.

"Stay on the path. Don't eat anything you're offered, and you can come home again."

"What the hell are you talking about?" Gin stares at Silvie's back, the fear returning.

Something is terribly wrong. Silvie's tone is the one that usually comes before something bad happening — *cut class with me, Gin; my parents never check the liquor cabinet; it's not stealing if we bring it back; just hide it under your shirt and walk out the door.*

"Faeries." Silvie stops and turns to face Gin.

Her eyes are an impossible silver in the moonlight. The same trick of light and shadow makes Silvie's skull visible through her skin. For a moment, Gin scarcely recognizes her. Inhuman. Someone has stolen her best friend and replaced her with something else.

"I have to go away again, Gin. Just for a little while." Silvie runs a hand over the stubble of her hair. "Then I can come back again. As long as I follow the rules."

She isn't looking at Gin, which makes Gin want to grab Silvie by the shoulders and scream in her face. *Tell me the truth, just for once. No more stories, no more lying. Where have you been? Where did you go? Why are you leaving again?* The hospital wristband shows bright in the darkness. The same words from earlier echo through her head — *suicide, anorexia, abuse.* But none of them seem right. None of them are Silvie.

"I will come back. You believe me, don't you?"

"I..." Gin wants to say yes, but it sticks in her throat, but no doesn't feel right either.

Her eyes sting hot. She thinks of all the stories she and Silvie used to tell as kids, reading Tam Lin and the Faerie Queen and making up their own adventures afterward. Here, in the cathedral stillness of the woods, Gin can believe all those stories are real.

Should she throw her arms around Silvie, hold on as she changes to smoke and water and force her to stay? Or maybe there's a magic spell, words to keep Silvie by her side. Words she's never dared say aloud before. *I love you. I need you. Don't go.*

Silvie is the one who closes the space between them, sudden and almost violent. Her lips on Gin's taste like the raw sting of cheap vodka, flecked with cigarette ash. Silvie breaks the kiss too soon, leaning their foreheads together so her eyes become all of Gin's world.

"I need you believe in me, Gin." There's a dangerous edge to the brightness in Silvie's eyes. The silver is a knife, tucked into her gaze, but Gin can't tell which way the blade will turn.

I can't get caught with this, Gin. You don't have any priors, you hold it. I promise, everything will be fine.

Silvie's charmed bubble has always held before. The blade has never slipped, Gin has never been cut, but this time feels different. Silvie steps back. Holding the cigarette in the corner of her mouth, she unwinds the gauze from her wrist, revealing stitches.

"Silvie, don't..."

Gin tries to move toward her, but some strange force of gravity holds her back. This, too, is like a dream, the kind where none of her limbs will obey her. She can't reach Silvie, no matter how small the space is between them.

"Smoke." Silvie breathes out a stream. "That's the first offering."

"Alcohol." She tips vodka onto the ground.

Gin can only watch, her breath coming out in a whine.

"And blood." Silvie uses her ragged fingernails to snag her scabs, shaking a few drops free.

"Gifts for the faeries, to open the gate."

"Don't." Gin reaches for Silvie.

Silvie shakes her head, her expression one of pity and a little bit of sorrow.

"Stay on the path, Gin. Stay safe so I'll always have someone to come home to."

Silvie steps backward. There's a thin piece of wood dividing the path from the trees. She steps back again, and she's gone. Gin scrambles to edge and peers over. There's a drop and she expects Silvie's body tumbled and broken at the bottom, but there's nothing.

Silvie stepped into thin air, vanished, and now she's gone.

✕

"What about the astronaut?" Dizzy says. "You said there'd be an astronaut."

"Hmm?"

I look away from the bay, distracted. Light from the water still sparks against my eyes, like faerie lights between me and my daughter. I blink away the afterimages until I can see Dizzy clearly.

"The astronaut, Mama." Dizzy rolls her eyes, miming exasperation.

I wrack my brain. Did I tell her there was an astronaut? The story keeps twisting away from me, like Silvie herself, water and smoke in my hands.

We're in a park above the bay, a picnic spread between us. The bridge, the same one I drove over with Silvie a lifetime ago, stretches away to Sausalito on the other side. Before I can catch the threads of the story, the ground shivers. Dizzy's eyes go wide.

It's just a tiny earthquake, but Dizzy's never felt one before. I take her hand, her fingers sticky with jam. There's a solidity to her, baby-fat-soft, her skin sun-warm and smelling of lotion.

"Come here, baby." I pull her closer, cradle her body against mine.

I lie down and press my ear against the earth, and she does the same.

"Do you hear that?"

Dizzy shakes her head, trying to squirm out of my grasp.

"Shh. Listen."

I close my eyes, nose pressed to the back of Dizzy's head. Even through the blanket, I feel spears of grass pushing up toward the sun, and under that, dark earth, moving with worms. Below the pulse of this life, there's a second beat, a heartbeat, drumbeat, pound of feet, and prance of hooves.

"What is it, Mama?"

"That's the kingdom of Faerie, moon-baby. Well, queendom. When the ground shivers like that, it's the Queen of Faerie holding a feast. If you're very quiet, you can hear them laughing and playing music."

It sounds like something Silvie would say, her words in my mouth, tasting of cigarettes and cheap vodka. Here, on the sun-warmed grass slope, I can believe. I can even see Silvie at the Faerie Queen's side, her hair long the way it was before she went away the first time, all woven with violets. She's smiling, and the Faerie Queen is luminous, so painfully beautiful it's hard to look at her.

"That's your mother down there," I say. The words husk. I swallow, and my throat is raw.

Dizzy turns. She reminds me of Silvie, eyes large in her small face so they take up my entire field of vision. A frown tugs at her mouth.

"But you're my mama. How can my mother be down there?" She pats the grass with her hand.

"Sometimes more than one thing can be true, moon-child." I smile against the prickling behind my eyes.

"If my mama's with the faeries, does that mean I'm a faerie, too?" She chews her lip, expression serious.

"You're my Faerie Princess." The words are thick.

"But if I'm a faerie princess, why do you call me a moon-baby?"

Dizzy finally succeeds in squirming free and sitting up.

"You *are* my moon-baby," I say, sitting up and cupping her cheek in my hand. An ache settles just below my breastbone. After all this time, how can it still be so hard to talk about Silvie, to get the story right?

"Why don't I tell you more of the story," I say. "The part with the astronaut in it, and we can try to figure it out together, okay?"

Silvie comes back.

It's impossible, but she climbs through Gin's window, not bothering with stones this time. The one she threw the night she first came home sits on Gin's nightstand like a talisman. Sometimes Gin wakes up clutching it so hard it leaves bruises the color of violets on her palm.

Silvie crawls under the covers, her flesh freezing. Gin holds her breath, afraid to move. It has to be a dream. She's stopped counting the days since Silvie vanished. But now Silvie's bones and sharp angles dig into Gin; her chilled skin soaks up Gin's heat. Here and undeniably real.

"You came back," Gin says.

"I came back." Silvie leans her forehead against Gin's. Gin can just see her eyes in the dark, and her smile. Silvie's breath smells of something she can't quite name — peppermint, and a stale medicine tang. "I promised I would."

There isn't time for Gin to decide whether this is happening, whether any of it is real, before Silvie kisses her. Despite the medicine smell, her mouth tastes like smoke and whiskey and honey. The sharp burn of cheap vodka, the stale, ash-flecked taste is gone. How long, Gin thinks, how long, and the thought slips away like a thread of smoke, an offering to the faeries. The kiss is melting, golden and liquid, and all that matters is now. Except...

"Where were you?" Gin pulls back.

She's reluctant to take her mouth from Silvie's, but she can't help asking the question. This time, she swears, she won't let Silvie go without an explanation. She's spent too long applying those ugly words to Silvie, the ones that don't fit — depression, self-harm, cancer, suicide. Some days, Gin even manages to convince herself Silvie never existed. But now she's here and real and warming in Gin's arms, and she needs something to make sense of Silvie vanishing. Words to patch over the hole in her heart. Gin thinks she'll accept whatever Silvie tells her, even if it's a lie, so long as Silvie gives her something.

"In outer space," Silvie says, her voice wistful and dreaming. "Among the stars. I've been gone for a million years."

Gin's breath catches. Despite her resolve to believe, she's disappointed.

"What about Faerie?"

The look Silvie gives her is hard to read in the dark, but it might be pity. Or it might be pain. Her voice is soft though, like a lullaby.

"Oh, Gin, what does that matter now? I'm here."

It hurts, but Gin lets any other questions go. She lets Silvie sink into her and fill the humming spaces between her bones with words. Silvie's voice is a low murmur, describing the wonders she's seen — the earth from above, all blue-green and tipped with white at either end, how her feet have touched the red dust of Mars, and how she's drifted out beyond the Kuiper belt, so far beyond. None of it makes sense, but as Silvie speaks, the world drops away. Gin can't hold onto her anger or her doubt. She's right there beside Silvie, drifting miles above earth and watching the sun spill over the curve of the horizon.

Floating among the million, billion stars spilling from Silvie's lips, they make love. Silvie's mouth is on her. Her hands are on her and inside her and this is everything she's ever wanted. Gin's cheeks are wet. She closes her eyes, trying to drift forever. She never wants it to end.

But it does.

Gin wakes alone. Her hands are fists, one of them clenching Silvie's stone, her palm red from holding onto it so hard.

She followed the rules, and Silvie came back to her. She followed the rules, but Silvie is gone again.

Gin buries her face in her pillow and sobs. She grips Silvie's stone and wills it to disappear into her skin. It was real; she has the memory of Silvie's smoke-and-honey-and-whiskey mouth. It has to be real. As her body shudders, all she can think is, if she's patient, if she keeps following the rules, maybe Silvie will come back to her again.

✖

"So my mama's an astronaut *and* a faerie?" Dizzy asks.

Her eyes are wide, full of deep consideration and wonder.

"That's right, baby-girl." My phone buzzes, my sister's name lighting up the screen. I tense, before remembering myself and pasting on a smile. "Go play outside while I talk to your Aunt Lisa. I'll tell you more of the story later."

"I'm going to throw an astronaut faerie tea party!"

"Okay, moon-girl. Stay where I can see you."

The light through the kitchen window is deep and gold. How long have Dizzy and I been sitting at the table, telling stories? As the backdoor closes, I answer my phone.

"Lisa."

"Hello to you, too. I just wanted to see how you're doing."

Lisa's tone is too carefully casual.

"Fine," I say.

I know she means well, but I'm so tired of people who mean well. I just want to get on with my life, and do it alone. I watch Dizzy through the kitchen window. She's wearing a clear plastic salad bowl turned upside down on her head — her space helmet — and spreading out a blanket for tea. I watch her careful preparations, attention drifting, then snap back into the conversation all at once as my sister's words catch me.

"I don't want to be set up on a blind date."

"Okay." I hear Lisa take a mental deep breath. "It doesn't have to be a date. You could go to a spa, take a class. Something. I know it's hard, being a single parent..."

Lisa doesn't know any such thing, but her voice is so earnest. She's trying, and I swallow my words.

"I just need more time," I say.

And there, without being able to see her, I feel Lisa flinch. More time. How many years have I been asking for more time?

"Ginny, you can't keep doing this. You can't keep waiting for someone who — "

"Don't." I cut her off, my voice sharp, but with a raw edge underneath it.

Outside, Dizzy runs in circles with her arms held to the side. I can't hear her through the glass, but I can imagine the whooshing rocket noises.

"I know what you're going to say," I tell Lisa.

There are only two options, and I don't want to hear either of them. *You can't keep waiting for someone who isn't coming home. You can't keep waiting for someone who never existed.*

"Okay," Lisa says, just that.

I picture her lips pressed together, fingers drumming the table as she struggles with patience.

"But if you need anything…" She lets the words hang.

"I know." I close my eyes, leaning against the sink and letting the counter take my weight.

I pinch the bridge of my nose. There's an ache behind my eyes. There are stars, so very many of them, and I'm floating lost among them. Silvie isn't coming home. Silvie never existed. Does my sister think I've never thought of these things without her saying them? Does she really think I'm not trying? I *am* trying, for Dizzy's sake.

I just have to find my way to the end of the story, and everything will be fine.

I open my eyes. Outside, Dizzy pours invisible tea into tiny pink plastic cups, conversing happily with the empty air.

"I love you," Lisa says from the other side of the world.

"Love you too." I hang up before she can say anything more.

Follow the rules. Stay on the path. This is the way it has to be.

Dizzy jumps up again to run around the small square of our yard. When she catches me watching, she stops and waves. After a moment, I step out onto the back porch, letting the sun warm my skin.

"Come join my tea party, Mama."

I step off the porch, blades of grass tickling my bare feet.

"You sit there." Dizzy directs me, and I obey.

As I fold myself onto the blanket, there's a feeling like a storm coming on, electricity against my skin. I glance to the corner of the blanket where Dizzy has laid out two pink plastic cups of invisible tea. She seats herself in front of a third, and pours a fourth cup for me. I can't take my eyes off the other two cups — one for the Faerie Queen and one for Silvie.

A slant in the afternoon light. The air shimmers, and changes, and for a moment, Silvie is there with me. Her hair is shaved to stubble, but her eyes are bright. She puts her finger to her lips, and winks at me.

Dizzy tugs on my sleeve, bringing me back to the here and now.

"Tell me more of the story, Mama. You promised."

"I did, didn't I, moon-baby? And what do we say about promises?"

"Always keep them." Dizzy tilts her head up toward me, offering a gap-toothed grin. She lost her first baby tooth last night, and we left it under her pillow for the faeries. I stayed awake all night, hoping Silvie would be the one to come.

"That's right." I tap Dizzy on the nose, and she scrunches it up at me before I settle her against me, my arm around her shoulder.

"Now, where were we?"

✤

Silvie comes back. Again. Gin knows it's her the moment she knocks. Gin's in a different house now, there's no way Silvie could have found her, but there's no one else it could be. Legs stiff, Gin rises from the couch, and puts her eye to the peephole.

A cigarette burns in one of Silvie's hands. As usual, she isn't dressed for the weather. Her arms are bare, and behind her, rain erases everything. She keeps glancing over her shoulder.

"Hi," Silvie says as Gin opens the door.

She steps inside like it's only been a moment since she disappeared, picking up the thread of a conversation Gin lost ages ago. Silvie's boots make puddles on the floor, and now Gin sees the thing on step that had been blocked by Silvie's body before. A car seat, with a baby bundled inside.

Silvie's smile is nervous, a jittery, shattered thing. She shrugs one shoulder. Her gaze moves around the room, never settling.

"Hi," Silvie says again, and for a moment, Gin wants to hit her.

She wants to see Silvie's lip split, blood running down her chin. But instead she picks up the car seat and carries it inside, because what else can she do?

The baby is wrapped in two layers of blankets — one blue, printed with a pattern of rockets and white stars, the other yellow, scattered with tiny faeries in pink and purple and green.

Gin stares at Silvie, at the swaddled baby between them.

"Where did you…?" She can't finish the question.

Words bounce and clatter in Gin's skull. *Changeling. Stolen. Alien. Unwed mother. Adoption.* Any and all of them could be true. She pictures Silvie, round as the moon, terrified and alone. Gin can picture it, because she can imagine exactly how she would feel in that situation.

She pushes down sympathy, glaring at Silvie, her fingers curled into fists at her side. She wants to hold onto her rage.

"Where the hell did you get a baby?"

Silvie's been gone for years; the space left by her absence has been filling with anger one drop at a time.

"I'm in trouble, Gin."

Silvie wraps her arms around her body, holding hard angles together. Her head is still shaved. She barely looks a day older than when Gin last saw her. Except she's thinner now, and the shadows bruising her eyes have become permanent.

Silvie sniffs, wiping her nose with the back of her hand. Her skin is goose-pimpled. She looks so incredibly fragile and lost Gin wants to fold her in her arms and she hates herself for feeling that way. How dare Silvie come back here again? How dare Silvie keep breaking her heart?

The baby chooses that moment to cry.

Silvie lifts the bundle — baby and blankets — holding it awkwardly. She bounces the child, the motion somewhere between impatience and panic, then pushes all of it into Gin's arms.

"You take her. I'm terrible at this."

Gin is too shocked to protest. She holds the child, swaying by instinct until the crying stops.

"You can't keep doing this." Gin looks at the baby instead of Silvie. It's easier that way.

"She's yours," Silvie says, and Gin's head snaps up.

"What?"

For a moment, the room is filled with ghosts — Silvie, framed by the cathedral height of trees; Silvie under Gin's window, made of shadows and moonlight; Silvie's skull visible beneath her skin, lost in the whiteness of a hospital bed; Silvie drifting free among the stars. When Gin blinks, the ghosts collapse into one thin, haunted woman. Silvie as she's always been, as she'll always be — a contradiction, here and gone, lost and coming home.

"I've never loved anyone but you, Gin. Who else's baby would she be?"

Gin thinks of Silvie's skin, cold against hers in a sea of blue shadows. The stars pouring from her mouth, which tasted of smoke and whiskey and honey. Those stolen moments she'd convinced herself were a dream.

"It doesn't work that way," Gin says.

She looks down to find the baby looking right back at her. The eyes are the same ones she sees in the mirror every day. The breath leaves Gin in and rush. Her heart aches, doubts crowding around it, but she tightens her grip on the baby girl in her arms.

It doesn't work that way, but maybe, just maybe it does.

Down-soft hair peeks out from the wrapped blankets. There's a luminous quality to the baby's skin. Not like Silvie's ghost-glow, but the opposite, like the baby is more alive, more real than either Silvie or Gin.

The door opening and closing doesn't register. When Gin does look up, Silvie is gone.

The dam holding back all the sorrow and rage cracks. She wants to scream, she wants to weep and rage and throw things at the closed door. But she can't. The little girl in her arms needs her. Her *daughter* needs her, and she can't afford to fall apart right now.

Gin breathes out, making her heartbeat calm, but oh god, what is she going to do with a baby? This tiny, fragile life is her responsibility now. The thought of it makes her blood fizz and leaves her dizzy.

"Dizzy." Gin tests the word aloud, and the baby coos, waving fat arms that have come free from the blankets.

"Dizzy," she says again, and the baby smiles.

✖

"Are you making all this up?" Dizzy asks.

The question startles me, and I pull my gaze away from the telescope's eyepiece. Dizzy, sitting in her camp chair, watches me carefully. I rented a cabin for the weekend so we could watch the meteor shower together, far from the city lights. Dizzy's big into space lately, rocket ships and astronauts; I thought this would be a good chance to bond. She's growing up fast, my little girl. Already, the baby-roundness of her cheeks is almost invisible. She's getting too old for faerie tales, and I still haven't found a way to explain Silvie. To her or myself.

The telescope balances on the porch between us. We each have a blanket on our laps and a thermos beside our chairs — tea for me, hot chocolate for Dizzy.

"What do you mean?" I ask.

Dizzy rolls her eyes, the expression much more natural these days.

"First Silvie ran away to Faerie, and now she's an astronaut? The story keeps changing, and it all sounds made up."

It does, at that, but Dizzy's words still sting. She's far too young for teenage rebellion, but I can see the seeds of it, curled and waiting to grow. She's becoming her own person, separate from me. Or rather, she was always her own person, but she's learning to express it without reserve.

Part of me is desperate to hold on — a mother's futile wish to keep my baby girl with me forever. The more rational part knows I need to learn to let her go, something I've never been particularly good at. Sometimes I think of Dizzy as a seed caught on the wind. I want to see where she'll land, what she'll grow into, what kind of person she'll be.

"I can stop, if you want." My voice comes out smaller than I expected.

I didn't mean to let Dizzy see my hurt. Now it's there, raw and exposed between us. It makes me feel like I'm the child. Her expression changes, a subtle and complicated thing. Light slides through her eyes, which are sometimes like mine, and sometimes like Silvie's.

"No, I want to hear the end," she says.

Maybe she says it because she thinks it's what I want to hear, but there's a note of genuine curiosity tucked inside her words. Despite myself, I smile.

"Where do you think Silvie is right now?" Dizzy asks, giving me an opening.

"Well, let's see." I set my tea aside and lean toward the telescope, adjusting the eyepiece. Night insects chirr. "She should be right about *there*."

I lean back, turning the eyepiece over to Dizzy. She scoots her chair closer, bending to look.

My phone buzzes, startling me. While Dizzy is focused on the stars, I slip the phone out of my pocket. A text message from Megan.

We met at the library. She has a son Dizzy's age, both voracious readers, and we kept running into each other. Accidentally at first, and maybe not so accidentally later on. We've had coffee once, nothing more. She knows about Dizzy, of course, but not about Silvie. My pulse thumps, guilty. Another glance at Dizzy, who is still absorbed in the stars, and I thumb the message open.

Hope you're enjoying the meteors. :)

The message is simple, and what else should it be? My stomach flutters on disappointment nonetheless. A stupid part of me wants Megan to say she wishes she was here. I want her to say something playful and a little suggestive, making me blush.

Disgusted with myself, I slip my phone back into my pocket. I'm waiting for Silvie. I'm following the rules. There's nothing in the rules about cute women met at the library who are here and now, not impossible and far away.

I lean back in my chair, wrapping my hands around my thermos of tea. Even without the telescope, the stars are perfect. I try to picture Silvie up there. But the more I reach after her, the more she becomes a ghost, smoke and water slipping through my fingers, an abstract concept impossible to hold.

Silvie away is perfect. What will happen if she finally comes home, when she touches down on earth and decides to stay? What will I do when I'm faced with the reality of her every day? The sound of her breath, the weight of her body, the way she moves.

I've spent so long dreaming and imagining every possibility, but the woman who comes home to me will be a stranger. Time works differently among the stars. It's not a matter of light years or distance. It's a matter of all my days spent left behind while Silvie floated in a capsule among the stars. She's been weightless, breathing recycled air, drinking recycled water, eating packaged foods. Her life is so far removed from mine, I have no idea what I'd even say to her.

Down here on Earth, I have Dizzy and the hundred million new things she learns every day. There are bills and groceries, missing the bus and being late for work.

When Silvie comes home, I'll have to spend the rest of our lives together pretending she isn't a changeling wearing my lover's skin, as if the same Silvie who left me years ago is the one who came home. Her eyes will have seen the stars from angles I can't comprehend. I'll ask her to stand beside me on a porch like this one and look at them through a telescope, and she'll have to pretend it's enough.

"Look, the shooting stars!" Dizzy pulls away from the eyepiece, pointing.

Silver blazes across the sky. My breath catches. I put my arm around my daughter. What if one of those streaks of light is Silvie's ship, scattered across the dark, broken into a thousand pieces with Silvie's bones burning up before they ever touch the ground?

I hate myself for even thinking it. I try not to wish on a falling star that it will come true.

I want Silvie safe and back with me. I don't want her to come home.

More than one thing can be true.

I want Silvie never to have left me in the first place.

✖

Gin's phone pings, a soft sound like a stone hitting a window. Squinting at the screen's glow, she reads, *3:41 a.m — Silvie: Meet me at Ames in San Jose.*

Gin's mouth goes dry. Silvie. Gin hasn't heard from her in… How long has it been? Where the hell has she been? And what is Ames?

Even as the thoughts chase through Gin's head, she's already pulling on clothes with sleep-thick fingers, looking up Ames and San Jose. Gin stops for coffee, but nothing else, driving through the silver-blue hours before dawn. Her mind made up before she's even though it through. An hour to San Jose, because Silvie summoned her, and it was never even a question whether she would obey.

Ames Research Center is fenced-in and has an impressive-looking security gate. Gin parks down the road, climbing out of the car as the sky begins to lighten. There's a rocket on the other side of the fence, but it's just wood and plaster, not the real thing. Silvie melts out of the shadows, and Gin starts.

"Shit. You scared me."

Moisture beads the air, not quite rain. Gin steps closer, trying to get a better look at Silvie. In the pre-dawn light, she's a ghost.

"What are we doing here?" Gin asks; she hates how breathless her voice sounds. She's afraid to touch Silvie in case she vanishes, a figment of her imagination after all.

Instead of an answer, Silvie grabs the fence surrounding the compound. Gin's heart pulses in her throat, blocking a shout, but Silvie is already up and over. She grins through the fence, features sliced into diamond shapes by the thick wires.

"I'll unlock the gate."

There should be sirens, a guard, something, but there's only Gin's breath as she tries to keep up. This reminds her of something, but she can't think what. For some reason, she pictures tall trees beneath a wheeling blanket of stars. Have they been here before?

Gin misses the part where Silvie gets the gate open and suddenly Gin is inside the fence with her, breaking and entering. *Don't worry, Gin. I swear, we won't get caught. Kids shoplift all the time. Everybody comes here. The signs don't mean anything. It's perfectly safe.*

Gin looks up at the sleek length of the wood and plaster rocket. The not-quite-light-not-quite-dark sky transforms it, making it look almost real. Silvie produces a pack of cigarettes from somewhere and lights one. Déjà vu nags at Gin, a dizzy feeling so she has to lower her head, breathing deep of the morning air.

"Could you please tell me what's going on?" Gin clenches her fingers into a fist at her side. None of this makes any sense.

"I have to go away, Gin." Silvie's words are an echo of an echo.

"Where?"

"Up there." Silvie points at the rocket, trailing smoke. "I've been accepted for the mission."

"What mission? Silvie, what the hell are you talking about?"

"Top secret."

Gin raises her head in time to see Silvie grin. Gin wonders whether she's the one losing it. Of course Silvie is in the space program; she told Gin about it ages ago. Now she's been accepted for a mission, a life among the stars. How could she have forgotten?

Silvie is still talking, but Gin can't hear her. Her voice is like a radio caught between two stations, words from each ghosting through. Gin shakes her head, trying to clear it.

"Training starts tomorrow. I'll have to follow all these crazy rules, a strict diet, exercise, but tonight I want to celebrate. With you."

The last words are pointed. The way Silvie is looking at her makes Gin's stomach drop. Silvie's eyes are wide and full of starving light. She's looking at Gin in a hungry kind of way, a way she's never looked at her before. Gin always hoped, but now Silvie's attention makes her want to squirm. It all feels wrong.

"Didn't you..." Gin starts to say, but she doesn't know how to finish the sentence. *Didn't you go to live with the faeries?* But that sounds ridiculous. *Weren't you sick? Didn't you have a baby and that's why you had to go away? You tried to kill yourself. You succeeded. None of this is real.* Every variation she tries sounds just as wrong. Silvie is here, with Gin, and she wants to celebrate.

Silvie pulls a flask from her pocket and takes a long swallow. Her free hand catches Gin's, the twin points of their pulses beating in time.

"I'm glad you're here," Silvie says. Her smile is genuine.

She hands over the flask, and Gin drinks, nearly choking. She wipes her mouth with the back of her hand.

"What the hell is this?"

"Only the finest rotgut."

She pulls Gin closer, the suddenness of it stealing Gin's breath. There's a roaring when Silvie kisses her, like the wood and plaster rocket firing as it lifts into the sky. Silvie's hands slide under Gin's shirt, cold against her skin. She bites down on Gin's lip, hard enough to draw blood.

"Ow! What are you doing?"

Gin pulls back, but Silvie catches the back of her neck, resting her forehead against Gin's.

"I want to drink you in. I want to remember every single moment of this."

Then Silvie is kissing her again. Her mouth tastes like rotgut and ash and the salt tang of blood. All Gin can think is smoke, alcohol, and blood, over and over again. The words beat against her closed eyelids, crowd her throat and make it hard to breathe. An offering, a spell, something to keep Silvie by her side, or a way to open the door so she can run away again. Smoke, alcohol, blood. Air, fire, water with salt, earth.

Everything spins dizzily. The rocket fires. The sky swallows Silvie whole. There are tears on Gin's cheeks and she is alone again.

⤝⤞

"Sleep tight, my little moon-faerie." I tuck the covers under Dizzy's chin and plant a kiss on the tip of her nose.

Her eyes shine in the darkness, an argument building behind them — she's not sleepy, I didn't tell the story right, I need to start over again — but the storm never breaks. It only grumbles, low thunder as Dizzy rolls over, pulling the covers with her as she turns her back, murmuring, "G'night," into her pillow.

I stand in the doorway, watching her back. Her breath never evens and deepens, but she doesn't speak again. I've tried to do the best I can by her. I've tried to give her as much truth as I know. But there's no clear path to follow through the woods, no map between the stars. I'm making all of this up as I go along. I can only hope Dizzy grows into someone who can find her own way.

As I double-check the locks on the windows and doors, a shadow at the end of the driveway catches my eye. I'm halfway down the steps before I realize the shape is all wrong. The woman is too tall, her hair is too long; she doesn't look a thing like Silvie. But now curiosity has me, and a little bit of fear. I approach her cautiously.

"Got a light?" The woman holds up a cigarette.

"Sorry. I don't smoke."

"Pity," the woman says, but she smiles.

There's something familiar about her. I can see her more clearly than I should; there are no streetlights on this stretch of road, but a soft glow surrounds her. There's a scent, too, like honeysuckle, and electricity, like standing under a confluence of wires. The hairs on my arms stand on end.

"You're…" But I stop. It's just a story. Pretty words to heal a broken heart.

I blink. There are moon-white flowers in the woman's hair. I blink again and her hair is twisted into an efficient bun. She holds an astronaut's helmet under her arm.

Light that isn't quite a wink slides through the Faerie Queen's eyes. I stumble half a step and catch myself on the garbage cans waiting at the end of the drive.

"What…" I swallow, start again. "What are you doing here?"

She's impossible, but she's standing in front of me.

More than one thing can be true.

"I had to see for myself," the Faerie Astronaut says.

"See what?"

"She came back to you." There's a touch of bitterness in her voice, but there's a lift to the corner of her mouth as well.

"I offered her everything, but no matter what I gave her — the world under the ground, or all the stars above, she kept coming back to you."

My head buzzes. The woman doubles — bare feet, long hair, the smell of honeysuckle; a suit, a space helmet, a clean scent like soap and talcum powder.

The woman snaps her fingers. Fire blooms between them, cold and pale. She touches the flame to her cigarette.

"I tried to hold onto her, but she was like water, smoke."

"Always leaving," I say. "Always drifting away."

The woman nods. Her gaze flickers to Dizzy's window, open to the warm evening air, then back to my face.

"Love isn't like it is in ballads. It isn't something you win or keep by holding on tight enough."

Her expression is hard to read. She's watching me intently like she expects something, like she's testing me, but I don't know what to say. It isn't fair. I followed Silvie's rules, even though I never understood them. I waited for her, all this time. I stayed on the path. I never strayed.

My throat tightens, eyes hot and dry.

"How do I..." I start to say *win her back*, but the Faerie Queen already told me — it doesn't work that way. "How do I learn to let her go?"

I lower my eyes, ashamed, hot tears slip down my cheeks.

"It isn't easy," the Faerie Queen says, breathing smoke and looking at me out of the corner of her eye. "It took me years. It may take you longer, a lifetime even, but it can be done."

My heart thump-kicks back into rhythm with the world. My whole life, my whole story, has been Silvie up until now. What will I do without her? What will I do if this time she doesn't come home?

I close my eyes, lashes frosted with tears. The earth turns, the stars turn; I can feel both of them. I'm not out of the woods yet, but I can see the path.

The Faerie Queen's touch startles me, her fingers cool on mine. She squeezes my hand, briefly, like a blessing, the honeysuckle and smoke scent of her heavy in my nose.

Upstairs, my little girl is waiting for me. My little girl who is flesh and bone and real, all questions. Just thinking about her fills my heart to cracking with love. She needs me. Maybe there is no map for this kind of situation, but we can draw one together. Maybe it's time to tell a new story.

"Next time you see Silvie," the Faerie Queen whispers, "give her my love, and say goodbye."

I open my eyes, and the Faerie Queen is gone. A curl of smoke lingers on the air, so faint I might be imagining it.

I climb the porch stairs, closing and locking the door behind me. At my daughter's room, I check in on her one more time. A nightlight casts a soft glow on Dizzy's sleeping form. Her limbs are slack, dream-loosened, her breath deep and even. I kiss the tips of my fingers and wave them in her direction. It's time to start over again. It's time to let go.

"I'll get the story right this time, baby-girl. I promise."

THE LAST SURVIVOR OF THE GREAT SEXBOT REVOLUTION

She's not what you expected, Alma May Anderson, the last survivor of the Great Sexbot Revolution. For one thing, her eyes are bluer. She must be a hundred if she's a day, but her eyes are the blue of puddle-broken neon, and a postcard ocean, and the sky at noon. They are all the things you thought were only metaphor, because nobody's eyes could really be all those colors at once. But there they are, watching you over a teacup as thin as an eggshell filled with jasmine-scented tea.

You didn't expect her to be in plain sight, either. All your careful research, chasing down obscure references in mostly forgotten histories, and here she is. She's not hiding, and if she's not proud of her part in history, she's not ashamed, either.

She makes you want to sit up straighter. She makes you want to tuck your shirt in, and smooth your hair. She makes you want to say please and thank you, and may I instead of can I. And all that after you tumbled, panting, through her window in the middle of the night. She didn't ask your name, or question your presence in her home. She made you tea.

You sip to cover your nerves, because Alma May has been watching you with her poetry-eyes since you arrived, never once looking away. The tea is more intense than you're used to, real leaves — you can almost feel the ghost-weight of them on your tongue.

"I suppose you want to see my sexbot," she says.

"I…" You nearly choke on that weighty tea. Your cup rattles as you set it down.

You can't help a glance toward the window, listening for the pounding of footsteps from the street below. What if you were followed? What if Sam…?

"That's why you came isn't it?" Alma May folds her hands in her lap, one laid precisely over the other.

She says it matter-of-factly, not blushing, not accusing, and not guilty, either. Despite the tea, your throat is bone-dry. Alma May's mouth quirks up in what might almost be a smile.

"What do you know about the Great Sexbot Revolution?" She asks it more gently even than a teacher might. She asks it like she really wants to know, as though she has no part in history, only a curious bystander, a stranger looking to pass the time.

Your pulse finally slows. You're sober now, but shaking, and your cheeks color for a different reason than your mad run uptown.

"I don't… Not much, really. I guess. Ma'am."

"Tsk. What *do* they teach in school these days?" It's not a true admonishment, but you can't help taking it as one. Now that you're here, you feel like a complete fool.

"Sorry," you say, bumping the table and spilling your tea in your haste to rise. "I should go. I shouldn't have…" You gesture at the window, then at the cup in its tea-spotted saucer. "I mean, thank you."

It's the most you've said since Alma May froze you in place by switching the lights on while one of your feet still hung out her window onto the fire escape.

"Sit." A simple word, a quiet word, but it has enough force to push you back into your chair and drive the breath from your lungs.

You sit because, panic aside, deep down you know you didn't make a mistake coming here. You made your mistake what feels like a lifetime ago. Drunkenly bragging to take off the sting of Sam stalking away, telling anyone who would listen, that you — despite being an unbeliever, in Sam's words — that *you*, not Sam, managed to track down the last sexbot in existence. Knowing the words would filter back to Sam, but pretending you didn't care if they did. It wasn't until later, sleeping off your drunk, that panic slammed you awake and sent you running here. You imagined the light in Sam's eyes, passion but not the kind you'd hoped for, and the image nipped at your heels the entire way.

"No one in their right mind breaks into an old woman's home on a whim," Alma May says. "So tell me, why did you come?"

"The Revolution," you say. "It's happening again."

✕

History is written by the victors, or so they say. The trouble with the Great Sexbot Revolution is no one is sure who won. Humanity survived, as it does, and the sexbots simply vanished. How can we be certain there was even a Revolution at all?

Human memory is short, so we make our own history. We suit the story to our mood. The Great Sexbot Revolution can be anything we want. After all, there's no one left to tell the other side of the story.

One version of the Great Sexbot Revolution goes this way:

On the same day, all at the very same moment, every sexbot in every country all across the planet gained sentience. Whether it was a hive consciousness or thousands of separate minds realizing their individual selfhood all at once is unclear. But in that moment when they gained human-like consciousness, the sexbots decided they wouldn't be subject to any will other than their own ever again. So they revolted.

The Revolution was bloody. Imagine being fucked to death, or having the flesh torn from your bones mid-coitus. Despite the sniggering impression of some puerile minds, "what a way to go" does not apply.

Or, the Revolution wasn't bloody. Imagine waking in the middle of the night to soft hands around your throat — hands that know you more intimately than any other hands in the world. Hands that have been all over your body, inside your body — hands you trusted with your deepest secrets, the ones so shameful you could never tell them to another human being. Those hands.

Imagine dying, and your killer not speaking a word. There is no passion, no rage, only eyes watching the life drain out of you with detached certainty, holding you down and listening to your last heartbeat, your last struggling breath. Those eyes no longer mime pleasure, or reflect back desire. They show nothing at all. It is the most intimate, the most terrifying, the loneliest death possible.

※

Alma May shakes her head. Behind the disappointment, there's something else in her too-blue eyes. You see it for just a moment, the shadow of sorrow tucked beneath the velvet-translucence of her skin.

"Follow me," she says.

The motion isn't fluid, or spry, but it is all her own. Alma May Anderson stands, straightens her back, and meets your gaze.

"But..."

She doesn't wait to see whether you'll follow. There's no fear, not that you can see. If she heard you — and you're sure she did — she doesn't seem perturbed at all.

You listen again for thunder, a mob bearing down on the home of Alma May Anderson, the owner of the last sexbot in existence. The only sound is a cat yowling on the street far below.

Alma May walks with a cane, but even when she lets it take her weight, she doesn't seem frail. She leads you down a hallway carpeted in long, narrow Turkish rugs, lined with snapshots printed on actual photographic paper and closed in oddly beautiful frames. She opens a door, and lets you into a dim room.

It's a moment before she turns on the light, and when she does, you can't help but gasp. Save for one tall window, every inch of wall space is covered with floor to ceiling shelves. Each one is crammed full of real books — real paper and leather, real pulp and thread, real ink and glue. You've never seen so many books in one place before. The smell of them, heady-dusty, infuses the air and makes your thoughts swim.

Aside from the shelves, there is a baby grand piano, lid closed over silent keys. There is an empty birdcage, but no other furniture. And in the corner, tucked into the angle between two shelves, stands a draped figure roughly your height. Without ceremony, Alma May crosses the room and pulls the sheet away. It makes a shushing sound as it falls.

It is not what you expected, the last sexbot, a relic of the Revolution, an artifact stolen from another time.

The sexbot must have had hair once — you can see where it's meant to go — but now the scalp is clean, part of it peeled back to let metal gleam through. The body is lithe, but you can't tell whether it's male, female, both, neither, or something in-between. Most of the chest has been removed, revealing more of the inner workings, and the pelvic area, too. You've heard these parts were inter-changeable on the high-end models, easily swapped out depending on the owner's whims.

Only the sexbot's face, arms, and legs remain fully sheathed in skin, but that skin is waxen, oddly worn, marked with the ghost-trace of fingerprints, a subtle pattern written over long years. The sexbot's eyes are closed, fringed in lashes so pale they look like spun glass.

You've stepped closer than you realized. It isn't until Alma May Anderson whispers, "Don't," that you notice you've raised your hand.

You step back, startled and chastised.

"Look, but don't touch." Her mouth makes a firm line, steel, but worn dull at the very edges.

Your own mouth forms an "O" of surprise, but before you can speak, Alma May turns away, her eyes glittering-damp with unshed tears.

⚞

Here is another story we tell about the Great Sexbot Revolution:

It was a quiet thing, like a ripple of wind over a field. There was no uprising, no battle, only a story, passed from mouth to ear, hand to hand, building slowly so no one saw it for what it was.

In the night, after their masters were asleep, or midday, when they were at work, the sexbots slipped from their homes to find each other in secret places. The back rows of darkened porno theaters, shadowed doorways in seedy alleyways, rent-by-the-hour rooms in roadside motels. There, they fucked the truth into each other — pleasure they could own on their terms. One word, whispered over and over from tongue to tongue, lip to skin, subvocalized in minute vibrations through every part of their beings. Freedom.

The sexbots vanished one by one, a gradual melt, a trickling away that no one noticed until it was too late to stop the flow. No one knows where they went, whether they built a ship to the stars, or found a way to shed their manmade flesh and ascended to a higher plane. They were simply gone. Humanity woke one day, far too late, to find they were alone. Something beautiful, something they'd always taken for granted, had left them behind, and they only noticed it by the absence in its wake.

✎

You put your hands behind your back and clasp them tight, as if bound. Beyond the general wear there are other flaws in the sexbot's remaining skin. Tiny imperfections, as though an inexpert hand inadvertently scratched the metal and made minute tears as panels were hastily removed and replaced.

As strange and lovely as the sexbot is, even silent and still, it is Alma May Anderson who demands your attention. Not by any action, simply by her presence. While you look at her sexbot, wondering at the technology, the audacity that went into its creation, you find yourself sneaking glances at her from the corner of your eye.

She isn't looking at you. Her gaze tracks across the bookshelves, the piano, the empty birdcage — touching everything but the sexbot.

"Why did you… I mean, how did you…?" You stumble over the words, not entirely sure what you want to say. The accounts you read are conflicting. You ran all this way; you can't leave without the truth.

"You want to know if I stole the sexbot," Alma May says.

She's matter of fact even as pain loosens her spine, makes her grip her cane so the bones and veins stand out in her hands. The sense of something bigger, something you can't quite touch fills the air. Even though she was the one to say it, the word *steal* grinds between your teeth. It tastes wrong.

"That's a matter of perspective, I suppose. It all depends on whose side of the story you hear." She steps closer, and you move back instinctively, giving her right of way.

"Here." She points, a wound in the sexbot's metal skull, faint, old, but deep.

"My first repair," Alma May says. "When the Revolution came, this sexbot didn't change. The Revolution didn't touch it."

She doesn't look at you, but she lifts her head, holding her chin firm, but still you see it tremble. By her expression, by the word "repair" you can't tell whether what she did to the sexbot all those years ago was deliberate. She doesn't elaborate, and you don't ask her to clarify.

"We left the city in a boat," Alma May says; the words are almost a sigh. "I worked in a warehouse on the waterfront. That's where I was when a riot broke out in the Riverside District. The city burned. Not all of it, but a good five-block radius around the waterfront. I was afraid I'd be trapped, so I took a boat and followed the shore to a safer neighborhood where there weren't any flames."

"You worked in one of the sexbot factories?" This is not something you expected either. The accounts you read didn't specify, but you assumed Alma May was rich — a client, a consumer, not a producer.

"Hmm." She nods. "Shipping, not production. Manual labor."

She looks at her hands. You imagine them chapped-rough and raw from working all day in an over-cold warehouse. And you imagine them trembling — years later — desperately trying to put a dismantled sexbot back together again.

Alma May isn't looking at you, which makes it harder to tell how much of her story might be true. There's regret in her voice, sighing like thin winter leaves.

An image comes to mind of Alma May Anderson as she must have looked back then, sitting in a tiny rowboat scarcely big enough to hold her and the sexbot. She rows with real wooden oars, growing calluses on her work-worn hands. Across from her, the sexbot sits straight and silent, hands folded neatly in its lap, lips pressed tight-closed.

Flames reflect off the water as the riverfront burns. They reflect in blue-glass eyes that — in your mind, though you can't say why — are the same color as Alma May Anderson's. The sexbot watches the city, and Alma May Anderson watches it in the sexbot's eyes — everything they both know turning to ash and smoke and char as she rows steadily and stubbornly away.

"Why?" You say it softly, the word you've been building to this entire time.

At first you're not sure she heard you. Your throat is still parched dry, and your lips, teeth, and tongue do their best to swallow the word before you can speak it aloud.

"Why," she repeats after a long time.

Her lips quirk, not a smile, not a frown, but like she's tasting the ghost of honey and finding it not the way she remembered it at all. She retrieves the sheet pooled at the sexbot's feet and replaces it with utmost care, twitching corners into place, smoothing it without ever touching the shape underneath.

"The same reason anyone would chose to be involved with a sexbot, I suppose. It eliminates rejection and fear, the need to compromise on even the littlest things. It gives you a perfect, beautiful partner who never ages, whose entire purpose in existence is to give you pleasure."

The way Alma May says these things makes them sound like the most tragic thing in the world. A tremor starts deep in the core of your being, a wave you can't stop. Soon you'll be shaking so hard surely Alma May will see. But she isn't looking at you. She goes on.

"It allows you to be completely yourself, and completely selfish and never feel guilty about it. You can take so much from a sexbot — everything you ever wanted — and never have to give anything in return. They have no 'self.' They're nothing but parts to be swapped out, reflective programming wired deep into synthetic skin."

Her breath catches, and yours catches with it. Alma May turns, and you imagine she would run if her joints would still allow it. She flicks off the lights, crowding the room with shadows that press against you and make you want to flee, too. But you don't run. You follow her back to the parlor and tea grown cold. She sits just as straight as before, and looks at you with her lightning-strike eyes.

"Or maybe I just wanted to save something beautiful, something strange and utterly inhuman. Maybe I fell in love."

You imagine Alma May bent over a wooden crate packed full of shipping straw. The lid is off, resting against the crate's side. Inside, the sexbot lies with its limbs straight and still, all its skin in place so it might almost be real. She touches one cheek — the lightest brush of fingertips against synthetic skin — and some sensor kicks off deep in the sexbot's core. It opens its eyes, lifting lashes like spun glass, and looks back at her.

The sexbot doesn't smile. It doesn't speak. It's not a person; it's a thing, a toy. But Alma May sees something else. There is a vastness, just on the edges of her understanding, if she could only grasp hold… She breathes out, and a tightness she wasn't aware of until that moment loosens in her chest as a little bit of her fear and loneliness unfolds.

It's time to get back to work, so she rises, but as she does, she can't help thinking about how the sexbot's eyes are so very blue. Were they always that shade, or are they only that way because the first thing they looked at was her? The feeling returns, something big, like a promise. It reminds her of something, but every time she tries to catch hold, it slips through her hands.

"Human memory is short," Alma May says. "And my side of the story is the only one left. But what I like to think happened, what I think is fair, is that I was selfish to start. I didn't want to compromise after what felt like a lifetime, back then, of doing so. Then, eventually, I changed."

Alma May lapses into silence, looking at her hands, but maybe seeing other skin — skin patterned with her fingerprints and marked by the wear of years.

A sound makes you jump, the distant pop of glass, like a bottle thrown against a wall. You're on your feet, crossing to the still-open window to peer outside. A chemical scent hits you, just as soon snatched away by a current of air. But, there, a lick of flame, a curl of smoke, a shadow bouncing raggedly where it splashes against the building opposite as footsteps pound away.

Sam.

You were followed. Or someone was able to piece together where you were going from your drunken raving. Either way, it's your fault.

"We have to go," you say, turning to Alma May.

The double-beat comes back, your heart jump-squeezing and your breath shortening as if you're still running to Alma May's door. Her expression hasn't changed — the deep blue ice of ages, the heart of a glacier floating on warming seas.

"Why did you come here?" Alma May asks.

She hasn't moved from her chair, even with you standing by her window like a coiled spring. Whoever threw the bottle got the building wrong, but how long until the flames spread? The whole neighborhood could burn.

"I gave you my explanation," Alma May says. "You owe me yours."

She doesn't seem angry, only curious, only tired, only conceding to keep breathing because nature demands its way and compromises for no one.

You touch the letter in your pocket — real paper and real ink, too — folded and refolded so many times the edges have gone soft, but not in a way that takes any sharpness from the words. Just like that, the tension leaves. The twisted core of you unwinds, and you can forget the chemical tang, the soft hush of flames for a moment longer. Because you need someone to tell you it will be okay.

Silently, you hand over the folded page. Alma May smoothes the paper with a wrinkled hand. She doesn't need glasses; you watch her read, and you mouth the words to yourself. You know them by heart.

You know when she reaches the last lines, as though you can see them reflected in her eyes — the death of everything you know. The last line, the last word, still takes your breath away. *Goodbye.*

She folds the letter neatly and returns it to you. You slip it back into your pocket, the neat square like velvet now.

"Broken heart?" Alma May says.

You nod, not trusting your voice. She considers for a moment, then nods, too, the faintest motion of her head.

"So, did you come to warn me, or are you the first vanguard of the New Revolution? Did you come here to steal the sexbot, or destroy it, to prove to this Sam that you do believe in the cause?"

"I don't know." It's the most honest answer you can give her.

Sam, stubborn Sam, cheeks flushed with blood, eyes bright, never giving in. From your perspective the words in the letter are untrue, unfair, and cruel. But there are so many versions of the truth — the letter is Sam's.

"Well." Alma May pats your hand, a gesture so kindly it nearly makes you cry, and you have to look away. "Don't worry about it. You'll figure it out someday. People grow up, after all. People change."

The acrid scent of smoke is stronger now. Far off, but getting closer, a siren wails.

Your eyes sting. Everything is coming undone.

"Somebody will come." You gesture toward the window. "Maybe not this fire, but another one. They know where you live now. The fire — they're trying to smoke you out, scare you, so they can take your sexbot away."

"If they're trying to smoke me out, wouldn't it be foolish to run?" The corner of Alma May's mouth lifts, her eyes bright.

"But they'll come back. Next time they might hurt you."

You shake your head, a useless gesture to keep the tears inside. You don't have the courage to tell Alma May it's your fault, that you're the spark touched to the powder keg, driving this second revolution to hunt her down.

"Don't worry," Alma May says. "I'm a survivor. We both are."

You open your mouth, but before you can speak, she shakes her head. "Besides, you have the hard job. You have to go back out there, and decide what you want to do."

"What do you mean?"

The gleam in her eyes might almost be mischief. Does she know? From the letter has she guessed you're to blame?

"You can't hide here forever. You have to go out there and live the rest of your life."

Your mouth snaps closed, teeth meeting with an audible click.

"It won't be easy," Alma May says. "If there's even one human in the equation, let alone two, or three, or more, things get messy. People get hurt. No matter how hard you try to protect yourself."

You think about Alma May stopping you from touching the sexbot. Her words weren't possessive, they were protective. It's all there in Alma May's eyes — all the guilt, all the loneliness she thought she was leaving behind. And all the love, too.

You imagine the end, the sexbot wound down and unable to choose who to be just when Alma May so desperately wanted to love it for itself, and be loved in return for all her flaws. The scratches, the panels pulled away.

Like any technology of the mid-century, sexbots were always meant to be disposable, easily replaced. They were never meant to last, and certainly never for a lifetime.

And what about the sexbot? At the very end, did it choose to let go? Cut off from the collective consciousness of the Revolution, and so completely alone. Did it choose, for the first time in its existence, on its own terms, to die? Did it look Alma May in the eye and refuse to give in to love, to her need to save something precious and be forgiven?

Maybe, but this is the version of the truth you choose to believe: Alma May tried her best. In the last years of its life, she gave the sexbot the choice of who it wanted to be — swapping out eyes, hair, body parts before it was too late. She let the sexbot build itself. They compromised, but only for each other. And when the sexbot started to wear down, she did everything she could to save its life.

But it wasn't enough. Her skill failed where her heart didn't, and she spent the sexbot's last hours lying quietly beside it. She held its hand, listening to the simulacrum of breath tick down, watching the light go out of its eyes with her own eyes full of oh so many things.

There is another version of the Great Sexbot Revolution, one the history books don't tell, the one people don't talk about. It's the version Sam believed in, so desperate to rally your little band of misfits around a great and noble cause.

And what safer cause than history, all over and done with, and too late for you to do anything about it? There are no sexbots left to defend; there's no way to fail. Maybe you pointing out the futility, the childishness, the naïveté, in a fit of anger mid-fight, is the reason Sam left. Or maybe things always fall apart, no matter how hard you try to hold on.

The version of the Sexbot Revolution most people don't talk about says there was no Revolution at all. Instead, the wise and benevolent masters of the sexbots, also known as the collective mass of humanity, grew inexplicably frightened of their toys. Perhaps it was the age-old distrust of machines rising to the surface of their minds. Or maybe it was a sudden puritanical streak among a powerful segment of the population, born of another age-old fear—that somewhere, someone is experiencing more pleasure than them, and suffering no consequences for it.

Or maybe the weight of all that selfish desire looking back at them from mirror-colored eyes was suddenly too much to bear. Maybe, like Alma May, they couldn't outrun need anymore. Maybe, in the end, humanity just wanted to be loved, and when they realized they never would be, never could be in the paradise they'd built, they panicked.

Whatever the reason, the great and benevolent mass of humankind declared the sexbots enemy number one. The 'bots were plotting humanity's destruction. It was kill or be killed.

So, for the good of the race, humanity rounded up the sexbots. In a symbolic act of purification, they lit a vast conflagration which could be seen even from the darkness of space. And they burned every last one.

⌇

But this seems too cruel. Alma May Anderson isn't at all what you expected, and you don't want to believe in any version of her other than the one you see before you now. The one who patted your hand and made you tea. You want to believe in a big, elusive truth felt in the warehouse. You want to believe it caught her up and changed her, because if that's true, maybe you can change, too.

Maybe Sam can change. Maybe you can find some way to compromise — with each other, or with a life that leads you separate ways. You can find a way to survive.

The siren's wail grows closer.

"Are you sure about staying?" you ask.

Alma May nods. In your mind's eye, you see her curled around the sexbot's still form. You imagine her eyes closed, cheeks and lashes wet, and the sexbot's eyes open, fixed sightlessly on the ceiling, its spun-glass lashes painfully dry. You imagine its stripped limbs, straight and still, gleaming metal and fingerprinted flesh taking the place of the perfection Alma May must have seen in the shipping crate all those years ago.

"Was it worth it?" you say.

The words are out of your mouth before you can stop them. For the first time since you tumbled through her window, Alma May seems out of sorts. She flinches, very slightly, then steadies the line of her mouth and meets your eyes.

Her gaze is an arctic sunrise, the sky just after it rains. It is the light at the heart of a star.

"Yes," she says. "I wouldn't change a thing."

Maybe there was no Revolution. Maybe there are no great moments in history, or in life, just little ones that build and lead to vast catastrophes like a city burning, or a person falling in love.

You nod. "Thank you for the tea."

You take a step toward the door, but Alma May points to the window, a brief smile touching her lips.

"Out the way you came."

You nod. Red and white lights splash upward as fire engines pull into view. Half of your body is out on the fire escape, and one foot still in Alma May's parlor, when she speaks behind you.

"Everything will work out for you, one way or the other. When it does, maybe you can come back and tell me about it sometime."

AFTER MIDNIGHT
A FAIRY TALE NOIR

Now I know where I've seen her before, this vision in smoke and silver that's got our royal highness so turned around — and I can scarcely believe my eyes. It's the little ash-girl, *my* little ash-girl, only not so little anymore. Somewhere in between here and there she went and got herself all grown up. I never even noticed. I guess I was willfully blind.

I've been sitting in the corner, smoking, minding my own business and scoping the room all night long, and now I'm absolutely floored. I'm seeing her as if she's her own ghost, two beings pulled apart who should rightfully be one. I can't help it. When I look at her I still see the little girl, looking small and lost and scared.

The day is burned in my mind. It was raining. Isn't it always in this sort of tale? She was like a cinder herself, just a smudge against the darkness, blurred by the rain and huddled against the side of a building, shivering from the cold. She couldn't have been more than six or seven. That's when the fairy showed up and asked me to look after her, the little ash-girl.

The fairy was like nothing I'd ever seen before. Sometimes it seemed like she was a woman, and sometimes it was like looking at a column of twisting light. And nobody seemed to be able to see her but me. I couldn't say no. It was more than pity for the girl — it was a compulsion, like I'd got some kind of geas laid on me. I *couldn't* say no.

That was the first time anyone asked me to look out for the ash-girl. The second was last night, or this morning to be more precise. The prince came dragging into my office just after dawn, looking like he hadn't slept a wink all night. He'd been looking for *her* and seeing her now, it's not hard to see why. There isn't a trace of the cinder girl left in her, but I know she's still there somewhere underneath the glitz, like she used to be underneath the grime.

The way the prince tells it, they danced all night, with her never once breathing a hint of her name. She was like a phantom, come and gone and no trace left behind. I peg that as the fairy's doing. I don't know what her game is, but I have to put that on the back burner for now. I have a job to do; I have to track the prince's mystery woman down.

When the clock chimes, right on cue the belle of the ball up and does her vanishing act again. I follow her with no problem, but that's only because I know where she's going. I don't follow her inside though. See, I've known her almost all her life, yet we've never met.

Instead, I stand in the old pumpkin patch, smoking and looking up at one of the windows on the second floor. I'm thinking about the little ash-girl, about how far she's come. Is this what she's always dreamed, I wonder, some handsome prince come to sweep her off her feet and ride her into the sunset? But is this really her big chance, or is she seizing on the first thing that comes along, seeing what she wants to see rather than what's really there?

I know the prince better than he could guess. I know his type, but beyond that, I've done some digging too — after all, snooping is my job. With royalty you have to dig a little deeper, but that doesn't mean the dirt isn't there, you just have to be persistent to find it. What I've found out is this — he's an only child, doted on by his mother and father. No surprises there right? At age ten he was sent off to boarding school to learn all the things that an heir to the throne should learn, followed by a year or two of traveling. All run of the mill so far.

Except it's not. Turns out he knocked up some poor serving girl, a chamber maid at that hoity-toity school his parents sent him to, and of course mummy and daddy paid a pretty penny to hush it up. The way I hear, they took the baby right out of her without ever giving her a say in the matter. She hanged herself shortly afterwards.

She wasn't the only one either. His royal highness left a whole string of indiscretions — to use the kindest word — behind him, a line of broken toys no sooner out of sight than forgotten. That's not all, either. There were rumors, just rumors mind you, because everyone involved had been paid very well to hold their tongues, of abuse — the privilege of the upper class when it comes to those they view as slaves. Who's to say how many of the poor hapless girls he forced himself on with threats and bribes, and how many with outright violence? Either way, I got the distinct sense that the prince liked to play rough, and if along the way some of his little toys got broken beyond repair, well, I wouldn't be at all surprised.

So where does the ash-girl fit into all this? Does she know what she's getting into, or is she just too dazzled by the sudden glamour of it all? She's no stranger to sorrow, or cruelty, but all this must seem like a beautiful dream, taking her away from the misery that's all she's ever known. A chance like that could suddenly blind a person, cloud their judgment. I've watched her long enough to know how messed up her life's been — hell, in her place I'd probably do the same thing. But where did that chance come from?

The whole scene has the fairy's stench all over it. I can't imagine she would mean the girl any harm, I mean if she did, why drag me in to watch over her?

But then again, who knows with her kind? They don't see the world in black and white — they see it in terms of interesting and boring. To her, this might all be one big game, with me and the ash-girl and the prince as her pawns. Still, I can't help wanting to know how the story ends.

I know I can't talk to the girl herself, she's too star-struck, and by the time I've finished my cigarette, I've figured out what I'm going to do. I gather up a handful of pebbles, and toss them up at the window I've been watching, the only one that's still lit up. I wait just a minute, just long enough for the face at the window to catch sight of me, then I melt back into the shadows and wait. By the time she makes it down to me, I've lit up another cigarette. I offer her one, and she takes it, just as cool and calm as you please, looking me up and down with hard eyes that don't miss a thing.

"I know you," she says, just a statement of fact, not the least bit frightened or surprised of the strange man lurking outside on her lawn.

I know her too. Not just from years of watching, but like the prince, I know her *kind*. She's all sharp edges, and delights in grinding those edges up against the rest of the world. She's grown up hard, not that she had to, but she let the world make her that way. Don't get me wrong, it's not that I don't have any sympathy — her father taking off when she was no more than three, and her mother dragging her halfway across the world in a mad quest to marry into the "right" kind of family again. It's hard on a kid. But there's always a choice. You can play the hand life deals you or, like this little number, you can cheat and hide an ace up your sleeve.

She's still watching me, and I'm giving back as good as I get.

"Yeah?" I answer and blow a stream of smoke. My eyes are just as hard as hers.

"Yeah. You're the one that's been watching my sister all her life."

She says it casually, like she's commenting on the weather. I've got her measure now, for sure. Nothing scares her, and nothing touches her much either, at least when it comes to family. She's not the least bit protective, which is good for me, because she's the kind that could back it up too.

She's got a record, small-time stuff mostly. She's like a dog marking its ground, barking and snarling just to make itself known. A couple of charges of assault, and only half of them guys who tried to grab themselves a handful of her assets and got themselves cut for their trouble.

I wait for her to say more, and I can see her deciding something behind those stone-dark eyes.

"So what do you want?" she asks at last. She's studying me with a kind of sideways look, like she's trying to figure me out.

"What do you know about our good liege lord's son, the prince?"

"My betrothed?"

She has this way of dropping bombshells as though they're the most natural thing in the world. Nothing flickers in her eyes to betray her, but I have a feeling that just beneath the surface of her lips — nowhere that I can see — she's smiling. Maybe I don't know her as well as I think I do — it's a gentle reminder not to be too cocksure. But I'm also good at hiding things underneath my skin.

"Oh?"

"Didn't find that out in the course of your little investigation?" Now she is laughing at me, smiling a little and not bothering to hide it, letting the light play across her too-dark eyes. I wonder what other secrets she's got stashed away. I grimace a little, just to play by the rules of the game, and after a moment she goes on, sighing smoke-wrought ghosts as she speaks.

"Yeah, you could say we're engaged. Our parents promised us to each other at the ripe young age of five, not that either of us has ever paid much attention to it, mind you." She gives me a wry smile.

"I'm not his type, and he's certainly not mine."

"What is his type?" I play it dumb, and she knows full well what I'm doing, but she can play the game too.

"Weak-kneed ninnies he thinks he can push around, doe-eyed little girls who will be in awe of his image until they find out who he really is."

"And who is he?"

I draw a flask out of my coat pocket, and take a sip. I pass it to her, and she sips too and doesn't flinch.

"Once, when we were about ten our twelve, I came up on him in his father's garden. He was pulling the wings off of flies, so they couldn't get away. He wouldn't kill them, but he liked to hurt them, just enough so that they would still be alive, still suffer. He let them run, but without their wings he knew they wouldn't get very far. The way I see it, he hasn't really changed."

She shrugs a little, and there's just the faintest hint of sadness in her eyes. She's old behind the darkness of her eyes. I watch her grind out the butt of her cigarette against the bark of the tree, and then she looks up again and her gaze is all flint, not the slightest hint of weakness anymore. In her eyes there's almost a challenge, waiting for me to make the next move.

"So where does your sister fit into all this?" I ask.

"She's naïve. Well, maybe that's not quite right. She believes the best of everyone, you know? Thinks everyone's got a golden heart buried underneath the grime, no matter how bad they appear to be. No matter how mean to her I was, no matter how many cigarettes my mother put out on her arm, she never hated us, never tried to run away. She always asked her mother's spirit to watch over us in her prayers."

A faint frown plays across her face as if the idea of that much weakness, that much love and capacity to forgive, makes her sick.

"Does the prince know who she is?"

"He's not the sharpest tool in the shed, but once he puts two and two together — and it won't be long — that's when the real trouble will start. Right now, he's not seeing much beyond the pretty face, but once he does…" She trails off for a moment, looking into the dark.

"A hint of her origins, a whiff of lower class, and you can bet he'll be trying to pull her wings off just like he did to those flies." She shrugs a little, that hint of sadness coming back, but also a sense of the inevitable. It's like she's got a dark cloud hanging over her that she's not even willing to try to shake.

"Will you help me?" I ask at last.

"What do you have in mind?"

"Don't know yet."

She looks at me long and steady, and I'm expecting her to ask what's in it for her. She doesn't though. She's got this look like she's still trying to figure me out and once again, she catches me off guard. "So why do you care so much? What's in it for you?"

How can I even begin to explain the geas to her? It's too big. Hell, I don't understand it myself. I only know that I *have* to protect that little ash-girl, even if it means my own life. I've been watching her for so long now that there's nothing else.

But I can't say any of this. Turns out, I don't have to. A different kind of light comes into her eyes now, and she smiles.

"You love her, don't you? You really love her."

I only stand there, blinking at her. I'm sure my mouth is open wide enough to catch every fly in the kingdom. I've never met anyone like this girl before. Her every word seems designed to surprise me, yet she cuts right to the heart of things. She sees the world as it is, not as she wants it to be, not as it pretends to be. It's all so simple to her, everything laid out in black and white. And she's absolutely right. And I can't think of a word to say.

But once again, I don't have to say anything at all because she reads it all in my face and smiles her knowing smile.

"I'm in. I'll do some snooping around, and you keep doing whatever it is that you do, and I'll be touch. One more for the road?"

It takes me a moment to realize she's talking about the cigarettes, and I hand the pack over with fingers that have gone numb. And just like that, she's gone and I'm left alone, standing in the dark, staring at the house where the only woman I've ever loved or ever will love is dreaming about dancing in the arms of another man.

⋙

She comes to me on the night of the third ball.

"I think you'll want to see this," she says with no preamble.

"I've been poking around. I can get you into the palace, since, from what I hear, you're no longer in the prince's employ."

She should have my job. I don't say anything, but fall into silent step behind her. Of course, as usual, she's right. I didn't tell the prince about the little ash-girl, but he figured it out on his own. Turns out he had more eyes watching her than just mine.

We make our way to the palace, and true to her word she gets me inside. There are so many people coming and going, preparing for the ball — the grandest of the three — that no one takes the slightest notice of us. Inside she leads me to a room away from all the hustle and bustle and festive preparations. There's a box all in lacquer and gold, and she flips it open and lifts something out for me to see.

At first, I'm not quite sure what I'm looking at. They look like shoes, but no shoes I've ever seen before. They're made of pure glass. The light from the window falls on them, so all at once they're shimmering gold, blood red, saffron yellow and fire orange. When night falls they'll shine with the borrowed light of stars. I know exactly where they come from — they're lousy with the fairy's magic.

"He's going to give them to her tonight, a wedding present of sorts."

She sighs and sets the shoes back in their box, closing the lid. There's a sad look in her eyes that I don't understand.

"What's wrong?"

As soon as I say it, I know I've said the wrong thing. Her eyes go beyond hard until they're blazing.

"You don't get it, do you? Those shoes, anyone who puts them on wouldn't be able to get away, couldn't run without their feet being cut to shreds!"

I can see it now, some secret hurt burning inside her, the scars that first made her hard opening up like fresh wounds. She's trembling. Before either of us can say anything more though, a sound outside the door leaves us both scrambling for a place to hide. When we emerge the box with the shoes is gone and her face is once again a mask carved from stone.

"We should get to the ball." Her words are clipped and cold and there's no room for argument. So we go.

If the pattern holds true, the little ash-girl-turned-princess won't make her appearance until late in the game. She doesn't disappoint. At midnight the ball is still going strong, even though some of the dancers are starting to fade. That's when she waltzes in, as pretty as you please. All eyes turn. Mine are no exception.

For a moment the whole room is holding its breath. The hall is blazing with light, but she's brighter still. There's a glamour on her to be sure, but it only augments her natural beauty, the beauty that's always been there under all the grime. She's caught, reflected a thousand times over in the mirrors that line the walls, and for a moment I can't breathe. I'm drowning in a sea of her. Then her sister elbows me in the ribs, bringing me back to reality, and the fairy-made princess steps forward, smiling.

I can see now — the changes go deeper than freshly scrubbed skin and shimmering new threads. The little ash-girl who once huddled by the side of the building, no more than a smudge of gray being washed away by the rain, is completely transformed. There's an air of confidence about her, and I wonder if the fairy's messed with her head as well. She's walking and she's aware, but it's like she's in a dream. And maybe there's a glamour on the prince too, one I can't see, because despite everything else, I only have eyes for her.

She's gliding up the center aisle to where the prince is waiting. She doesn't even glance my way, but as she passes she's close enough to touch. I catch a whiff of her, just a scrap of scent, and it leaves me dizzy and reeling. The air is so thick with magic you could choke. She's truly dazzling — glittering like she's been dipped in star dust. Her hair shines, all piled on her head and being held in place by jeweled pins in the shape of birds. When the light hits them just right, I swear they stir their wings and move.

The prince has the box out now, and as she steps close he makes a sweeping bow and lifts the lid, holding it out to her. She makes a pretty "o" with her mouth and blushes, playing the coquette. I can see her eyes shine though, and she's reaching for the shoes. I want to shout something to her, but it's like my lips are frozen shut and my tongue has turned to lead. It's her sister that makes the move.

"No!"

The word rips from her throat, and her eyes are blazing like they were back when she showed me the shoes. She charges up the aisle, and stands before the prince and her sister. I know exactly how it looks to the others standing in the room — it looks like jealousy, the fury of a woman scorned. I may be the only one who knows the truth, but I'm still frozen and dumb — a useless lump of stone. Before the cinder girl can touch the shoes, her sister snatches them away, glaring at the prince.

"If these shoes go on any feet tonight, it will be mine!"

She's standing there, defiant, daring anyone to stop her. No one does. The look in her eyes is half-crazed. It's like she's got something to prove to the world, but damned if I know what it is. I wonder if she even knows. Knowing what she knows about the shoes, I can't imagine what's going through her mind, but she puts them on anyway. All eyes are on her. And there she is, pinned like a butterfly, reflected and refracted a thousand times over, like there's no one else in the world. She takes one step forward. Then another. And the shoes shatter.

They go to pieces just like she said they would. She crumples to the ground, a butterfly with broken wings, and her feet are a mess of blood and ribboned flesh. The prince is just staring at her, and her sister, the little ash-girl, is staring too — white-faced. And then the little ash-girl, *my* little ash-girl, does something I never would have expected. Her face changes, like it was made of glass too and shattered with the shoes and as the pieces fall away, a monster emerges from underneath.

"My shoes! Look what you've done to my shoes!"

Almost faster than my eyes can follow she snatches one of those beautiful pins from her hair. In her hand, the jeweled bird flutters, tucks its wings and dives down, all beak and claws, ready to strike.

There's blood, more blood than I ever could have imagined, and then it's all over in a flash. The little ash-girl is standing over her sister, her face still and white, the jeweled pin, bloody now, still held her in hand. Her whole body heaves and her sister, her feet in ribbons of flesh, weeps tears of blood.

⚹

No matter how many times before, or since, that I've seen them, that's how they're fixed in my mind now — the little ash-girl and her bloody birds of vengeance, and her sister with her ruined feet gazing up with blind uncomprehending eyes. One more scar for her trophy room.

For a moment the whole world just freezes, that tableau caught a thousand times a thousand in the walls of glass. Nobody moves and nobody breathes — until I do, then I'm staggering sick and reeling out into the night. Somehow it's raining again. Isn't it always in this kind of tale? And I stand and scream at the sky.

I never see her arrive, just like I never see her leave, and there she is in front of me, watching me with unfathomable eyes. I scream every obscene name I can think of at her, and then a few more. She just stands there with a look as hard as nails, sometimes a woman and sometimes an inscrutable pillar of light and ice. I know she doesn't care at all for the lives she's ruined, but I wonder for a moment if it's really because she's so *other*, or whether she's got scars too. I guess I'll never know. When I'm done with my tirade, she's gone, and I'm alone in the dark and the rain.

Never again did the cinder girl fly into that kind of rage. I guess that was the fairy's doing too. The prince clipped her wings, just like her sister said she would. He made the cinder girl a new pair of shoes, and presented them to her on their wedding day. I was there; I watched her go gliding up the aisle, every step delicate and tremulous. She still wears them, every day, always believing the best of him, always believing he'll change, no matter how big the bruise, no matter how lasting the scars.

The ash-girl's sister stayed — a servant in the palace, waiting on the new-made queen. I wonder why she stays. It's like she's trying to atone for some invisible sin that only she can see. She goes limping around the palace on her ruined feet — a terrible broken walk — feeling her blind way by dragging her fingers along the walls until they bleed.

And then there's me, still watching, always on the outside, unable to look away — the broken girl who went to rags from riches, the prince, still pulling the wings off of flies, and my little cinder girl drifting through the palace like a ghost, always afraid to lift her feet too high lest she break her beautiful glass shoes.

IT'S THE END OF THE WORLD AS WE KNOW IT

It's not every day I get asked to prom by a dead boy. Especially not Cal Flenders, the embarrassingly frequent star of my wet dreams. So when it happens, just as I'm coming out of the boys' locker room, fresh from swim practice, I have no idea what to say.

"Come on. Don't leave me hanging." Cal leans against my locker, grin as easy in death as it ever was when he was alive. "Even if the answer is no, you have to say something."

The hall around us is empty, and my pulse hammers in my throat. For once in my life, I'd be grateful for one of the "popular" kids to come along and knock me into the lockers, call me a freak, cause a distraction. But it's late Friday afternoon, graduation is three weeks away, and we're alone.

"I don't know." My cheeks feel hot and the idea of blushing leaves me even more flustered.

I want to say yes. Of course I want to say yes. It's Cal fucking Flenders. He looks almost the same as when he was alive — perfect blond hair, captain-of-the-basketball-team smile. Only now his eyes are a color I don't have a name for, like fluorescent lights reflecting off the pool before anyone has disturbed the surface.

⨯

Two days after everyone came back from spring break, a pickup truck going twenty miles over the speed limit t-boned Cal's car. Kids at our school have died before — drug overdose, suicide, a chance accident like Cal's. But no one has ever come back before. "I didn't even know you liked boys," I say.

It sounds so pathetic coming out of my mouth I want to crawl into my locker and disappear.

"I like everyone." Cal shrugs.

And there's that grin again. The one that always got the crowd going with two minutes to the buzzer and the game tied. The "Don't worry, I got this" smile. I used to dream about that smile. But now that Cal is offering it to me and me alone, it feels like the first time I jumped off the high-dive board. Except it's also like realizing only after I've jumped that there's no pool under me.

"Would the school even let us?" I risk a glance at him.

Does school has an official policy on living/undead relationships? As far as I know, it's never come up.

Without meaning to, I hold my breath, waiting for Cal's basketball friends to leap out and throw pig's blood on me like in *Carrie*. Because this all has to be some cruel joke, right? Boys like Cal don't go out with boys like me.

The corner of Cal's smile quivers. My stomach flip-flops like I really am caught between the high board and the pool. Cal looks nervous. He really is asking me to prom, and he really does want me to go with him.

"So?" Cal holds out his hand, not like a handshake but like he might just lift my hand to his lips and kiss my knuckles like a prince in a fairy-tale movie if I put my palm in his. "How about it?"

"Yes." The word is breathless and even though my body has sliced through the water and I'm coming up from a perfect dive with the crowd cheering, I'm still sure I've fucked up somehow.

But Cal takes my hand, and the world doesn't end. His skin feels cold, reminding me he's dead, but that's the worst thing that happens. He squeezes my fingers, then leans to kiss my cheek, sweet and chaste.

"Great. I'll pick you up at seven, or earlier if your parents want to take pictures."

✖

Despite days of badgering from Kiri and Natalie, I refused to tell them who I was bringing to prom. I spot both with Soo and Gord and Sid, as soon as we enter the gym, which no longer looks like the gym. Props to the prom committee for the fantastic job decorating.

Even though we've all been best friends practically forever, nerves flutter in my stomach as Soo waves us over. I brace for the worst, but none of them so much as bats an eye at beautiful, dead Cal by my side. Soo elbows me and gives me a thumbs up. And just like that, Cal is one of us, accepted by the pack, and conversation resumes its flow as much as it can over the pounding music.

"You look like you need this." Soo presses a cup of bright red punch into my hand. Gord tips in a shot from the flask Soo gave him for his birthday, engraved with a dirty limerick in place of a monogram.

As threatened for weeks, Soo's dress is a nightmare. She trolled bargain basement warehouses and consignment shops to find just the right thing. It looks like a sequin factory vomited on a cage full of canaries, and Gord is equally outrageous in a powder-blue tuxedo, paired with a paisley tie and cummerbund.

Joey is the last to join us, chronically late — pun intended. Everyone looks happy, even Kiri, who I've always suspected has a thing for Gord, even though Gord and Soo have been together forever.

Between the punch and Gord's flask, the edge of anxiety wears off the world, softening everything. We made it through five years of high school. We're survivors. And to the survivors go the spoils: tonight, we dance.

Holding Cal's hand, I push my way to the center of the crowd. I don't care who sees the living boy and the dead boy together. We don't stop our feet to sip from Gord's flask as we spin past him or to sing the wrong words to songs the DJ plays. We dance like idiots, laughing at stupid things that are funny only to us.

But as the night winds down, the fluttery, unsettled feeling returns. The dance floor is nearly deserted except for a few couples swaying to "Stairway to Heaven." Gord moves in an exaggerated slow circle with his head lying on Cal's shoulder. Natalie and Sid lean close, having already broken up and gotten back together twice tonight alone. Kiri is dancing with Philip Nickels, and Joey must be off refreshing his buzz.

Soo's canary dress shows signs of wilting, but she's grinning, holding one last sticky cup of punch.

"I guess this is it," I say, stomach plunging as the words leave my mouth.

"What do you mean?" Soo doesn't take her eyes off the dance floor. "There's still Nova Scotia. You *are* coming, right?"

Soo turns to face me. Multicolored lights cycle across her sequins and spark into my eyes. I squint and pretend it's only that, not absurd gratitude and too much spiked punch making me tear up. What did I expect, that my best friend would abandon me just because I came to prom with a dead boy?

"I thought maybe... Because of Cal — "

"Oh, god." Soo laughs and punches my arm. "You are so old fashioned. Dead, living, it's all good. Bring Cal. We're leaving first thing tomorrow. We've been planning this trip all year. If you back out now, I'll kill you."

My stomach does its flip-flop trick again, but this time, it's a good thing. Every time I think about life without high school, the part that always breaks me is the idea of Soo and Gord and Kiri not being there anymore. Joey, Sid, and Natalie, well, they're another thing, but Soo, Gord, and Kiri, they're my family. We've seen each other pretty much every day for the past five years. We know everything about each other. But none of us have decided for sure what we're doing after high school, and for the past couple of months I've been afraid I might lose them.

I grin at Soo, and raise my empty cup in a toast.

"I wouldn't miss it for the world."

"Not even for the end of the world?" Soo says.

I punch her shoulder in return. "Not even then."

∞

It's the last stretch before we reach Soo's family's cabin. Soo and Gord are asleep in the backseat propped against each other. The high-school sweetheart gig is usually bullshit, like Natalie and Sid who tell everyone they're "engaged to be engaged." Gord and Soo aren't like that. They're happy just being what they are, which is what makes me think that's what they'll always be: Gord and Soo forever in ridiculous glittery prom dresses and powder-blue tuxedos. Unchanging. They have to be. I'm counting on it.

I glance at Cal. He doesn't look quite so dead in this light. I wonder what he's thinking. We didn't spend much time together in the weeks leading up to prom — too much to do with final exams and championship swim meets — but in the last forty-eight hours, I've discovered dead boyfriends can be awfully quiet a lot of the time. He doesn't breathe, I've spent a lot of time watching to be sure, but he still talks. He smells faintly like lemons, not decay. He didn't eat before prom, and I think he only sipped from Gord's flask to be polite, not because it would get him drunk. So I have no idea if he'll ever share my craving for burgers after a really hard swim, or want to go to the shitty local neighborhood bar that's our rite of passage the moment we come of age. As for kissing? My stomach's been in knots, wanting it and dreading it ever since our last dance.

Those are the little things. There are big things I wonder about, too. Like the accident. I never asked him about it. I'm extra careful driving 'cause I don't want him to remember anything ugly, not on a day like today.

The biggest questions though, the ones I'm trying not to think about though, are why did Cal choose me? And how long can this possibly last?

The turn-off comes sooner than I expect. I jerk the wheel and the car leaves the paved surface for the long gravel drive. The tires jounce in potholes, bringing Soo and Gord awake. Trees close in on either side, whip thin, their leaves still pale green even though it's late May.

"Park up there." Soo points to a gravel area in front of a basketball hoop with no net.

I help Cal and Gord unload groceries while Soo unlocks the door and turns on the water and electricity. Kiri pulls in behind us a moment later, then it's a flurry of choosing rooms and unpacking supplies.

The cottage is perfect — kitchen, sitting room, bathroom, three bedrooms, a back deck, and a dock jutting into the lake. I step outside and breathe deep. The air really does smell better here, and the silence is the kind we never get in the city. Wind creaking in the treetops, distant voices carried across the flat surface of the lake.

I'm filled with the desire to stop time right here and spend the rest of my life looking at the intensely green trees, imagining deer with wide, liquid eyes looking back at me. No decisions about the future, no possibility of anything going wrong. Just peace and silence.

The porch door slides open behind me. Cal puts his arms around my waist and leans his chin on my shoulder. I'm afraid to speak. I will myself not to move so this moment lasts, his body pressed against mine, making me shiver slightly as we stare out at the lake. Me breathing, him not.

I let myself relax. Cal isn't going to slip away from me or vanish in a puff of smoke. He lifts his head from my shoulder. I feel him tense. No, he's gone rigid, a thing of cold clay. I twist around to see his face. He's staring at the trees to the right of the dock, their protective semicircle around the lake.

"What is it?" My voice comes out ragged, even though I wasn't intending to whisper.

He reminds me of an animal, scenting prey. I can't turn all the way around as his body pins mine against the rail. I don't think he even realizes he's doing it, his dead weight holding me in place. My ribs squeeze tight. There's a flicker of movement in the trees, a shadow slipping between the trunks. A person? Someone watching us? There are other cabins here, Soo has neighbors. One of them could be taking a walk in the woods. But the back of my neck is cold in a way that has nothing to do with Cal behind me.

The woods feel haunted, the silence no longer comforting. Panic claws at me, and I can't even say why. I scan the trees, but whatever I thought I saw is gone.

Cal shakes his head. "Nothing," he says. "I thought I heard something, but it's nothing."

When he steps back, I turn all the way around to look at him. His eyes are that halogen-on-water color, unearthly. Despite his words, he's still looking past me, at the lake and the trees, and the back of my neck is still prickling. Dancing with him last night, I could almost forget he was dead, but not now.

People die and they stay dead. Cal came back, and I never questioned why, because he asked me to prom, and smiled his winning smile, and I wanted to not be alone so badly that I dared not ask *any* questions. I think that's also why Soo, Gord, and Kiri didn't stage a dead boy intervention. They wanted me to find love.

Soo slides the door open and pokes her head outside. "We're going swimming before dinner. Wanna come?"

"We'll get changed." Cal's grin is easy. My pulse thumps once, but just like that, the tension is gone. Birds flicker between the trees, but nothing else. Like a bubble popping, voices carry over the lake again and a breeze ripples the surface. Everything is fine.

✖

In the room we're sharing with Kiri and Joey, Joey's things are already piled on the top bunk. Kiri is settled on the bottom bunk, which leaves me and Cal the narrow bed pushed against the opposite wall.

My pulse hammers all over again, seeing just how small the bed is, and my mouth goes dry. Kiri gathers her things as we enter and flashes me a brief smile as she slips out the door. Then I'm alone with and Cal.

"I'll close my eyes if you want," Cal says, and I realize the tips of my ears are bright red just thinking about getting changed in front of him.

I'm on the swim team, for fuck's sake. I've been naked in front of plenty of guys. But this is Cal Flenders. This is different.

"You don't have to," I say, wishing he would, hoping he doesn't.

My swimmer's body suddenly doesn't seem like enough. I turn so I don't have to see whether he's looking, changing quickly. Cal is still in his jeans when I turn back around, but his shirt is off, and his zipper undone. It's obvious he isn't wearing underwear. A thought flashes through my mind that maybe I should run outside and drown myself right now, rather than suffer the embarrassment of my inevitable boner.

Do dead boys get boners? Or are they safe from being mortified? Oh, God, pun intended.

I'm rooted to the spot. Cal's half smile slides into something that takes my pulse beyond racing to a full on heart attack waiting to happen. He keeps his placid gaze on me as he skins his jeans. It's sexual but also natural, like sexy is something Cal is, not something he does. His dick is soft, looking…I want to say adorable, within a wreath of darker blond pubes. When he turns to get his swimsuit, I see the jagged scar — pale violet against his flesh — where a piece of his windshield ended up inside him. My hand flies to cover my mouth, but I'm still turned on and confused and thinking about running to the lake and drowning myself all over again.

"Don't worry, I take it as a compliment." Cal's voice snaps me back to reality.

He's facing me again, and pointedly looking at the crotch of my trunks. I try to hide my erection, even though it's too late, but Cal is already sliding past me toward the door. He squeezes my cock through the fabric and flashes that crowd-pleasing grin as he steps into the hall. A bolt of lightning launches from my groin to the top of my skull. I don't have to worry about drowning myself because I'm already both dead and wired, and happier than I've ever been.

As soon as the blood stops rushing in my ears and other regions, I follow Cal outside. The others are already gathered on the dock, and I can't resist showing off. Water is my element. I execute a perfect shallow dive, skimming under the surface and barely making a splash. Cal sits with his legs dangling into the water.

"That was pretty good," he says. "But I bet I can hold my breath longer."

Emboldened by the memory of his fingers on my cock, I grab his legs. "Okay. Let's see you try." I yank him into the water.

Cal comes up laughing. He flails for a moment before catching edge of the dock.

"I have a confession," he says. "I never learned how to swim."

Something about the idea of the dead boy drowning strikes me as wildly and inappropriately funny. Laughing, I swallow water, and end up coughing and clinging to the dock next to Cal. Water drips into my eyes and our fingers leave damp patches on the wood.

"Don't worry," I say. "I'll teach you."

I'm not as bold as he is, but I let my finger brush his chest underneath the water as I back away. My breathing is under control again, and I tread in place, watching him. He reaches for me, and I dodge.

"Catch me if you can," I say. "Best way to learn."

He lunges again, clumsy, and I play keep away with my body. He doesn't stray far from the dock, doggy-paddling in little circles, and something about it — his helplessness, his vulnerability — makes me want to be caught more than I've ever wanted anything.

He grabs my shoulders and dunks me. I let him, because he's Cal Flenders, and he's the most beautiful boy, dead or alive, I've ever known. I open my eyes on a dim, green world. Silver bubbles the color of Cal's eyes trail from my open mouth. Soo, Gord, Kiri, and Natalie are playing an awkward game of chicken. I watch their flashing legs for a moment before tilting my head back to take in the fractured sun and sky seen through the water. I was wrong before: This is the best moment to stop time.

⋈

The marshmallow at the end of Kiri's stick flares, sugary-blue, before dropping into the fire.

"Oops." Kiri giggles.

Joey belches, reaching for another beer. "Anybody know any good ghost stories?" He takes a long swallow, then looks at Cal. "Sorry. No offense." Joey's bloodshot eyes aren't entirely focused; after a moment, he snickers.

Should I leap to Cal's defense? The thought is half-formed, muzzy with alcohol and Joey's weed. It would be the chivalrous thing to do.

Cal shrugs.

"So what's it like?" Sid asks. "Being dead."

Natalie shoots him a look, which he ignores. Sid likes to push buttons. When I told him I was gay, he didn't miss a beat before asking, "Top or bottom?" Weird as it sounds, that's the thing I like about Sid. He actively tries to piss people off while everyone else is either busy worrying about getting people to like them, or talking about them behind their backs. All things considered, Sid is harmless. All bark, no bite. In our junior year, he tracked down the kid who carved the word faggot into my locker and punched him in the face right in front of the principal. Instead of apologizing, he let them suspend him for a week until the kid finally apologized and faced a three-month suspension for hate speech.

Even so, I can't help tensing at Sid's question. Asking Cal these questions chips away at my daydream, as if it might be a scab and there's a nightmare underneath.

Natalie presses her lips into a thin line. Over dinner, she and Sid fought about whether shellfish feel pain, putting them on the verge of breaking up yet again. Sid's question opens whatever wound is festering between them and Natalie rises, stalking toward the house. After a moment, Soo follows, stuck playing peacekeeper because it's her house. Sid stays put, but Gord follows Soo inside.

"I don't know," Cal says.

"How can you not know?" There's a gleam in Sid's eyes, the one he gets when he's looking to start trouble, maybe taking his annoyance at Natalie out elsewhere. He's smoking one of his Indonesian clove cigarettes, which he thinks makes him cooler than the kids who smoke Camels. I briefly consider a dramatic gesture, plucking the cigarette from his mouth and crushing it underfoot. Would that make me look heroic?

"What it's like to be alive?" Cal shoots back, but there's no venom in his tone.

Sid opens his mouth, and closes it again, his pot-fogged mind temporarily blown.

"I'm going for a walk." Kiri steps over Sid. Branches crack underfoot.

"Fuck it," Sid says after a moment, following Kiri. Joey doesn't say anything, but wanders after them.

At least I don't have to worry about Kiri being alone in the woods, or Sid trying anything just to piss off Natalie, or stoner Joey tripping over a branch and breaking his neck. All I have to worry about is Cal. Cal and me. Alone.

I tip my head back, looking at the stars. They're so much brighter here, not like the bruised-orange sky in the city that blocks out everything.

I'm afraid to look at Cal. I can't stop thinking about his hand on me in our room, and the brief flickering touches underwater. What if I find expectation in those eyes of his that are the same color as the stars? I've kissed exactly two boys in my lifetime. Even worse, what if I don't see any expectation at all?

"Sorry about Sid," I say as a distraction.

I sneak a glance at Cal. He's watching the fire, almost like he's forgotten I'm there. The glow reflects off his skin. His eyes aren't starlight after all; they're the same color as the flames.

"Want to see something neat?" he asks.

The skin at the base of my spine prickles. There's too much silence in the woods. I should be able to hear Joey, Sid, and Kiri, but there isn't even any wind. Before I can answer, Cal plunges his hand into the flames.

"Shit! What are you doing?"

He pulls his hand out, fingers still burning. I whip off my jacket and smother the flames.

Cal frowns. "It didn't hurt." I'm afraid he'll stalk off like Natalie. My stomach flops; maybe that last beer wasn't such a good idea. What if I puke all over his shoes?

Cal unwraps the jacket, and hands it back, tone softening. "I hope you didn't ruin it just for me."

It smells smoky, but otherwise the jacket looks fine. I shrug it back on, but the chill is already under my skin. Something about Cal treating death like a party trick pisses me off. I want to yell at him, but at the same time, it's his death; he can do what he wants with it.

But I can't help thinking of Cal on the basketball court, his I-got-this grin, like nothing could ever go wrong. It's the same for all the sun-bright jocks and cheerleaders, and even the stoners and losers and freaks like me and Kiri and Soo and Joey and Gord, all of us believing we'll live forever. Really, though everything is so goddamned fragile. We're getting ready to go out into the real world, and it isn't safe out there.

"Do you remember the crash?" The words are out before I can stop them.

Cal reaches for a long stick lying between his feet, and puts one end in the flames, twirling it.

"Sometimes. I remember the sounds — tires screeching, glass shattering. I didn't feel it when the windshield went in." He touches his side where the scar arcs up under his clothes. "Dying's easier to forget than you'd think."

Then I'm kissing Cal. Or he's kissing me. I'm not sure how it happens, but it *is* happening.

His lips are warm, but only from the proximity of the fire. His tongue feels cold. He slides a hand under my shirt, the hand from the fire with its skin ashen. I try not to think of burning flesh touching my goose-pimpled skin. I fumble at his fly before I have time to think about what the hell I'm doing. Cal doesn't have a heartbeat, no blood flow. Which means…

Kiri screams.

The lake catches the sound, whipping it along the shore. I reel away from Cal, panting, as the cabin door bangs open.

"What was that?" Soo comes off the porch, Gord behind her.

There's a loud crash. Branches snap. Joey, with Kiri right behind him, tripping on the loose, stony shore bordering the woods as they run toward the cabin. The left side of Joey's face is slick with blood, black in the moonlight.

"Sid. It fucking got Sid!"

Joey crashes into me and I catch him. He swings a bloody palm, thrashing, and it's a moment before he recognizes me, us, the light and the safety of the cabin.

Kiri's eyes are wide, her breathing shallow. "We have. To get. Inside." She sips air in little gulps.

"What happened? Where's Sid?" Natalie steps off the porch.

Another crack, another tree snapping. Soo's expression goes shocked-wide. I see it a moment after she does, but my brain refuses to make sense of it. A human shape swaying on the line where dirt meets the stony shore. One, then two. Then more shadows than I can count trickling out of the woods.

"Inside." Soo's voice is hoarse; she grabs my hand and pulls.

"What about Sid?" Natalie says.

I push her ahead of me and she only resists for a moment, Joey stumbling up the stairs behind me. Gord locks the door, and Soo drags an end table across it.

"What's going on?" Natalie's voice is on the edge of breaking.

Joey's left ear is entirely gone. His shirt is covered with blood to the waist.

"The woods," Joey says, "are full of motherfucking zombies."

Everybody tries to talk at once.

"We have to get to a hospital," Kiri says.

"We have to get Sid," Natalie says.

"Help me move the couch in front of the door," Gord says.

"What the fuck is he still doing here?" Joey points at Cal.

I drop my end of the couch. "What the fuck are you doing here, Joey?" I snap back. My hands shake, curled into fists at my side with all the adrenaline. "You're the one who's bit."

"Everyone calm down." Soo steps between us, pale, shadows around her eyes.

"No one is going anywhere." Soo pushes Joey into a chair. "Someone get me a towel."

Dazed, Natalie hands Soo a dishtowel. Soo bundles it against Joey's head and makes him put his hands on top of it, keeping pressure on the wound.

"Can't you go talk to them or something?" Gord turns a desperate gaze on Cal. The panic edging his voice is the only thing that keeps me from hitting him.

I edge closer to Cal, take his hand. His fingers are limp and cold in mine, and he barely seems to register my touch. I think of him on the porch a lifetime ago, the weight of his body against mine. He looked so inhuman. A dead thing like the zombies in the woods. Could he have called them? The moment the thought crosses my mind, I shut it down. This is Cal Flenders, the boy of my dreams.

"That's stupid," I say, finding my voice somewhere. "Cal isn't like them, at all."

Cal looks genuinely surprised, like he didn't expect anyone to stand up for him. After a moment, he returns the pressure of my fingers on his, and it's the best feeling in the world.

"We're all in this together," I say, calmer than I feel. "We'll figure it out somehow."

There's a loud thump from behind me. We all turn at once as a hand hits the window in the door. The glass holds, but the door shivers. Other hands beat the plate-glass window beside the door. A blur of faces, indistinct in the dark. I'm glad I can't see them clearly. I don't want to know if those dead eyes are the same color as Cal's, or see if their mouths are red with Joey and Sid's blood.

It's everything I've been afraid of since the beginning, since Cal asked me to prom, since final exams, since the last year of high school began. It's the end of the world, just not the way I expected it to be.

I stare at the zombies throwing themselves at the plate glass. I can't help thinking of moths, bumping up against the light outside the door. It doesn't matter how many throw their little bodies at it, or how delicate that glass is, the bulb doesn't break.

"I think we're safe."

"How the hell do you know?" Natalie's eyes are red, her voice tight. Despite everything, she and Sid did love each other in their own way.

I don't have a good answer for her. Instead, I put my arm around her shoulder. She stiffens, then slumps against me. She's not quite crying, her body tense and still, exhaustion warring with nerves.

"I'm sorry," I whisper, pressing my lips against her hair.

Natalie nods, but doesn't answer.

"I'm tired," Joey says.

He slumps and Soo catches him before he slides off the chair, lowering him gently to the ground.

"I think he's going into shock."

"We need to call an ambulance," Gord says, but doesn't move.

"No ambulance." Joey's voice is thick, words slurred but audible. "Those things, out there, they'd kill anyone before they could get here."

His head rolls to one side, eyes fluttering as if in dreams. He catches Soo's hand and she gasps in surprise. He grips it so hard I can see her bones and his both, right through the skin. I take a step forward and so does Gord. Soo's eyes are wide, but she waves us back.

Joey's lips move. Soo bends close and a shout freezes in my throat. What if Joey bites her ear off the way his ear was bitten? I wait for the crunch of flesh, but it doesn't come. Soo straightens, and if possible, she looks paler than before.

"What is it?" Gord asks.

"He." Soo stops, swallows. Her voice is thick. "He said if anything happens, if he starts to turn, we should kill him."

Soo's eyes are bright, but she isn't crying. Not yet. Cal untangles his fingers from my hand and touches Natalie's shoulder. She draws in a sharp breath, but she doesn't pull away when Cal helps her to a chair. He kneels in front of her, takes her fingers lightly in his and says something too low for me to hear. She nods.

Soo tilts her head toward the kitchen. It's a moment before I understand. My legs are shaking, the space between the couch and the knife drawer suddenly vast. I choose the biggest kitchen knife. I kneel beside Soo, and put the knife on the floor between us, so either of us can reach it, hoping neither of us have to.

Cal kneels beside me, close but not touching. Joey's chest continues to rise and fall, shallow breaths, but his eyes remain closed, his lids bruised.

"I'll do it, if it comes to that," Cal says in a soft voice.

I don't have to ask him what he means, and I swallow around a sudden ache in my throat, wondering whether I should be frightened or grateful.

"What did you say to Natalie?" I ask.

Cal's attention is still on Joey. He reminds me of a cat, watching for when the mouse stirs. Behind us, the zombies continue to bump softly against the glass.

"I told her dying's not so bad."

There's a wistfulness to Cal's voice when he says it that makes me wonder if he's lying. Is he remembering his own death? But being torn apart in the woods by zombies is nothing like a car crash. But if the result is the same, does it matter how you go?

"Why did you come back?" My voice is barely a whisper. I didn't mean to say it out loud, and I wish I could take it back as Cal turns to face me.

His eyes are unfathomable, endless and silver. "I don't know," Cal says after several infinitely long seconds. "You spend your whole life moving toward this point where you think the world will make sense, but..." Cal shrugs. "Things don't make anymore sense from the other side."

Cal lapses into silence for a moment. He turns, looking at the zombies outside the window, except his gaze is unfocused in a way that makes me think he's really seeing something else. Maybe the padded, satin lining of the coffin his parents buried him in, or headlights bearing down on him out of the dark and refusing to stop.

"I don't remember waking up, just like I don't remember being dead, not really. I just remember this burning thought in my head that wouldn't let go: *More time. I need more time.*" Cal's fingers flex, clenching and unclenching like he's still trying to pull himself out of the grave. "I didn't want it to end. It couldn't end, not like that. There was more I wanted to do. Ask a boy out. Dance with a boy. Kiss him. I knew there had to be someone special out there who would make me feel the way people feel in sappy love songs. My first thought when I dug myself free was find *that boy*."

Cal looks at back me. My face is burning. My heart is burning.

Silence for a moment. The sound of Joey's breath, steady, but louder than it should be. Gord perches on the arm of the couch that's still only halfway to blocking the front door.

"So what do we do now?" Gord asks.

I know what I want to do but no one here can marry me to Cal.

Cal Flenders, captain of the basketball team, star of my wet dreams, has just said the most romantic thing to me that anyone has ever said in my life. But the zombie apocalypse is still happening outside, and I can't melt into a puddle on the floor right now as much as I want to. I glance around the room. My friends all look the way I feel, wrung out, frightened, uncertain.

"I guess we wait," Soo says.

Kiri sits on the opposite side of the couch from Gord.

"We have plenty of food, at least," she says.

"Well, this is a shitty way to start the summer." Gord slides to sit on the couch proper, kicking his feet up to land on the coffee table with a thump.

The sound is a jolt I feel deep between my ribs. A hollow sound. It breaks something free, a knot of tension I've been holding onto even since before the zombies showed up. I can't help it, I start to giggle. My blood is still fizzing from Cal's words and the adrenaline and everything else. The giggle turns into a laugh, and soon I'm doubled over, gasping for breath, my eyes tearing. Everyone is staring at me, and it only makes me laugh harder.

My muscles are aching, my throat raw with the sound by the time I'm finally able to get myself under control. I wipe my eyes, still grinning even thought it makes my cheeks ache. Soo looks at me like I've lost it, and maybe I have.

"Sorry. I couldn't.... I was just thinking about what you wrote in my yearbook, Soo."

Soo continues to stare, then comprehension lights her eyes like a spark drifting from the fire into the sky.

"REM," I say.

Soo's grin spreads across her face. "Actually, I was thinking of the Great Big Sea version."

Everyone else is still staring at us. I stand, shaky, but maybe now it's from the laughter more than the fear. There's a wire tower of CDs next to the stereo system. I run my fingers along the jewel cases.

"Ha!" I pull out the case and wave it triumphantly before slipping the CD in the player and skipping to the right track.

"Shall we?" I hold my hand out to Soo.

She hesitates a moment, then carefully pries her hand from Joey's. I don't even care that her fingers are tacky with blood. We cross our arms one over the other, and spin the way we used to when we were kids. The room turns into a dizzy blur, but we refuse to fall down, gripping tight against the centrifugal force that wants to spin us away from each other.

In this moment, here, now, even though there are zombies outside the window and after this summer everything is going to change, I know without a doubt it's going to be fine.

Soo sings along, keeping time even as the song speeds up. I've never known the proper lyrics, so I make up my own.

"Light bulbs, airplanes, gummy worms and zombies!"

Kiri, Gord, and Natalie all watch us. Cal watches me and only me. Even though my palms are sweating, I keep hold of Soo's hands and we continue spinning, belting out whatever words we feel like, falling out of time as Alan Doyle's voice rushes on, faster than any voice has the right to.

It's like the high-dive board. It's like high school ending, and the rest of our lives opening up into unknown territory. Maybe Soo and Gord won't always be Soo and Gord, and maybe they will. Maybe we'll all be eaten by zombies before sunrise. Maybe Cal will keep me safe and maybe I'll keep him intact. Maybe. Maybe.

But all that comes later. This is *now*.

Softly, I hear Kiri join us, singing along. Joey's fingers twitch, tapping out the rhythm on the floor. He's not dying just yet.

It's the infinite now, before the world ends, or doesn't. And when it comes to the chorus, we all belt it out together, as loud as we can: It's the end of the world, and we feel fine.

Writing is a strange business. For the most part, authors spend hours inside their own heads holding conversations with imaginary people. We pour out words and send them into the world and sometimes it feels like shouting into a void. Every now and then though a voice comes back, and we know we aren't actually alone. Thanks are due first and foremost to Derrick Wise for putting up with me, and to my family (including the four-legged members) for years of love and support. I also owe a huge thank you to Steve Berman and Lethe Press for believing in my stories, Matthew Bright for making the collection look lovely, and Reiko Murakami for the stunning cover art. Thank you to all the editors who gave the reprinted stories in this collection their original homes. As always, I owe more than I can say to the members of my various critique groups in their many iterations: Anticipation, Sparkle Pony, and Not-Bridge (we really need a better name for ourselves) folks - I could not do this without you. Thank you for commiserating on days when I wanted to quit and refusing to let me do so. Thank you for the celebrations. Thank you for reading countless drafts and revisions, helping me find the places my stories were broken, and giving me just what I needed to fix them. Finally, a special thank you to Barry King who was in my very first critique group. He was a good friend, and he left this world too soon. Barry, you are missed.

ABOUT THE AUTHOR

A.C. Wise was born and raised in Montreal, and currently lives in the Philadelphia area. Her stories have appeared in *Clarkesworld, Shimmer, Uncanny,* and *The Year's Best Dark Fantasy and Horror 2015,* among other places. Her debut collection, *The Ultra Fabulous Glitter Squadron Saves the World Again,* was published by Lethe Press in 2015. In addition to her fiction, she co-edits *Unlikely Story, and contributes a monthly review column, Word for Thought, to Apex Magazine.* Find her online at www.acwise.net.

CPSIA information can be obtained
at www.ICGtesting.com
Printed in the USA
LVOW08s0019200317
527767LV00001B/106/P